AFTER
THE
PRETTY
POX

Book One: The Attic

AFTER THE PRETTY POX

Book One: The Attic

August Ansel

LOOK MA NO HANDS
EUREKA

ISBN-13: 978-0-9861717-3-4
ISBN-10: 0-9861717-3-5

After the Pretty Pox, Book One: The Attic is a work of fiction. Names, characters, businesses, places, events, and incidents, including those of a historical nature, are products of the author's imagination or are used fictitiously. Any resemblance to actual persons, living or dead, events, or locales is entirely coincidental.

The following lyric excerpt is from a work in the public domain:
"The Water is Wide." Scottish/Irish folk ballad, traditional, c. 1724.

Cover by Inspired Cover Designs
www.inspiredcoverdesigns.com
Copyright © 2016 Dominika Hlinková

Look Ma No Hands Publishing
P.O. Box 84
Eureka, California 95502
lmnohpub@gmail.com

෧ ෬

For news and upcoming books from August Ansel, subscribe to the newsletter:
www.carlabaku.com

Dedicated to

Andrew, Jeffery, Benjamin, and Luke

*"My goodness, how the time has flewn.
How did it get so late so soon?"
--Dr. Seuss*

and to

Mildred, Doris, Mary, Olive, and Ellie

A strong woman is a force to be reckoned with.

A long tale, like a tall Tower,
must be built a stone at a time.

Stephen King, The Dark Tower

Nature, as time, is erasing this wound.
Time is unstoppable, and it transforms the event.
It gets further and further away from the day.
Light and seasons temper it in some way.

Joel Meyerowitz, Photographer

PRAELUDIUM~ POSTSCRIPTUM

by Tuli, c. 2052

An after-reckoning about how it shook out.
Supposition, hypothetical, considering everything, etc.

What happened?

This is how we create a history, as passed from lip to ear. The birth of rumor, legend, long nights around a fire while the moon rises and the log burns to embers.

The quickest way to spread information: telegraph, telephone, tell a secret.

The world came apart.

That may not be true. It may only have been the country. Or the continent.

The cavalry did not arrive. No assistance was forthcoming. Perhaps that means something?

I doubt it.

For a long time the disintegration was recorded. Data was downloaded and consumed. The unraveling was spectator sport.

There was probably a tipping point. One last margin of error, a hair's breadth, a held breath, right before the moment of no return, an accumulation of trouble, enough to make us stand still, to look around at each other and say *we should change this.*

That is not what happened.

Who did this, damn it?

Finding a Responsible Party was more important than standing down.

We already knew *we* were responsible.

For a time, we knew everything, had all the information.

That is not true, either, but we thought it was.
I search, therefore I am.

Once upon a time, a hole opened in the great web of connection. The filaments broke loose. The old forgotten quiet poured through.

What happened?

History is what we remember. Real-story is what we forget.

I can only write a history. But for you it may be a real-story.

I will write.

Not today. My hand fails.

Let us begin with a reminder: *Carpent tua poma nepotes.*

Your descendants will pick your fruit.

1

SOMEONE WAS INSIDE. All the way inside, pushing past the overturned furniture and trash she had scattered strategically around the entryway and the living room. *Bear*, was Arie's first thought. It had happened before. But there was a quality of hurried stealth. No bear would try to step around the bottles and cans, the old cellophane and silverware, broken glass and dead leaves. Lying face down on the attic floorboards, weight on her forearms, not moving a muscle except to turn her head ever so slowly, Arie hovered, put her ear as close to the slats of the old heating register as she dared. Panting down there, broken and whistling. A person, then. A person in the house with her. Someone frightened. Arie could smell it, without even putting her nose to the grate. The sour, dank odor of a body in extremity, familiar to her as a rat's nest or a string of possum shit.

"Please don't." The words floated into Arie's ear, a scrim of sound so high and wheezy it seemed like imagination. No longer directly below her. The sound now drifted up from around the corner, in what had been a kitchen. "Hurry. Have to hurry." Female, probably. Or child. Arie knew better than to look.

Then something else inside, down there. Quick and scrabbling, not minding the debris, claws loud on the wood of the floor, despite its soft and patchy rot. The whistling breath of the intruder, the human, had gone silent. But the fear smell was loud and louder still. The clawed thing panted and snuffled directly under the grate. Arie held her breath until it passed under, following its prey. The sky panel was open above her, had been all day, and the cool smell of evening fell through. Her mandala was visible in the late twilight, a circular labyrinth etched into the attic wall, its path dark where her finger had traced again and again. Lying on the attic floor, silent, she followed the spiraling line with her eyes, outside to inside. Slow breath in, slow breath out.

The growl below became an open-throated snarl. There commenced a great crashing and floundering, things thrown, something heavy cutting the air with a quiet whoosh, a squall of pain or surprise. Arie's eyes moved through the mandala, now from the center back to the outside. While the animal's clawed feet tried to gain traction in the debris on the floor, the human made a break for the front door. She made it outside, sobbing. Arie heard and felt the door hit its frame when the intruder tried to pull it shut. But the latch mechanism was long gone, knob utterly useless. The animal slammed against the door on the inside, raging, clawing, biting, effectively keeping it closed for a few extra moments. The woman fled, her footsteps fading in the direction of the gulch. Down in the entryway, the animal commenced a deliberate, clatterous digging.

Arie rose to hands and knees, waited. The instant the scratching ceased, she leapt to her feet. The ladder leaned against the edge of the sky panel. She scurried up two rungs and poked her head and shoulders through the opening in the attic roof, just in time to see the dog racing into the tree line at the bottom of the cracked asphalt cul-de-sac. Dog, not wolf this time. The legs were bulky and not long enough for wolf, tail not a wolf's heavy brush, but a bald knob, hacked off by a human in the time before the Pink. Presently, two voices rose—the woman's first, pitching upward until it splintered in some high register. Then on top of it the dog's bay, smooth and delighted. An immediate response came from all around, a multitude rejoicing. Dozens of canid howls. Scores, perhaps.

Arie stepped off the ladder and laid it lengthwise against the wall, pulled the guy rope out of its spring cleat and paid the cable through her hands until the sky panel dropped solidly into place. She shot the flat bolts through their brackets. The animal singing continued, but was muted now, fading as each voice dropped out of the chorus. The attic was entirely dark. She took a lighter from her apron pocket and lit her way to the work table, set the flame to a stub of candle.

A single shriek somewhere near the river, then silence.

At the basin, she dipped her hands, dipped them again, laving the water up and through her fingers. "Rest is not mine to give," she said. "My life is my own." She put her wet palms against her cheeks, smoothed them back and over the crown of her head. Her silver hair darkened where her wet hands touched. It was the middle of fall by her reckoning. Despite weeks of warm days a chill came at night, one she now felt on her damp skin.

Normally she ate a little something before sleeping, some dried berries and jerky, perhaps a carrot or chunk of flatbread, but she had no appetite. She opened the bedroll and got ready for the night, slingshot tucked into the ammo bag at her right hand, short spear under her pillow. She double-checked the sky panel bolt, peed into the compost bucket. Finally, she stood before the mandala and kissed the null signs etched on her inner forearms. She touched her finger to the outside of the labyrinth and began to trace the smooth rut, back and forth, inward, outward, eyes closed, her breathing slow and rhythmic. Eight times her finger traveled to the center and out again. On the ninth and final circuit, she recited her full catechism.

"I sojourn," Arie said. The words were old. She was older. They fell from her mouth like polished agates. "I sojourn. My life is my own. I shall not give, neither shall I receive. Rest for me. Rest for the Mother." She slid into her bedroll, a thick pile of sheets and blankets layered over a plastic shower curtain. All was silence in the attic. All was silence in the rooms of ruin below. Beyond, in the ravaged streets and burgeoning timber, the crumbling buildings and bounteous estuaries, there were only the sounds of the rightful inheritors.

She slept later than usual. The sun had already cleared the horizon when she opened the sky panel and looked out. An enormous flock of geese passed overhead, plying their northern route. It was early fall and the weather still warm. "October," she said aloud, then again, stretching the word out on her tongue:

"Oc-to-berrrr." It was another language, a word that connected in her mind to other anachronisms, like "school" and "jack-o'-lantern" and "shoe store." Odd, since Arie hadn't attended a school until she was close to grown, nor ever carved a pumpkin—that being the devil's work—and as a child she only wore shoes that her older siblings had outgrown. "Collective unconscious," she said. More devil's work, according to Daddy Mack.

The second rung of the ladder put her barely head and shoulders above the roofline. She raised the binoculars for a quick scan of the street. There was only a raccoon disappearing into a neighbor's window, into what had been Peter and Rachel's house, and baby Gabe's. Gabe—fine and happy when Rachel put him in his crib so she could catch a shower, but five minutes later slumped onto his side, clutching a stuffed penguin and struggling for breath. Rachel came tearing into the street with Gabe in her arms, screaming for Arie. The baby was the first one Arie saw dead with the Pink, the shocking color making his little round face look not only alive, but radiant. They both tried to breathe for him, crouched between the raised garden beds in Arie's front yard, taking turns. Arie had not taken up the catechism yet, but it rooted in her then, the wisdom of it, as she tried to blow life into her neighbor's child.

The sky panel let out on the south side of the house. The pitch and angle of the roof created a protected space there. She could ease out, and unless something was directly beneath her in the weedy tangle that had been her backyard, she could not be easily seen. It wasn't until she was all the way out and moving around that she was visible from the street, so she stepped onto the top rung and emerged inches at a time, watching, listening.

Clear.

First, she hauled up the bucket and emptied it into the plastic laundry basket that served as her compost bin: meager food scraps, river muck and dried grass. She kept coons and rats from disturbing the basket by adding her night urine. Then she made a quick pass through her checkerboard of small garden boxes. She gathered carrots, a few leaves of kale, some pea pods, munching while she pulled a few small weeds. The soil in one box was especially dry; she dipped into the gray-water bucket and wet around the beets and chard.

That done, she dropped the bucket back into the attic and lowered the sky panel. The ammo bag and slingshot were in her apron pocket, the short spear in her belt. She strapped on a woven carry basket she used for gathering firewood and other bulky collectibles, and crept to the edge of the roof. The yard was still empty of everything but overgrown amaranth weeds and trash. To one side of the decayed chimney was a narrow space formed between the wall of the house and a matted screen of rhododendron, jimson weed, blackberry, and English ivy. She dropped a rope ladder into the gap. Once she was down, the contraption retracted by means of a pulley line; this she threaded deeply into the brush, rendering it all but invisible.

She picked her way out from behind the bushes. She followed an occluded path in the tall weeds and through a place in the chain-link fence where the gate once stood. Most of the windows in the house were broken, some roughly patched with cardboard but most left jagged and gaping. The front yard was also overgrown, the lawn now a shoulder-high prairie. She moved out to the street, watchful, hand on the shaft of the short spear.

It was another beautiful day, with the kind of huge clouds meant to be watched while lying back in a field, looking for familiar shapes. Arie preferred to walk close to the street rather than in it, the shrubs and weeds flanking the hoven and cracked asphalt providing a certain amount of cover. In many places the chunks of asphalt were so blasted and invaded by plants growing up from underneath and from seeds falling or blowing into every microscopic crack, it was already hard to see that it had once been a tidy suburban street, even though it was barely two years since cars stopped driving on it.

The tree line was also much closer than it had once been. It happened. The rains recommenced, city maintenance workers—whose job had been to cut back branches and briars—were dead or disappeared. Now every time Arie came outside, the gulch seemed to have crept a little closer. At the edge of the woods, she went down on her haunches and looked back at the house. It looked utterly derelict: the front door standing most of the way open, broken windows on every side, hugely overgrown yards. And on that open front door, a faded red X painted. Pox inside, that X meant. The Pink Plague lives here.

Satisfied, she took the path into the woods. It had been a packed-dirt thoroughfare when she was a little girl, the favorite way for disk golfers and skateboarders to cut through the trees and into the Cooper Gulch Family Park. A favorite shortcut of derelicts, too, mostly meth-addled homeless who raved back and forth, shouting down a windrow of invisible foes, their skin haggard with sores, their teeth gone or going. That was the neighborhood her grandparents had lived in, a different one than they had moved to in their middle years, but still familiar, still wreathed in a certain tattered normalcy. This version, though, they would not recognize in any particular. Storms had blown over a great many trees, more than a few power poles (which had been trees once, too) and dragged useless lines down into snarled nests. All those entertaining pulses of data and power, all those houses tethered like angular fetuses on twisted umbilici, all silent now. There was more of everything alive, and less of everything constructed by the interlopers. And the interlopers themselves, of course. Not many of those left.

The path showed the outline of the woman's tracks, where she'd fled from the dog last night, the faint whorls from her shoe soles more pronounced through the toes because she had been running. These were the first human footprints she'd seen in a great while. Close to a year, maybe longer. She uprooted a handful of horsetail and brushed away the mottled prints as she walked alongside in the weeds.

Arie hunched into the underbrush, angling her way south away from the trail until the alder saplings and huckleberry bushes got so thick she was practically on hands and knees. The woods still smelled of summer skunk cabbage, ripe and acidic, and the fading perfume of blackberries, mostly rotting on the branch now—those that hadn't been eaten by birds and bears. And by Arie, who had gotten gallons this year and reveled in them. Fruit leathers and bowls filled, she with seeds lodged between her molars, fingers and mouth stained deep red. Straight from the bush, the fruit was often sour—they'd used so much sugar on berries before the Pink—but fresh and delicious anyway. She'd even created a rough version of pemmican from a mix of things she half-remembered from a childhood reading assignment: berries, finely minced fat and meat saved from a duck she'd managed to snare, and blanched acorn mash. The resulting pemmican had been chewy and variable in taste, gamey. But edible after having dried in the sun. Thinking about it now made her mouth water.

When she got to a particular stone (one she'd set alongside a tree herself), she turned toward the river and came out very near the bank. Here, in a natural horseshoe clearing that was virtually invisible from up or down the riverbank, she had set four fish snares. It was passive fishing that required neither her presence nor the need for her to get down into the water, like a fish weir or gill net would do. Each snare consisted of two sticks with notched ends. One stick was pounded into the ground, notch up. A willow sapling, connected to the un-notched end of the other stick by a length of monofilament, acted as a spring. Arie would carefully fit the notches together; a bait line trailed out into the water. When the fish nibbled, the notched sticks came apart and the sapling sprang upright, pulling the fish from the creek. If she was lucky, she got to the dangling fish before a rightful inheritor did. Today she'd been very lucky. Three trout hung above their snares, the gills of one still opening and closing as it tried in vain to breathe the air. Water dripped from its tail, making a dark spot on the duff below.

Arie pulled the fishes free and walked several paces down the creek to clean them. She threw the entrails into the shallows and washed her hands, then rinsed the rocks clean of fish blood and any trace of guts. She wanted to leave as little evidence as possible and to avoid luring a hungry animal to her catch. A big-leaf maple was in the process of throwing off its massive cargo of brown and yellow leaves. She picked several that were still clinging to the branches and wrapped the little trout before stowing them in her basket. She returned to bait and reset the snares, hooking the notched sticks with particular care.

She worked her way back to the path and followed it down to the creek. She hung back in the brambles, again squatting and scoping the bank, first south and then north. Satisfied, she ducked under a low-hanging manzanita and out into a miniature meadow. It was risky here—she was terribly visible— but this was an area the rabbits loved. Set around the edge of the clearing, her traps were almost identical to her fish snares, catching small game that ran for the trees when spooked by predators. These required taller saplings to lift the captured animal out of reach of hungry opportunists—dogs, wolves, raccoons. Arie walked the perimeter of the clearing and found the first snare still set. She'd have to relocate it soon, since it had only ever caught a small partridge, one with no more meat under its feathers than a pigeon. The second trap was twenty long paces from the first.

Before she got halfway there she could see it was sprung, and hoped for something edible.

But the snare line was empty. She examined the trip wire. In the loop, a bit of sticky blood and scrim of soft fur. So something had been in the trap, but then? Had a rabbit somehow managed to work itself loose? She'd seen one twist and thrash until its ankle was rubbed to the bone by the trip wire, but the slipknot worked too well, tightening relentlessly no matter how slick with blood. Arie held the loop in one hand and looked around at the ground for some clue to tell her where her prey had gotten to.

"I had to take it."

She turned, the short spear in hand before she was all the way around. The man stood five yards into the trees, both hands slightly raised (and empty, she was glad to see) so that she could see the palms. He crouched just slightly, springy through all his limbs. The look on his face was wary but curious, ready for her. In the fraction of time it took to register his presence, it was clear that he blocked her way back to the path, and even if she managed it he could outrun her. She stood bolt upright, returned the short spear to her belt, and pulled open the laced front of her blouse. The skin over her heart had the same tattoo as her inner forearms: a deep-red null sign.

"I am only a sojourner. Pilgrim, will you give me rest?"

Uncertainty flickered over his face, and he looked away, staring into the middle distance. "I, uh—" he hesitated. "I can't." Then he snapped his fingers. "Rest is not mine to give." Triumphant, as though he'd found the answer to a difficult examination.

Arie pulled her blouse closed and rested her hand on the shaft of the short spear. "So where is that rabbit?"

"We ate it for breakfast. Nothing left over, either."

"It's your rabbit now, then. If you filch my traps, you've interfered a good deal with my journey," she said. "Reckon the woods are big enough and bountiful elsewhere for you and yours." She fought a hair-prickling urge to glance around her for others.

"I had to feed the girl."

"Whose is she?"

He shrugged. "Nobody's, I'd say, from the state of her leg. Dog-chewed. She may live yet."

"Not long, likely, if she hasn't yet learned to climb a tree to get a dog off her. Others?"

"Only her and me."

"She's yours then."

"Not until I found her, bit that way."

"Will you keep her?"

"I can't leave her. She took a fever."

"That's your path, I suppose. I have my own. Go off a ways, is my request." She kept her hand on the short spear and adjusted the straps of her carry basket as she eased to her left, aiming for the path. "Let me work this bit of dirt in peace, if you mean well. Do you? You haven't murdered me yet." Her whole attention was on the shape of him in the corner of her eye and the sounds all around her as she backtracked, one deliberate step at a time, not turning her back, but not obviously watching him as she went.

"But I've come for you, Arie."

How long since her name was spoken to her? A few times here and there during the short days of ravaging, and likely not at all since. She faced him again. "How is it you call me by name?" He took a step toward her, but she lifted a hand to stop him. "Just tell it."

He cocked his head and blinked at her. "I suppose you wouldn't know me. I was born six years after you left Daddy Mack."

She saw it in him, then, in this young man. It was the square set of his face, the eyes narrow as any animal peering out of its den. High cheekbones and thin, straight hair and long beard the color of strong tea. It was his father's face, made over more kindly perhaps, the mouth set in a straight line rather than fat-lipped and self-satisfied. "So," she said. "My brother." She calculated a moment, thinking back at the state her mother had been in when Arie'd left God's Land. "You're William."

"William that's called Handy," he agreed. "I've come to find you."

"You've found me. It's no secret where—I've been in Granny and Pop's house since I struck out from God's Land."

He nodded. "But no way to know if you survived."

"I did. And you."

"Daddy Mack says it's in the blood."

"So he lived."

"He did. Not all of us, though. Some took it quick."

"Everyone who died took it quick. And the rest?"

"Some gone. Some not gone. Daddy Mack sent me for you."

"To bring me back there?" She chuffed laughter. "Not on the best day, nor on the worst. I shook the dust of God's Land off my feet a long time hence, though you're too young to have seen it happen."

"Sister Ariela—"

She held up a palm again. "Arie is enough. I'm old enough to be your mammy, and a perfect stranger." She turned from him and made for the path. "Go well, Sojourner. You and her. Rest is not mine to give, nor succor either." She looked back only once. William was moving into the trees. His hair hung down his back in a stringy plait, its pale color blending with the no-color of his shirt. "Appears you turned out fine," she said. "A good one, maybe. Not like him." He ducked into the scrub without another word.

Up the path, a quick scan, and into her yard. She let down the rope ladder and hauled it behind her when she was on the roof.

The three fish were small. She cooked them all on the fire inside. She could have fried them out on the roof; she had a low-slung steel fire pit up there. It sat on a heavy scrap of corrugated sheet metal, and in it she could build a deep bed of coals for cooking, out where the risk of fire was smaller. But right now she wanted to be inside, in the dark of the attic again.

When the house had belonged to her grandmother, the trash burner on the kitchen range vented through a small central flue. In the attic, Arie had rigged a tiny makeshift fireplace to vent through that old pipe. The top of the flue was partially screened by trees, so smoke was less visible and the smell of cooking dissipated above head-height. Even so, she laid only a tiny portion of dry wood. With these little trout the cooking was a matter of minutes, and she smothered the fire with sand immediately. She sat on the floor under her mandala, eating with her hands. The light from the sky panel was dappled in the afternoon; the shadows of an ancient plum tree moved in a freshening breeze. A tiny wind chime sounded, a remnant that still dangled somewhere on the block and indicated a change in the weather, southerly winds usually a harbinger of oncoming rain and storm. Arie relished the crackle of the trout's crisp skin, and she sucked the brains and eyes from their heads.

The rest of the afternoon she spent setting things tightly in order. The possibility of storm always impelled her to double down on housekeeping matters, although today her sense of an oncoming problem was much more acute than her sense of rain. Knowing William was in the woods, out there close enough that if she were to step on the top rung of her sky panel, she could whistle loud enough for him to hear. The girl was a cipher to Arie, so she considered her not at all. She wanted to know that he was gone. Having him nearby gave a sense of an unwelcome conduit yawning open. Every few minutes, she conned the street with her binoculars. She saw only birds, mostly gulls defying the freshening onshore wind, hovering in place like tethered kites.

On the roof, she checked the water supply. A fifteen-gallon plastic jerry can was snugged beneath a special length of downspout that diverted from a rain gutter. Down in the yard, at the back of the house, was a full-sized rain barrel, sixty gallons. She hadn't checked it for over a week, but with all the wet weather, it was likely brimming—there if the jerry can failed her.

At the garden boxes, she picked all the green beans still left on the vine, stuffing them into the deep pockets of her apron. The sky was already gray, a stack of dark clouds massing overhead, and the temperature dropped precipitously in a matter of minutes. Rain for sure, then. The smell of the ocean was cold and heavy.

Inside, she lowered the sky panel. The beans she set aside to string later and hang for drying. The only light was a silvery ripple on the far wall from the revolving turbine set into the peak of the roof. The windows set on either end of the attic were heavily curtained to prevent anyone seeing her candlelight or cooking fire, and she hadn't pulled them open that morning. She could see well enough, once her eyes adjusted. Before she could settle down for the end of the afternoon, she needed to go below. Into the rooms of ruin. The bitten girl had been in there, and the dog. Arie had to check things and put it to rights.

In the center of the attic floor, there had once been a drop-down ladder that could be accessed from the hallway below. One of the things Arie had done when her grandmother passed was dismantle that little door, replace it with drywall and paint over it. She created a new way into the attic. It was a hidden hatch, set into the ceiling of an unused closet. It could only be opened from above, and she left it ajar when she had to go downstairs. When closed, the hatch was virtually invisible, its edges neatly fitted behind narrow trim that ran around the closet's upper perimeter. Arie first bolted shut the sky panel, then unlatched the inside hatch. She lifted the panel aside and stepped down onto the built-in shelves, which served as her ladder. The closet door stood partway open, as did all the doors down below. Her face went into a spider web as she stepped out of the closet, and she wiped it away, blinking.

This had been her own bedroom, from age fifteen—when she came to live with Granny and Pop— until Granny's death one year before the Pink. There was very little left in here from those days, only the torn corner of a poster of Mount Everest and the gnawed remnants of her mattress, home now to mice or rats. She inched her way silently out of the room.

It was all chaos in the rooms of ruin, a perfectly orchestrated symphony of disorder that Arie had spent as much time planning and constructing as she had the smooth-running systems she now lived in up above. Every room showed ample evidence of having been utterly ransacked. Burnables were gone, and the truly useless remnants of the time before were bashed into corners and the middle of the floor: a television set, a metal file cabinet, a seascape painted in oils on canvas, its wooden frame gone; a leather loveseat lay on its back under a thick skin of mildew, the overstuffed back torn and bleeding stuffing. Her grandmother had collected antique mirrors, and there were shards everywhere, making the floor a mosaic of reflected wreckage. Anything that could make noise and discourage the weary from taking refuge, Arie used. Besides the glass, there were empty cans and bottles, a certain amount of pea gravel from the alley behind the house, her grandmother's music and movie collection, the slippery plastic discs in an unexpected scatter around one corner. There was even a mound of bear scat in plain sight near the middle of the dining room floor. This had been provided for her one day by a young black bear that had come foraging and left with an empty belly as well as empty bowels. The shit didn't smell much anymore, not to Arie, but it did seem to act as a deterrent to smaller animals. When it dried completely she could burn it for fuel if she needed to, but when that day came she planned on scouting for a new pile that she could bring in from the woods herself—provided no bear made a second special delivery.

The girl's footprints were there, same as they had been in the dirt of the path, but on the rotting hardwood floor they had no strong definition. The dog's tracks were there too, overlapping, the striations of its claws like comb marks in the grime. In the kitchen the mess was exponential, broken dishes and useless kitchen rubbish tossed everywhere. A bashed-open garden window above the sink was full of vegetation blown in from the yard, the sink itself a foul-smelling mess of standing water, rotted plant matter, and a dead robin floating half-submerged. Stainless steel flatware littered the floor, especially in front of the partially boarded back door. There was a cudgel in one corner, a twisted metal chair leg it was, blood on the heavy end. This was what the girl had swung at the dog, swung and connected, clearly. Some windows were still intact, but Arie had made sure that there were enough broken panes to convince any would-be intruder that the house was unfit, even as a way station, even if they saw the red X slashed on the front door and weren't scared off by threat of the Pink. Was anyone who'd survived it still worried? Probably not. Two years was enough to dull the edges of that particular panic, she thought. She was sure, though, that with all the empty houses running up and down the streets, and what seemed to be damn near all other people dead, one look at the mess she'd made in here would be a discouragement. The biggest impediment was in her grandmother's room in the middle of the house. That door stayed closed. It was ruined, too, in a much more fundamental way.

The day was pushing dark now, and the rain had started. It gusted in on the south side of the house, mostly along the kitchen walls, commencing a clatter above her, the exhaust vent for the kitchen range. It thrummed a bright, uneven tattoo. Arie looked all around, trying to see it all through the eyes of a stranger, and found it believably awful. Without even glancing at her grandmother's bedroom door, she went back through her former room, into the closet, and stepped onto the first shelf. Deep dust and the crispy carapaces of desiccated flies covered them, gritting under her fingers. It was a challenge getting over the lip of the hatch—harder by far now than it had been when she was fifty. Once up, she leaned head-down and swiped randomly at the filth on the shelves, getting rid of anything that resembled handprints. She fitted the hatch lid back into its space. This hatch, like the sky panel, had its own homemade bolt, and because it was more vulnerable from inside the house, she blocked it with her 'sofa': the bench seat from the rear of a car. Gods knew how it had ever ended up in the attic—probably something of Pop's.

Covered with hideous thick fabric, the car seat was a relic of steel from an era of automobile frenzy at least a hundred years in the past, when the combustion engine beat like the heart of the world, pumping forever on a supply of crude oil thought inexhaustible. The thing probably weighed in the neighborhood of a hundred pounds, and if someone from below managed first to find the secret opening and then to break through, the car seat might at least give Arie a head start to escape through the sky panel and onto the roof. She put her back to one side and pushed until the old bench seat sat squarely over the hatch.

At the table she lit two candles tonight, one for light and one for heart. She dropped onto the car seat, the worst of its holes stuffed with Pop's clothes and covered with her old bedspread. The rain had picked up urgency and beat down on the old asphalt shingles. She was exhausted. "Not young as I once was," she said to herself, and laughed. Her grandmother used to say that when she was in her middle eighties. "Not young as I once was, and not nearly old as I'm getting to be."

Her brother William.

She'd heard that a fourteenth had been born to Mammy Delonda, but by that time Arie had been twenty-one and not much interested in yet another sibling, one among the herd of them. Arie had taken the vow, taken the marks of the vow, years before. Her parents' continued antipathy to the bitter reality of life was no direct concern of Arie's. It wasn't the physical fact of this young brother appearing that she was caught on. Was it? No, not him. He's a stranger. On his own path, like all men, she thought. No, her snag, the thing nettling her now, was hearing of Daddy Mack alive. So many dead, and Daddy Mack still walking the face of the planet. If ever there was an argument against the possibility of the terrible deity they'd kowtowed to, that was a feasible one.

She got off the sofa seat, struggling a bit from that low position. With the rain here in earnest, the parts of her that felt the damp most keenly muttered pain— knee, ankle, left index finger. The bang and flutter of the hood vent kept up a small, bracing racket that Arie liked. It was a thin metal sound from the past, when all was snug and yellow with lamplight inside, and all was gray, blowing wet outside.

Order, order, order. She began with the table; all-purpose work spot that it was, it tended to clutter. The bowl of green beans she'd picked earlier she placed next to the sofa, for stringing later. Her many candle stubs were scattered around and she hadn't washed her bowl and spoon since using them...when? Two days ago. A stray carrot was here, too. She stowed it in her apron pocket along with various lighters and her folding knife. The candle ends and lengths went into their own bowl like fat crayons discarded by a distracted child. She dumped standing gray water out of her washbasin into the piss bucket and—a treat— refilled the basin with fresh water, even though she'd only used the old water twice. There was plenty of rain filling the jerry can on the roof, so she'd break her own rule of using the basin at least three times before dumping. She rinsed her face, grabbed a chunk of soap and scrubbed her hands. Finally, she cleaned the dishes, picking bits of dried oats off the spoon. Before drying the dishes and covering them with the towel,

Arie wiped down the whole surface of the table and everything on it. The attic was constantly shedding itself everywhere, sending down a steady blanket of dust and cobwebs, dead spiders (or living ones), and crumbled bits of asphalt shingle and outside dirt. Her few clothes she shook out and refolded, and the same with her bedding and the cover of the old car seat.

"A 1950 Packard," Pop used to say. "Hell of a car. A tank." It had been up in the attic as long as Arie could remember. Every so often, Mammy Delonda had gotten a wild hair and brought Arie and her two older sisters, Mercy and Lulu, into town for a secret visit with Granny and Pop Merrit, who were her parents. Daddy Mack thought they were going to the co-op and spending the afternoon on Clam Beach. But they only stopped at the beach for a few minutes, just long enough to gather up little bits of ocean flotsam and get sand in their shoes. Then they'd pile back into the truck and drive into town to this house, the house their mother had grown up in.

Granny would get tears in her eyes and make a terrible fuss over them all, with a lot of extra hugs and kisses for Mammy Delonda. After a minute or two, Pop would give each of the children a dollar, and they'd walk two blocks to Pat's Market for a treat. The unheard-of novelty of having money in hand was eclipsed entirely by the strangeness of being in a store all by themselves. The possibilities had seemed vast to them—shelves of candy, chips, cookies, the cold case with rows of sweetened drinks, and a freezer filled with ice cream bars. Choosing kept them busy for a good long time. Back at Granny and Pop's, their mother would be sitting at the kitchen table with

Granny, smoking a cigarette. Her big smile, conspiratorial. With the taste of chocolate in their mouths, there was no question that everyone's secrets would be safe when they got back to God's Land, when Daddy Mack said, "Well, Treasures? How was your road trip, what adventures?" They would tell him about going to the beach, would empty their pockets of stones and gull feathers and the desiccated claws of Dungeness crabs. He would laugh his enormous Daddy Mack laugh and say, "Good you drove back to God's Land, after all that. You and your mammy, too!" Mammy Delonda would look sweetly up at him, and she'd have her little voice back, not like the calm, level voice she spoke with at Granny's kitchen table. And when they went to bed, all of them at once—girls in the loft, boys on the living room floor, Mammy and Daddy in their curtained alcove—there would be the Sacrament of Life for ever so long, the restless thumping of the bed, finally Daddy Mack's sacramental groan, followed moments later by their mingled post-coital benediction, a prayer asking the Lord for increase. And the Lord increased. The Lord was ever so generous with the giving out of babies.

The storm pounded the attic roof, rain like a hose turned on, pouring in great blowing sheets. Arie gathered up tools and weapons and spread them out on the floor, sitting cross-legged before them: short spear, extra spear tips, pocket knife, bowie knife, sling and sling ammo. Every three days she did this, usually before dark. Checked the knots on the sling and ensured the lacings were not frayed or nicked. Put the blades of the two knives to the whetstone. Double-checked the lashing on her short spear and the edges of the blade for cracks. There were no visible cracks, although she couldn't be completely sure in this light. The stone was sound, fantastically thin on its cutting edge. It was a Daddy Mack original, given to her when she turned twelve. All the children were trained in the art of stone knapping, first by observing and mimicry, and then in earnest on their twelfth birthday. Daughters and sons each had their own rites of passage, but being allowed to knap stone for the protection or provision of the family was a universal. Arie had a half-dozen other blades for her short spear, and all of the others she had made herself.

Everything set right now, she took up heavy thread, needles, and scissors and sat on the couch with the bowl of green beans. She knotted the thread around a small stick and began to string the beans, skewering each one crosswise. Each bean gave off a sweet, lightly musty scent when she ran it down the thread, stopping when it barely touched the bean before it. When she was finished, she had a string three feet long to hang from a joist in the roof, close to the gable vent where the air circulated. The beans would dry and keep for months. Leather britches, her mother called them, best when cooked with fatback, but Arie hadn't had pig in years. Thinking about a salty bit of ham or bacon was a train of thought best left unmolested.

The wind spun the roof turbine so fast that it started to hum, and the range hood vent rattled like a snare drum, and the front intermittently slapped itself against the frame. The feel of damp air found its way into the attic. Even with a sound roof above and ancient pink fiberglass insulation covering a great deal of the attic floor, there was no way to keep things snug—all those broken windows down below, and the old walls around her with their hairline splits and fissures.

With all her things seen to, she decided to attend her own self, too. She took her hair out of its braid and brushed it. That was a feat of some doing; there were not only small knots at the nape of her neck, but bits of leaves, from crawling through the underbrush to care for her snares. Her hair was thick and wavy, so she had to work the hairbrush hard. The arthritis in her wrist began to thrum. She tied up her braid again, and felt some cheered, back in the center of her life. At the mandala, she took three deep breaths. The fabric of her apron rippled slightly in an errant fillip of wind. She set her finger in the path and traced it around, back, toward the center. This was the time when she allowed memory to meld with the life at hand, all in images. She judged nothing, applied no sense of judgment to any of it, let all of it run through her and snag on nothing. This was simply life, passing through her. She was fifty-two years old, and she was alive—still alive, for some reason that didn't matter. Finger circled to the left, then up, down and around to the right, always moving toward the center. All the years on God's Land—fifteen—and after that her years with Granny and Pop. Then Pop died, and Arie stayed on with Granny, to be of help. Then Granny died. Then everyone died. Finger at the center now, and she followed the path back out. If she'd been able to see herself, she would know that her face was slack and her pupils large. All her muscles were soft and her breathing deep and slow.

The front door banged again down below, and she hardly noticed, but then heavy, dragging footsteps. She immediately bent and blew out the candles, waited. More steps inside. A female voice, slurred, hard to hear above the storm sounds. Arie counted on the noise outside to act as camouflage; she took three strides to the heating register, landing gingerly on the sides of her feet. Crouching, she waited.

"This is a bad place," the girl said, sounding both frightened and petulant. "It can get us here." More heavy footsteps gritting through the mess on the floor. He was carrying her.

"We have to have shelter, Arie," Handy called. He waited. "I am going to put us up in here. If you don't come down, I'll do it myself. But I need help with her."

She said nothing, just laid down so that she could look through the grate into the room below. He held the girl like a baby and glanced around in the dark. He'd never been here in his life, not that Arie knew of. He stepped carefully to his right, toward the hallway and the bedrooms, inching along flat-footed to avoid tripping over something. Arie could no longer see him through the vent. She got up and tiptoed directly over his head, listening. He stopped at Granny's bedroom door. She didn't hear the door open, but she heard him shuffle into the room. With all the windows intact in that room and the curtains drawn, it would be quieter, darker than the other rooms. A step, two, feeling his way. He bumped into the foot of the bed and stumbled. The girl moaned. Then a harsh cry from William, his footsteps now hurrying to the door, heaving it shut behind him.

"Fuck, Arie. What is that?" he cried at the ceiling.

Arie smiled. "Was," she said. "Not is. It was your grandmother." She spoke aloud, not knowing if he could hear her above the din outside, not caring now. He knew where she was.

The girl's moan had devolved into thin and breathless weeping. "All right," Handy told her. "Hush, now. Shut up, and we'll find a spot for us." He made it to the end of the hall and into Arie's old bedroom, where the mildewed and mouse-eaten mattress hulked and the closet door stood open. Arie lay down on the old car seat, her sofa, to add her slight weight on the barricaded hatch, and to listen. After some bumping around, Handy said, "Lie still here. I have to close things up.

"You're leaving me, Handy," she wailed. "You're leaving me to die." Arie stiffened. In a house so quiet of voices for so long, the shout was like an assault.

"Shh," he told her. "Hush up the noise. I won't leave. You'd be dead already." Moving out of the room now. There commenced a lot of effortful commotion downstairs, dragging and thumping in the entryway, so probably he was blocking the front door shut. Then the crunch and shuffle of his footsteps. He made a methodical circuit of the house, opening cupboards and cabinets, looking in the broom closet, where there was nothing but cobwebs and the dead, empty hot water heater. It was a fruitless search, Arie knew, for she'd ransacked the place herself, with utmost attention to detail, not leaving anything that would make the house seem likely to yield comfort. It was meant to seem fully picked-over and useless, and it did look so. That not a single intruder had ever so much as glanced at the ceiling, had not apparently thought to look for an attic or crawlspace despite the deep angles of the roofline outside, always surprised her—the survival instinct didn't seem to include an overload of common sense, it sometimes seemed to her.

After finding nothing of use, Handy hesitated at their grandmother's bedroom door again. In there, he might just find something. The bedding was still intact, all of it—mattress pad, sheets, blanket, comforter, and pillows. Trouble was, of course, Granny was there too, and a great deal of Granny had gone into the bedding. After three years the smell was nothing like it had once been, but her body and her bed were mostly of a piece now, melded like one thing, the liquid parts of her fused forever with the fibers of her nightgown and pillows.

Handy opened first one and then another of the drawers of Granny's highboy chest. Now he would find something worth having: most of her clothes were still folded inside. In the closet were more clothes, and even a suit of Pop's—the suit he'd worn when they'd married, which Granny had saved back when she gave away all the rest of his shirts and trousers and neckties. Everything in the room was exactly as it had been when Granny died, the framed pictures and electric alarm clock on the bedside table, her diploma from Humboldt State University over the antique desk, a mirrored tray on her vanity, filled with bottles of lotion and perfume and eyebrow pencils. The only thing Arie had taken away was Granny's dressy winter coat, because it was heavy boiled wool, shin-length and black. Handy was apparently gathering things together, by the sound. After a couple of minutes, he went out and shut the door behind him. Not superstitious about the dead. Good.

The storm was letting up some, especially the wind, although it was still raining a pretty good clip. She gave a slight thought to the garden boxes over her head—they'd be getting good and heavy in this wet— but it didn't worry her overmuch, small and evenly laid out as they were. She could hear her brother with the girl again, doing whatever he needed to tend her. She seemed to mostly start up her whining when Handy was right in with her, but he spoke to her now in a more tolerant fashion, soothing. Whatever he said and whatever he may have found to make her more comfortable, she did finally let up and go quiet. After a while, he went into the bathroom, and it took her a moment to puzzle out the sound she heard—pissing, into the empty bathtub, directly into the drain, by the sound. It was a funny thing, to hear that. Handy, who had grown up with never more than a hand-dug latrine on God's Land, putting the defunct sewers to some use, now that they were just a hole in the world that would someday collapse, forgotten and un- mourned.

"Sister."

She startled. He was standing directly beneath the heating duct, and she hadn't heard him go there. He was obviously gaining his bearings and creating a quieter path for himself down there. She didn't move nor answer.

"We can't go out again, not now," Handy said. "Not for some time, maybe. Renna's feverish and needs mending." He paused, as though considering his next words. There was a slight lisp in his speech, and his voice was pitched soft, as if not much used. "You know that I'll have to come up, Arie. Tomorrow." He seemed so close. She fancied she was feeling the draft of his breath on her face. "Maybe you'll come down, though. It would be better."

She strained to hear him say more, but there was nothing, not even the sound of retreating steps. The door of her former bedroom clicked shut, and silence from below. She fetched the short spear and a blanket from her bedroll and settled back onto the couch.

Tomorrow, then.

2

S HE HAD A WIND-UP CLOCK, one that had seemed an important part of her prep gear in years gone by. It was perched high on the west wall on a cross-member and had been all these years, gathering dust and resting forever at 3:27. It amused her in a weird, reliquary way. How could she have imagined any scenario in which keeping an eye on the hours could matter? Now it was a mute reminder that her sojourn was limited. Tonight, though, she kept glancing up toward the clock, wondering if it was hours or minutes that had passed each time she roused and listened. The weather was done with its howl, and only a few animal voices made any noise outside. After a while those were quiet, too. She wanted to get up and work or walk or trace the mandala, not just lie on the couch, hand resting on the haft of her short spear.

Finally, after what seemed like a fortnight of hours, she got up and opened the sky panel, holding the rope until the weighted counterbalance touched down on the roof without the least sound. Cool damp poured into the attic. It smelled deeply of the ocean; perhaps there had been a storm surge at the beach. Her earlier thoughts about going to the beach returned. How she'd love to walk down to the bay and over the spit to the ocean side. It had been such a long time since she'd seen it. Too long a journey, maybe three miles by foot. She'd reconciled herself to the fact that the ocean wasn't hers now, except the smell. None of it was hers, out there, and never had been. Whatever came into her hand was a gift, and when she was unable to accept the gifts, her sojourn could end.

She put the ladder out and scanned. No movement below, but a little light in the east, just the least bluing at the horizon she could see through the trees. Up and out she went, stretching until every vertebra crackled. The shingles were wet, and she stepped carefully around puddles to squat over the compost basket for a piss.

The previous night's rain had filled the water supply to brimming; she cranked shut the overflow valve, opened the lid on top, and put her face right down in the water to drink. It tasted sweet and mildly vegetal, having run off the branches of trees, across a partially moss-covered roof, and through a rain gutter with more than a little organic debris along its length. Everything passed through a simple filter of polyester batting that kept the gross matter out but allowed the invisible green taste through.

Belly full of cool water, she faced east again. The skim of dawn was now brightening, thin yellow showing on the bottoms of the moving clouds. It was a beautiful morning. Ariela McInness, who was now just Arie, lifted her arms toward the oncoming day and chanted the words taken by the Null Folk for a creed, something from some old dead poet.

"Swear, in the pale wine poured
from the cups of the queen
Of hell, to wake and be free
From this nightmare we writhe in,
Break out of this foul has-been."

Her voice was neither loud nor soft. Any human ears could hear her if they were nearby. Perhaps some reprobate would take the words to heart and give her rest, but Arie thought that only the rightful inheritors were listening just now—raccoon, possum, screech owl, mourning dove. Dog, probably, and bear. So she repeated the words. A glorious thing, to wake.

She went back into the attic energized. Her habit was to never have the upper hatch to the roof and the lower hatch into the house open at the same time, so she closed the sky panel. She got herself fully armed, put her back to the Packard bench seat, and shoved it off the inside hatch in three big pushes. She slid the bolt and lifted the board out of its place. It was quiet below—she could almost believe she was alone. But when she looked down, Handy's face appeared.

"Good morning," he said. Quiet and formal as any houseguest. Another thing gone with the Pink, she thought: casual visitors.

"Can we get her up?" Arie said.

"Is there another way?"

"None any easier than this."

"Then we'll have to," Handy said. He motioned with two fingers for her to come down.

The first thing she noticed was the changed smell. It was rank. The broken window—Arie had knocked out only one small pane —was stuffed with a hunk of clothing. Nevertheless, Handy had fixed things up a fair bit with items from their grandmother's room. By tearing down the flowered drapes from in there, he'd managed to make a passable bed. One big panel covered the mattress. The girl wore Granny's favorite quilted bathrobe, and the other drapery panel was laid over her like a blanket. She was asleep, mouth open, breathing ragged. Even next to the shiny peach of the bathrobe, her skin had a sallow cast. The marks under her eyes were bruise-dark, and the worst of the smell in the room emanated from her. Arie laid her wrist on the girl's forehead; it was hot and sticky.

"Any ideas about putting her up above?" Arie said. "It would help if she was conscious."

Handy stood in the closet, looking up at the open hatch. "That's fine work," he said, "hiding the hole this way." He looked at Arie. "Wouldn't Daddy Mack be proud of that?"

Arie shook her head. "I doubt it. I only ever knew him to be truly proud of himself."

"Oh, now," he said, a mild reproach.

"He's perhaps changed in his dotage. Is that it, Handy?" She laughed lightly. "A better man now that his worst fear is come upon him?" She moved to one side of the mattress and peeled back the makeshift blanket. "Come on, let's get her up between us and see what's possible."

"It's her left leg that's worst," he said. "It can't bear weight."

"You'd best get on her left, then."

She came to with a wail when Arie pulled her to a sitting position. "Don't hurt me!" she mewled.

Arie paid no attention, just nodded at Handy, and together they lifted her to semi-standing. She tried to protest again, loudly if incoherently, and Arie slapped her across the face. The yowl ended abruptly.

"I don't like to do that," Arie told her, "but you'll not put us all in danger because you can't keep quiet." Her voice was mild, almost pleasant. "Shut it up now, or I'll strike you again." The girl stared, shocked eyes welling tears, but she made no more protest. "If we're to really help," Arie said, "in just a minute, we're going to have to hurt you quite a little bit more. It can't be helped. Do you understand?" The girl nodded. The tears moved slowly through the grime on her face and her nose began to drip. "So," Arie continued, "what's your name, child?"

"Renna," she croaked, voice barely more than a whisper.

"I see. My name is Arie. My life is my own, Renna. And your life is yours. If you don't want me interfering, you say the word. If you stay on down here like this, you'll soon be out of it." She fell back easily on her morning prayer. "Down here, alone, you'll 'wake and be free from this nightmare we writhe in, break out of this foul has-been.' I won't stand here and tell you that coming up above with me is the better bargain."

Renna's glazed eyes rolled toward Handy, looking for some sign. Her breathing was chesty and labored as a wind-broke horse, probably from sleeping on the fouled mattress, wrapped in the dusty drapes from Granny's room. Gods knew what she might have inhaled during the night.

"It's all right," said Handy. "You're coming up with us."

"Where?"

"Up to where I can have a look," said Arie. "First, let's get you out of this slippery thing." She tugged off the satin robe and tossed it into a corner. The smell of mildew and thick dust, combined with the smell of Renna herself, was powdery and pungent.

"Walk her to the closet," Arie said. "I'll be right back." She clambered into the attic and fetched the ladder, lowering it through the floor hatch. From below, Handy braced it against the closet wall. He got Renna's stronger leg onto the first rung and then positioned himself behind, with his arm tight around her waist. When he was able to wrestle her onto the second rung, Arie leaned down and got hold of her under one arm. There was simply no way to get her up without hurting her. She wept steadily, but Arie could see that she was trying not to yell. Halfway through the hatch, almost up and in, she turned the wrong direction and scraped her bad hip against the edge. She let out a warbling cry. Through the open sky panel an answering howl ignited—two voices, three. Renna covered her mouth with her hand. Her eyes rolled up and she passed out, whether from pain or fear or exhaustion, Arie wasn't sure.

"Well enough. It's best she's out of it for a bit," Arie told Handy. She took a sheet from her own bedding, snapped it once, folded it in half lengthwise, and laid it across the rough board floor, directly under the sky panel. Handy took Renna under the arms and Arie took her under the knees, and they laid her there on her back. "Get the ladder," Arie said. "And put the hatch closed." While he did this, she opened the sky panel. The inside surface of the big panel door was painted with high-gloss white paint, and the morning sun slanted onto the surface and reflected down into the attic, directly where Arie had put Renna. In the clear light, she looked gray and corpselike. "She's just barely here, William," Arie said. "Don't set your attention on her making it."

"What now, then?" he asked.

"Up there," Arie said, gesturing at the sky panel. "You're mostly visible when you first climb out, so go up slow and check the street before you do." She handed him a yellow plastic tub that had once held several pounds of margarine. "You'll see my water in the angle between the gables. Fill this." Don't spill, she almost added, but held her tongue. A son of God's Land might be soft-headed enough to entwine his life with a stranger's, but he would never be careless with a draught of water.

While Handy went on the roof, Arie tossed a large handful of dried chamomile and calendula flowers into a bowl with water and rubbed the wet herbs between her hands to make a quick tea. She grabbed a pile of rags and bent over Renna, who hadn't roused in the least. Arie put her fingers to her carotid artery; the pulse was there, faint and racing along. She took off her shoes, old sneakers with no socks underneath; her feet were black, with toenails grown long and thick. She wore wide-legged cotton trousers closed at the waist with a drawstring. Arie untied and started to peel them down, but the fabric stuck fast to the larger wound on Renna's right hip and wasted buttock. The pants had acted as a sort of bandage and barrier, but they would have to be removed for her to heal. Handy walked overhead, and the sound was disorienting. Arie's own pulse rushed in her ears, body primed for the worst. When his feet dropped onto the ladder, she had to take several deep breaths. Her fingers had strayed to the haft of the short spear. He put the margarine tub on the floor next to Arie.

"I'm going to have to cut these britches off to clean her up, and then take care of these wounds," she told him. She'd already gotten the smaller of her scissors. "I doubt she'll wake up while I'm laying waste to her trousers, but chances are good she's going to scream bloody murder when I try to get the remnants off."

He looked distinctly uneasy for the first time since Arie had clapped eyes on him in the woods yesterday. "William," she said quietly, "this child is in terrible shape. Did you not think to clean and cover these open spots?"

"She's no child," he said. "I had no business uncovering her." He shook his head, as if Arie had asked him to do something repugnant. "She didn't want to be touched, anyway. Told me no three times. More than three, even when I just tried to see where she was hurt."

She felt a hot stab under her breastbone. *Told me no three times.* Daddy Mack's Rules. Number 24: If a man would lie with a woman, even if it is a woman whom the Lord has provided into his hand, if she should refuse him even unto a third time, he would not lie with her.

"I don't believe you were trying to ravish her, were you, William McInnis? Was it fuckery you had in mind? In your worry over defrauding, you've left this woman's wounds to fester directly into her clothing." Her voice was even and low-pitched, despite the fury blowing through her. "Perhaps if I'd told you three times no to coming into my home you'd have turned aside?" He did not reply, nor make eye contact. "You're going to help me here," Arie said, "and you're going to see a great deal of her body, much of it fouled and some of it torn, and you will not look away. Not once."

While she spoke, she ran the shears in long strokes up one pant leg, then the other. She left three sections, one on each side and one in the center. The panel on Renna's unhurt left leg fell away easily; on her right leg, Arie snipped slowly around the stuck places. They had to roll her onto her left side so that Arie could snip around the wound on her buttock. At each bite, the fabric was raggedly torn and stiff with dried blood. Careful as she tried to be, a few times the fabric pulled at the dog-bit spots, and Renna would make a little moan. The flesh under Arie's hands was swollen and stiff, hot.

Through it all Handy stayed mute, but he didn't turn away. In fact, he seemed to anticipate Arie's movements and made the difficult task a little easier. It was only when Arie pulled away the center panel of Renna's pants and handed him the whole ragged mess that he hesitated.

"Put these over by the floor hatch. We'll toss them downstairs later. Then I'll need plantain," she said. "You know it?"

"Yes. How much?"

"It's all over in the yard, particularly out by the back fence. Take that," she said, pointing to a heavy burlap sack. "Fill it if you can." She told him where to find the rope ladder. He was clearly glad to be sent out.

Arie watched, some relieved when he paused at the top and scanned the street. She turned her attention to getting Renna as clean as she could before debriding and tending her wounds. When she'd told Handy the girl was fouled, she meant it quite literally. She wore no underdrawers, and Arie couldn't imagine how long it was since she had properly bathed. She washed her as she would wash a neglected child, a task she'd been trained to perform when she was only a child herself. Mammy Delonda loved being pregnant. She did not love mothering. When each one was born and mostly weaned from the tit, she'd pass it off to the older girls. I'm centered in my purpose, she'd say when full of a new baby, giving Daddy Mack her eternal doe eyes and caressing her belly in a way that made Arie and her sisters decidedly uncomfortable.

"Does she think it's a crystal ball?" Lulu said one night, when she and Arie and Mercy were whispering together in bed, the younger children finally asleep. This had caused a great deal of snickering. "Look into my crystal ball," crooned Lulu, always determined to act out her role as chief instigator among the three of them. "I will tell your future. You will...you will..." She moved her hands mystically over the surface of her own flat stomach. "You will marry a dark stranger—"

"Picked out by Daddy Mack," Mercy interrupted.

"Oh no," said Lulu. "This stranger lives in town. He drives a car. He will make you the mother of millions. Oh dark stranger," she whispered, and now she cupped her little breasts in both hands. "Give me a baby."

Arie and Mercy put their faces down in the pillows to stifle the laughter, but even laughing Arie felt sick at her stomach when Lulu said things like this. The fact was, Lulu's little charade was not awfully far from the truth that was passed to them from their parents—except for that part about a car, and Daddy Mack not picking out the husband. Every night at bedtime the girls received the laying on of hands.

After their teeth were brushed and they were lying in bed—Arie, Lulu, and Mercy in one bed, the three younger girls in another—Daddy Mack and Mammy Delonda would climb into the loft. The quilts were folded down to the foot of the bed. Daddy Mack would bless them one at a time, because he needed both hands. One big, rough hand would rest on her forehead, and one would rest on her pubic bone. When nightly blessing had first started, back when Arie was much younger, the second hand would be on her tummy, but over time it went lower and lower. It couldn't get any lower now without getting up to mischief.

"Bless this vessel," Daddy would intone. He would look at the ceiling during the blessing, and it always seemed to Arie that he was trying to convince someone of the rightness of the blessing by speaking in a deep, commanding voice. "See this, your daughter, feeble in her ways. Make her womb strong and worthy of bearing your seed. As you did with your vessel Mary of old, redeem, dear Savior. Make her the mother of millions." The last part was a kiss on the forehead. Mammy Delonda would crouch by the loft stairs throughout, silent. After all the blessings were given (even to Creigha, who was four and asleep), Daddy would go down to the boys, and Mammy would follow, giving the girls a little wave as she turned out the overhead light.

Downstairs, where the boys bedded in sleeping bags on the floor, Daddy Mack said a single prayer for all. The boys were exhorted to look forward with joy to the day God provided them a woman, the weaker vessel made worthy by receiving his seed. They were told to be mighty in exploits and multiply God's children upon the earth, that the faithful might once more subdue creation as Second Adams. There were five boys then, aged twelve to nineteen.

Arie had crept from bed once and peeped over the railed edge of the loft. The boys received their blessing standing up, arms crossed over their chests, feet planted wide apart. Daddy Mack stood the same way while he prayed over them, and often he sat and chatted awhile afterward. Mammy Delonda was nowhere to be seen. Sometimes they'd beg him to arm-wrestle, and Daddy would laugh and say no, no, no, until they finally pleaded long enough. They'd all wrestle, starting with Morgan, the youngest. With Morgan, Daddy would pretend to struggle for a long time before pinning his arm over. It took a little longer with Beckman and Harold; with the two oldest boys, Thomas and Zachary, it really was a contest. Zach was about to turn nineteen around this time, and the wrestle was hard, both he and Daddy with red faces, bulging muscles and tendons. But Daddy beat Zach. That night and every night.

She took up a bar of soap and several rags from a box under the table. One by one she dunked the rags, wrung them out, and laid them over Renna's wounds. Once those places were covered, she washed her from waist to knees. The smell of her was noxious. The rope ladder rattled against the side of the house, and Handy crossed the roof. The burlap tow sack bulged under his arm.

"Wash a double handful of that," she told him. She lifted one of the wet rags and pulled gingerly at a shred of bloody cloth. It peeled up a bit. Renna whimpered but didn't wake. Arie counted silently to three and yanked the ersatz bandage off. It went with a slight tearing sensation, and Renna's eyes flew open. "Don't!" she shouted.

Handy knelt next to Arie with the mass of pulpy plantain in the yellow bucket. Renna was naked from the waist down, but he didn't avert his eyes, which gave Arie hope that he'd be of use to her during the unpleasant task ahead. "Girl," she said to Renna, "I know you're in pain, but if I don't do this right the first time, you may just as well be dead." She leaned close to Handy. "Talk to her a minute while I get something to help take the edge off." When he turned a blank face, she shook her head. "Quiet and kind. It doesn't matter what the words are."

Handy took one of Renna's hands. He leaned close to her face and began to murmur. Arie couldn't quite hear the words, but it was the sound of a man soothing a white-eyed horse. Her protests fell a notch into intermittent quiet crying.

On the east wall of the attic under a gable, a set of shelves ran nearly floor to roof joists, filled with canned food, bottles of whiskey, vodka, and moonshine, boxes and baskets of candle ends, chunks of soap, matches, salt. Herbs hung upside down in bunches. Arie retrieved a brown bottle capped with a dropper.

"What is it?" Handy asked.

"Tincture," Arie said. "The herb. Indica, mostly." She removed the stopper and lifted Renna's head. "Drink this," she said. "You'll feel a little better." Feverish as Renna was, Arie wasn't certain this was true, but she wanted her to believe it. Handy continued to stroke her hair away from her face and speak low words of encouragement. When she pursed her lips, Arie tipped at least half the bottle into her mouth, a great deal more than she would ever take herself. It was a bitter dose and made the girl grimace, but the effect was almost immediate. Her head lolled back over Arie's arm, and her eyes glazed again.

"Let's do this quick," she told Handy. "We need the plantain bruised hard, but don't mash it all the way. Just break down the fibers some." The three biggest wounds were soaking under wet cloths. "I'm going to pull away these pieces of her pants," she said. "I'll rinse the hole with tea and then slap the plantain on it. Ready?"

"Yes," he said in his quiet way, almost as though speaking to himself. His was nothing like the voice of Mammy Delonda—kittenish and fluttery—or the voice of Daddy Mack—everything a proclamation. His pale eyes looked dark in the low light of the attic.

She started with the smaller wounds, reckoning that the larger one would hurt more and make Renna fight harder. Without hesitating, she took hold of one corner of the soaking fabric and ripped it free. Renna grunted and her head jerked to one side, but she didn't try to pull away. There was a row of punctures, fat and raised at the edges like a set of tiny red atolls. They immediately began to seep blood in the center, and Arie let them bleed a little before pouring the tea over the spot. Before she could ask, Handy held out a limp leaf of plantain. It gave off a bland smell and was slightly slippery between her fingers, fibrous and cool. She evened the plantain over the bite, pulling the edges out like a thin green bandage. Renna breathed evenly and laid still, eyes closed. Arie tended two more bites similar to the first, neither of them exceptionally problematic. She moved squarely in front of the largest wound.

"Better put the bucket here by me," she told Handy. "Get ready to hold her." He did as she said, setting the bowl next to Arie's knee. He had spread the plantain leaves out across the edges of the old margarine container so that it was easy to see how large each one was. Positioning himself next to Renna's head, he crossed her arms over her chest and held each wrist lightly.

"Ready," he said.

This time, before tearing it free, Arie tested the edges of the dampened shred of trousers stuck to Renna's thigh. The area was hot to the touch and stank. She poured more tea over the place and patted until the whole thing was saturated. Then she grasped the fabric in two places and yanked. Renna lifted her head from the floor and howled.

"Yes, I know," Arie said. "That must hurt like hell. Hold her," she told Handy. The dog had been able to set a deeper bite here, and the flesh was badly torn. The sticky yellow scab that had grown into the fabric of Renna's pants had pulled mostly away, and the wound bled freely. Strands of the cotton pants clung in the edges of the mess. All around the bite, the skin was humped and swollen red. She tipped the pitcher; cool tea drizzled over everything. Tendrils of blood traced down the girl's white thigh. Arie looked at Handy.

"Do you have a good hold?"

He braced his feet and snugged his grip on Renna's wrists. She cried steadily now, sounding like a child who has lost all hope of comfort. "I have her," Handy said.

Arie didn't hesitate. She laid her fingers flat on either side of the wound and pressed down. Renna's chin tipped at the roof, and she loosed another guttural cry that petered out into soft sobs. She couldn't move under Handy's grasp, though, and seemed not to even try to break loose. White-yellow pus oozed from the ragged edges; Arie rinsed it away with tea—once, twice, three times, until only clear fluid and traces of blood filled the gashes. She did her best to pull free the random strands of fabric that stuck fast, like coarse hairs. Finally she was able to cover the spot with plantain. She layered three large leaves there, patting, thinning, spreading them so no part of the wound was left uncovered.

"Here," Arie said. She handed over a plastic water bottle. Renna panted now in gasping little whimpers. "Give her a drink. That tincture's helping, but she's got dry-mouth." She drank greedily, coughed a little, drank more.

"That's enough," Handy murmured. "Hold on to me. Almost done."

Renna belched loudly. "Sorry," she croaked. "That was rude."

Arie laughed. "Aren't you polite," she said. "Not to worry, girl. More room out than in." She was already wetting the last and largest wound, this one straddling Renna's lower right hip and buttock. She set her jaw against what she would see underneath. "Almost done," she said. "Ready?" She held Handy's eye; this was actually a question for him, because there was no earthly way Renna could be ready for what came next. He nodded once and set his grip again on her.

It was awful. Getting the last gash uncovered seemed to take forever, so embedded was the cloth and dirt in the places where the dog's teeth had sunk deepest. This time the pain broke all the way through the effects of the weed tincture. Renna screamed herself hoarse and tried desperately to writhe away from Handy and Arie, threatening, promising, begging. Arie finally straddled her knees, doing her best not to dislodge the already-poulticed places. Handy knelt right at Renna's crown, cradling her head snugly between his thighs while maintaining his hold on her arms and hands. It was no good trying to verbally calm her—she couldn't have heard them over her own howls, even if they'd been speaking directly into her ear.

The gash in Renna's hip told its own story. There the dog had struck more than once and torn a plug of flesh right out. Under the muck of half-scab and filthy fabric, the skin and fat layers were flayed down to muscle in grisly striations. It was a miracle she had been even marginally ambulatory. The smell was awful. Arie tried not to hurry this, even though the cries bouncing wall-to-wall in the attic room were shockingly harsh after so many months of solitude. Sweat trickled between her breasts and down her lower back. By rights this wound should have been stitched up. Arie had the means, but closing the wound now would trap the incipient infection. So she prodded and pressed and rinsed, while Renna yelled and pleaded for her to stop.

Then Arie realized she was hearing another sound, this one even louder than Renna, coming from downstairs. Harsh, hysterical barking.

"Damn." She elbowed sweat off her forehead and tossed a look at Handy. "We have to shut that thing up."

"You almost done? I can go down." The barking was deep and chesty, breaking on a high note. Bull terrier in its voice—favorite pet of the time just prior to the Pink, and well suited to the new world.

"Give her some of that," Arie said, gesturing at the bottle of moonshine. "Not too much. A sip, or she'll puke it." Handy shifted his grip to hold Renna's wrists with one hand, and he uncorked the bottle. "Pour a little in here," Arie said, holding out the plantain container. "Hold on now." She tore one of the smaller leaves and chewed it vigorously, pulled a chunk from her mouth and rolled it into a plug. This she dipped into the moonshine and then pushed the dripping mass into one of the deep punctures that ringed the edges of the wound like a ghastly bracelet.

"God," Renna screamed. "Fuck you. God will fuck you!" Down in the rooms of ruin, the dog redoubled its frantic barking. It seemed to be carrying on directly under the heating grate.

Arie spit another hunk of chewed plantain into her palm. "It'll be worse than a fucking," she shouted above Renna's howls, and the dog's. "God will ignore us entirely. Elvis has left the building, is what my grandmother liked to say." She packed four more punctures with the plant material, working as quickly as she could, then rinsed with tea and spread the last of the bruised leaves onto the red and wretched mess.

"All right," she said to Handy. "Get rid of it." He released Renna. She put her hands over her face, weeping, but had quit bucking about. "I have her," Arie said. "Hurry, before more show up."

She thought he would go down the inside way, but instead he crossed soundlessly to the sky panel, up the ladder and out. "Easy now," she told Renna. "Hard part is over but for healing." Below, the dog had paused in its barking and was pacing beneath the grate, whining and growling. Arie stood, stiff from crouching over Renna for so long. She purposely stamped first one foot then the other on the attic floor. The dog immediately threw itself at the wall under her, snarling and digging at the rotting drywall.

"It's here," Renna wailed. She lifted her head and stared around the attic with huge and frantic eyes, as if the dog were about to leap out of the shadows under the eaves. Arie didn't try to quiet her now. Instead, she started singing at the top of her lungs. "Bye low baby, bye low baby, bye. Papa still loves you, still loves you.

Bye low, baby bye." The dog whirled in a fury below them, and Renna moaned.

There was a sudden shift in sound, a surprised snarl that ended in an abrupt yelp of pain. Then quiet.

"What is it?" Renna whispered. "Did it go?"

"Shh," Arie said. "William has sent it away."

"William?" Renna rubbed at her eyes.

"Yes. Are you thirsty again?" She lifted Renna's head and helped her drink. "That's the herb at work. Here—a little more." Down in the house, something large slid across the floor, then thudding sounds came from near the front door.

"I have to pee," Renna said, her voice starched and querulous. "But I can't get up."

"Hold on. Don't wet yourself, or you'll foul those bandages. Do you understand?" She hurried to the work table and grabbed up the shallow tin basin she used for washing dishes and shelling peas. There was more thumping and dragging downstairs. "I'm going to help you lift your bottom," Arie told Renna. "Try to use your good leg to lift up." She managed to slide the basin under her in the nick of time.

Renna moaned roughly. "Burns," she said through clenched teeth.

"I imagine so," Arie said. When she'd bathed Renna, she'd seen for herself the raw flesh between the girl's legs. It would be a blue-eyed miracle if she wasn't suffering a urinary tract infection as well. She trickled the last of the cool chamomile tea over Renna's genitals, blotted her dry with a clean rag, and helped her lift up enough to slide the basin free. As she did, there was a knock that made her jump a little—

Handy at the inside hatch. She hurried over and pushed the car seat-sofa aside.

Handy pushed aside the hatch cover. He was compactly made and muscular through the arms and shoulders, and when he put his palms flat on the attic floor he was able to hoist himself up in a single easy motion. "I threw it out front," he said, "and I blocked the door shut." There was blood streaked across his palms and bare forearms.

"Good."

"In case anyone heard the noise."

"Anyone or anything," Arie said. "Did it get at you?"

He shook his head.

"Help me here." Together they barricaded the inner hatch again. "Go up top and wash," she told him. "I'm going to get her settled for the night. And take that basin with you," she said. "Empty it into the compost. She'll need it again before morning." He climbed up, balancing the piss pot with a finicky care that made Arie turn away to hide a smile. She checked Renna's pulse. Still too fast and feeble, but she was breathing deeply, exhausted from the day's trauma.

Stowed under the eaves was a mildewed wooden crate that held a remnant of their grandfather's belongings. Her hand found a compact bundle wrapped with a stiff nylon cord, and she pulled out an ancient down sleeping bag—from Pop's backpacking days as a young man. Despite its advanced age, the manmade fabric was some sort of indestructible plastic and was in one piece, even though the goose feathers inside had deteriorated to dust. This she set out for her brother to use. From her own bedroll she removed the coverlet and pillow. She arranged them on the Packard seat for herself, meaning to move Renna off the damp spot where they'd doctored her and onto the remainder of her bedroll when Handy came inside. When he didn't come back, she climbed onto the ladder and poked her head out.

He was squatted down on the balls of his feet, profile low in the early-afternoon light. He motioned with two fingers that she come to him, and pointed out at the street. Arie crab-walked to him and looked down. Two dogs were down below, sniffing at the carcass of the dead one Handy had thrown into the street. The more aggressive of them was pulling mightily at the rear haunch, bracing its front paws, and jerking back and forth so that the dead dog jounced on the broken asphalt as though convulsing. The other one darted intermittently forward, intent on the torn belly, but each time it did, the alpha dog, wide face matted with gore, swung around on it with a single low snarl. There was clearly no contest; the secondary animal fell back, rump held low. Its ribs stood out like a washboard under the filthy pelt, and it drooled profusely.

Arie pulled the slingshot from her pocket. Handy smiled. She hesitated for only a moment before handing it to him. Her aim was excellent, but her eyesight wasn't, not anymore. "Here's more," she whispered, and gave him the three stones she always kept with the sling. He loaded the pouch and moved closer to the edge of the roof, angling himself for a more direct shot. Arie crept to her ammo pile, smallish heavy stones, sharp edged, that she collected on the regular every time she was out. She stuffed a large handful into her apron and moved next to Handy so that he could grab more at will. He cocked his head slightly to the right, sighting with his left eye, same as her.

The rock flew with an electric whisper of sound, but the missile went slightly wide. Neither dog noticed. Handy chose another stone, hefted it in his palm before loading the sling. Getting a feel for his weapon, she thought. The lines of his body were terribly familiar to her; if she'd never seen his face, she might have known his posture. He was her brother Beckman all over, though Beck was long dead, in the ground for decades.

Handy pulled the sling again, shoulder and upper arm bunching, straining the black bands taut as they could go, and the stone whistled down. When it struck the alpha dog behind one ear, the animal staggered sideways without a sound, losing purchase on the haunch it had torn almost free. The other dog jerked in surprise and then rushed forward. It buried its face in the dead dog's guts, growling. The alpha dog swayed, holding its head low, shaking it as if to clear its vision. Suddenly its front legs buckled and it toppled over. The instant it was on the ground, the lone survivor rushed it and went for the throat. The wounded animal tried to thrash away, kicking its hind legs, but the strength of the jaw clamped on its throat was too much. In the manner intended by centuries of breeding, the attacking dog held fast, taking every chance to set its teeth more firmly and bear down harder, waiting for its victim to bleed out or suffocate from a crushed windpipe. While the alpha dog succumbed with a few final spasms, Handy reloaded.

The dog now muzzle deep in the guts of his fellow took the blow in his shoulder. He leaped away with a howl and a yip and snapped savagely at the air.

"Shoot," Arie said. "One more time."

Handy loaded, standing this time, and let fly. When the stone struck its ass, the dog ran for the trees behind the house, silent, head forward, heavily-muscled chest and shoulders straining.

Watching it go, smiling to herself, Arie caught movement from the corner of her eye, something between the houses over there, down in the shrubby brush at the tree line. Another dog. Not a pit bull, this one. She scrambled to the sky panel and grabbed the binoculars from their nail just inside. Handy was crouched again; Arie got next to him and raised the glasses. It was a German shepherd, hunkered low in the brush, and when she got the binoculars focused Arie was startled to realize the shepherd was looking not at the street, where there was now an unattended meal to be had, but up at the roof, directly at her. The focus of its brown eyes was so clear and close through the binoculars that it caused her to duck slightly.

"What is it?" Handy asked.

"Another one," she said. "Not a pit, though. See it? Between the houses over there, under that scrub alder."

Handy squinted. "I do now."

"It's in good shape," she said. They both spoke in low voices, almost a whisper. "Why isn't it going after the dead ones?"

"Smarter, maybe."

"Smart doesn't matter when they're hungry. Hey—" The shepherd had looked suddenly over its

shoulder into the wooded shadows, then turned away
so quickly it seemed to melt into the brush. As it did,
Arie saw a form, back in the dark. Barely discernable,
but tall. Up on two legs. Definitely human. It was there
and gone, the shepherd clearly following its lead.
"Shit. We have a watcher."

Handy dropped low. "I don't see anything."

"Already moved into the trees," she said. "Let's
get inside." She automatically glanced at the rope
ladder—it was up. "Get a full bucket of water. I'll grab
food."

They wrestled the five-gallon bucket down the
ladder, and Arie filled her skirt with carrots, kale, and
tomatoes. Her aim was foods they could eat raw.
While Handy bolted the sky panel, Arie lit a few
candles and stooped to check on Renna.

Her dark hair lay in matted clumps across the
makeshift pillow, and she gave off a smell of sour
musk, but it was nothing like the powerful stink she'd
thrown earlier. Dark circles ringed her eyes like
bruises. She lay on her unbitten side, hands tucked
beneath her cheek like a child's, sleeping deeply. Arie
touched the poulticed wounds with the lightest
pressure, checking that they were still damp. The
smallest one was starting to dry, and Arie dampened it
with a few drops of tea. Renna didn't stir in the least.
"She's sweating some," Arie said. "That's a good
thing."

Handy was at the work table, wiping down
carrots with a damp rag. "Maybe the fever will break?"

"Maybe." Arie knew the problem was deeper than
a little fever, but if the plantain could draw out the foul
infection in the larger wounds, Renna might live.

"We'll eat a cold meal," she said. "We don't dare make fire right now with someone maybe around."

"Are you sure it was a person?"

She glanced at Handy. "It's been awhile, but I haven't lost the difference between person and beast. Hungry?"

He nodded, barely visible in the dim attic light. The spinning vent above him circled over his features in a dizzy spin of half-moons. "I'll eat," he said.

"There's jerky. Rabbit." She told him where to find it. They sat side by side on the Packard seat sofa and ate. Handy rolled the stringy meat in a leaf of kale and popped cherry tomatoes one at a time.

"So you don't see people," he said.

"Almost never anymore. At first, yes. A few. I know there were some right around here who lived through the first week of the Pink. I could hear voices now and again. Crying." She washed down a bite of the salty meat with some water and wiped her mouth on the back of her hand. "Hardly anyone came down around here, though. Why would they? Dead-end street."

"Scavenging."

She bit off a chunk of carrot. It was sweet and earthy. "Yes, there was some of that for a while. I tried barricading things, but it never kept anyone out. Bolt a door and they bust a window. I was forever running up here and hoping no one would think to look. Scared all the time."

He looked at her levelly. "Are you scared now?"

She leaned into the old seatback. "Fear kind of burned out. Every time I came through, I felt the One Thing come over me."

"One thing."

"We're an anomaly," she said, and hesitated. "You know the word."

He nodded once.

"Humans used to be part of the One Thing."

He wiped his hands on his heavy jeans and said nothing.

She shook her head with a little snort. "I imagine you're holding onto Daddy's teaching, though. 'Exercise dominion over the bounty of creation.' That it?"

"You want more water?" he said. He fetched them each a fresh mugful.

"What would you give for coffee?" she said, and sighed.

"Coffee. Well hell, I barely remember it."

"I remember," she whispered. The dark bitterness, the rush. "There must be something you dream about," Arie said. "What comes back to you at night? What shows up?"

There was a staccato clittering across the roof peak. They both went still. It came again. "Raven," Handy said.

Arie stood, took his mug. "Let's hope it stays awhile," she said. "It will sound an alarm if something ugly turns up." She rinsed the cups in her little enameled pan and set them aside.

"With the dead down there, it will stick around."

"There'll be feasting."

"There's a whetstone here," she said. "I assume Daddy Mack taught you to use it?"

"That fell to Mother."

"You must be kidding," she said. "I never saw Mammy Delonda lay her hand to the stone in my life." She handed him her blades. "Nor to much else. Here, sharpen yours, too."

He moved to a spot on the floor that had a little extra light from a porthole window set in the west wall, far up under the peak of the gables, and began to work the edge of Arie's knife first, deliberate in all his movements.

Watching him, having another breathing soul in this space—two of them besides her—rubbed at her mind. She'd forgotten the everlasting distraction of other people. It was like having an itch crop up, a relentless, restless gnawing of possibilities—where is he? what is he doing? what will happen next? Her eyes sought the labyrinth and began to circle. She longed to stand up and trace it with her finger, but didn't want Handy watching. Back and forth her eyes went. The raven's talons skittered across the roof, then it croaked from down in the street. Into the center. Reverse and travel out, as the thin and gritty sound of the whetstone rose and fell. In, around. Out, around.

She slept.

It was full dark when she woke, hearing footsteps below. She held perfectly still. She opened her eyes. The attic was black inside and smelled of people. It took moments before she thought to wonder where Handy was, whether he heard the intruder. Rolling onto her stomach, she positioned herself over the heat exchange.

It was too dark to see anything. To her right, several feet away, Renna was breathing deeply, making a little snore on the outbreath, and Arie wished she could put a hand over the girl's face to stop the sound. The intruder in the rooms of ruin was being exceptionally furtive, moving in a slow circuit and managing to avoid the noisiest debris. She clutched the shaft of her short spear and listened, willing Renna and Handy to stay silent.

When the footsteps moved down the hallway and into the back bedroom, Arie rose into a crouch, balancing like a sprinter waiting for the starter's pistol. She took a deep breath and walked swiftly and softly on the balls of her feet to the car seat sofa, meaning to add her weight to the top of the inside hatch. As quiet as she meant to be, the attic floorboards seemed to thud and creak under her. She had her hands stretched into the dark, feeling for the sofa's steel frame, but when she got there the seat was pushed aside.

Heart thudding dully at the base of her throat, Arie squatted and felt her hands around the edge of the hatch. It was unbolted and slightly ajar. The intruder was right below her, almost in the closet. Her eyes widened in the dark. The pale wooden rectangle of the hatch was visible to her; she stared at it, breathing shallowly through her mouth. She waited there, short spear raised. Just as the intruder entered the closet right below her and fumbled at the shelves, she moved onto the hatch and knelt. There was a nudge from underneath, just the slightest feeling of pressure under her, and a hesitation. Her mouth had gone dry. Another push under her feet, harder this time, and a little grunt. The thick plywood lifted and dropped minutely, not more than an eighth of an inch. She breathed shallowly. Her right hand trembled with the effort of gripping the short spear. She didn't weigh much, but with her weight on it the hatch would be tough to move from the confines of the closet below. There was a little hesitation beneath her, and for one awful moment Arie imagined a gun aimed at the hatch, could almost feel the bullet punch through the wood and into her lower body. "My life is my own." She mouthed the words soundlessly. "I sojourn."

Knuckles rapped the hatch. Softly, a gentle enquiry.

"Ariela."

She dropped the short spear. It hit the floor with a thud and clatter.

"Let me up." It was Handy.

She stood and yanked the hatch open. Shaking, she clasped her hands together to keep from grabbing hold of him. "What are you thinking?" she whispered. "I was ready to put my spear into you."

He pulled himself up and slid the hatch cover back in place. "Checking," he said. "A look at the doors, to see if anyone was creeping around."

"Only you," she said. "You're the creeper." She felt around for the short spear and tucked it back into her belt. She made her way to the work table and lit a tiny stub of candle that was stuck by its own wax onto a plastic plate. She positioned it among shelves and dishes and tools so that it threw only the smallest glimmer of light.

He touched her shoulder. "Sister," he said.

"Don't." Arie took a sideways step so that his hand fell away. The weight and warmth of his fingers was a shock. The kindness in it seemed a threat. She felt invaded from all quarters.

"You were sound asleep. I figured if you woke you'd have to know it was me down there."

"I've only had grubbers and defilers and animals down there for years. And her," she said, gesturing at Renna, who had slept through everything.

"And now me." His face was half in shadow, half lit by the candle.

"Why would you be my first thought?" She went to the washstand and splashed her face. "Do you understand, William, that I have a way of being here? It's my calling." She stepped into the puddle of candlelight and held out her forearms. The raised scar tissue was deep purple. "You know this?"

"Deaders," he said. "The voluntary extinction."

"You wanted to say 'the heresy.' Didn't you?" She could see it on him.

He hesitated. "It's called that."

"By some." She laughed and pushed her silver hair back from her face, retied her apron. She'd been wearing the same clothes all day and longed to change into her night things. "There was an extinction anyway, wasn't there. And nothing voluntary about it." She peered at him in the dim light. "Was that one a heresy? I imagine not." She made a dry little spitting sound. "That one was chalked up to deific punishment, I'll wager. Though I haven't heard it called that firsthand." She swept an arm to indicate the space around them. "I don't have much chance to hear what's wagging on tongues these days, eh? What tongues there might be left to wag."

"Nor do any of us, I guess."

"I guess." She sighed. "Let's us tend this one and have it behind us awhile." She picked up the plate and little candle stub and knelt beside her. "Renna," she said. "Are you with us?" She touched her forehead, her neck. "Can you speak?"

Renna rasped something unintelligible and swatted feebly at Arie's hand.

"There you are," Arie said. "Talk to us a little."

"Shouldn't we let her sleep?" Handy asked.

"She could sleep herself right to death. She's burning up again," Arie said. "We need to cool her. Get water and rags." She pulled back the sheet so that Renna was bare. The poulticed wounds were now sticky, almost gooey to the touch.

Handy brought the water. He kept his face turned partly away.

"Come on," Arie said. She handed him a wet rag. When he hesitated, she took hold of his wrist. "William," she said quietly, "she's your project. I'm not doing all the work for you. Start with her face and neck." He knelt and wiped tentatively at Renna's forehead.

"That's it. Sponge her down, or she'll cook for sure." Tiny rivulets of water dripped down the girl's face. "Keep the cloth wet," Arie said. "Really soak her. Good. Now work your way down—chest, armpits, inside the elbows and knees." She stood.

Handy hesitated, the wet rag dripping onto Renna's neck. "Where are you going?" he said. His face was hard to make out in the low light, but Arie thought he looked next door to terrified. She patted his cheek. A spark of pity lit inside her. "Brother, there is nothing to fash you here. You want to help her. So help her. I'm getting more plantain."

"Yes," he whispered. He chewed a corner of his lower lip as though tackling a monumental task, and wetted the cloth again. He lifted one of Renna's arms to swab into her armpit. Her poor body was so emaciated and torn, Arie was astounded that he could feel anything but pity to see it. An ancient snatch of song flitted through her head: He's just a poor boy from a poor family. Daddy Mack's progeny. Son of a quiver-filler and a glassy-eyed breeder. She grabbed a double handful of the plantain from the bag Handy had filled earlier and squeezed, lightly breaking the tough fibers. The bland green smell rose up to her, clean and redolent of the summer just past.

Handy stroked the wet rag down Renna's front and flanks. Water trickled sideways, making a dark spot on the bedding beneath. She reached up as if to wipe her face, but her hand fell back. "I'm cold," she said thickly. "Get me a sweater, Kara."

"Good," Arie said. "We'll cover you in a minute, Renna. Squeeze a little over the poultices," she told Handy. "Easy, just get them damp." She fetched a kerosene lamp and brought it close enough to show what she was doing. She wetted her fingers and wiped at the edge of one wound. The old poultice was sticky and thickened with draining fluids. She rolled it away, taking care not to touch the wound if she could help it.

The three smaller bitten places looked much better, the swelling having gone down considerably and the puncture wounds already knitting together at the edges. Plantain was good that way, for the mending process. Renna growled a little in her throat, sounding more peeved than pained. Handy ran the damp cloth over her face again. Her skin looked almost translucent, blue veins clearly visible under her pallor. She put out her tongue and pulled a corner of the wet rag into her mouth, sucked on it.

"Give her a little to drink," Arie said. "Not too much at once." She laid fresh leaves over the clean wounds while Handy steadied Renna with one hand behind her head and helped her drink. He seemed to have forgotten his own discomfort again, and when he laid her head back, he brushed his thumbs across her brow. "Close your eyes," he said. "Almost done." He looked at Arie to confirm it; she nodded.

"This last one now," Arie said. She touched the edges of the large poultice spread over the mess on Renna's hip.

"I have her." He took her wrists, as he had that morning. "Go ahead."

Once the poultice was cleared away, the large wound was still ghastly, almost harder to look at than it had been. Clean now, no longer oozing blood and pus, the outraged flesh beneath looked like a fresh butchery, meat ready for the cook fire. Long tags of skin, pale as a dead fish, lay useless across the flayed and garish muscle beneath. The central wound looked much deeper now. Arie once more packed the plantain into the hole and covered it all with several damp leaves. There was no more smell of infection, but there was heat and swelling all around the bad spot.

"I don't know if it's these bites making her fever up," Arie said. "It could be something else." She went to the shelves and felt around in the dark until she found what she wanted: a plastic bottle of aspirin, a little everyday miracle they'd taken so for granted before the world ended. Even past their potency date, they were precious. She crushed two and swirled them in a cup of water. "Renna," she said, "drink a little more." She grimaced at the bitter taste, but swallowed it all.

"She needed those sooner, it looks like," said Handy.

Arie shook her head. "I was worried she might bleed. Help me turn this."

Together they flipped the sheet and covered Renna again. It clung to her wet skin. Arie gave her another small dose of Indica tincture while Handy cleaned things up. "Let's put out the lamp," Arie told him. "Candle, too."

"It's dark," Renna whined. "Night light." The childish quality of her voice made the hair on the back of Arie's arms prickle.

"We're right here. Sleep."

"You never do it," Renna said, her voice trailing out. "You're always mean."

Arie nodded in the dark. "I am."

ล้า ฬ์

Since she'd had some rest, she took first watch. Handy stretched out on the Packard seat sofa, but Arie knew he was awake.

"What did you see down there?" she asked him.

"Downstairs? Nothing."

"Nothing?"

"Nothing much," he said after a moment. "The dead dogs. Something at them."

"The raven?"

"Nah. Bigger. Not too big."

"Raven probably got enough. Coon, maybe," she said. Talking to him, she found herself falling into the cadences of family patois, a certain squatty rhythm that they all used, being short on outside influence and long on their father's daily rap.

"Maybe. Something smallish and hungry is all."

It was quiet for a few minutes, nothing stirring, only Renna's small snore.

"William, why did you come?"

"Handy," he said. "I prefer it, if you will."

"Sure, then. Why are you here in the bottoms, Handy, running after the black sheep?"

"The family," he said. "The old man wants you. He had a vision."

She snorted. "Yes, that's his way." She was on the floor, leaning against an upright post, not quite trusting herself to lie on her bedroll. The spinning turbine vent hummed in the darkness, showing the slightest glint of silver at its edges, a moonlit flicker show.

"You're not a black sheep, anyway. More like—" He faltered there.

"A cautionary tale."

"No. A fable, I suppose."

Arie started to laugh, quietly at first, then harder, until her head was thrown back and tears were on her face. "A fable," she repeated. "One more famous harlot, is that it? A middle-century Jezebel? Famous reprobate and prodigal." She wiped her nose and eyes on her sleeve. "Or would I have to come back to God's Land to be a prodigal, do you reckon? Will Daddy Mack order up a fatted calf?"

Handy stayed mute, and the silence rose up around them.

"Who's left of them?"

"Garrett," he said. "Jubilation. They live in the big house with Father. Auntie Lulu is alive, and Morgan and Big Zach."

"Tallula's your sister, not your auntie."

"I've been calling her that right along."

"I suppose. She's old enough to be your ma— might as well be an auntie. Like me." She thought for minute. "You didn't say Mercy."

"Mercy's gone. Thomas and Harold, too."

"Ah," she said. It was a little arrow in her heart. Her last memory of Mercy was the day she, Arie, bugged out. Mercy and Tallula were her only confidants, and Mercy had stood at the south gate in tears, watching her go, early sun brilliant on her blond head. "Awful hard for Morgan," she said, "losing his twin. And the other pair? What about Hanna and Gerta?" Mammy Delonda had had two sets of twins and claimed it was lucky, like rolling double sixes when they played Monopoly. Since Mammy didn't actually do much with babies but birth them and nurse them awhile, Arie supposed that was as good an analogy as any.

"Hanna is...she's still alive. Gerta's gone a long time ago. I never knew her."

Arie sighed and rubbed her eyes with the heels of her hands. "I didn't know," she said tiredly. "That's a terrible shame. Little Gertie-birdie—she and Hanna were just sprouts when I left. Creigha, too."

"Pretty Pox took Creigha the very first."

"Pretty Pox—that's what you call the Pink?"

"Big Zach heard a doctor call it that."

"Zachary saw a doctor?" She felt stunned. Daddy Mack had always vilified medical providers in the extreme. Arie hadn't seen a doctor until she was sixteen, when Granny had insisted she have a physical.

"He was down the hill the day it started, picking up a tank of fryer oil at the Snack Shack. He had a couple of his grandkids with him. When people started dropping, some park rangers set up a sort of clinic at the forest service office. The fry cook at the Snack Hut is on the volunteer fire crew. He and Zach ran the grandkids over there. Probably shouldn't have."

"They didn't make it."

"No. He couldn't even take them home. Their bodies. They kept all the dead in an equipment shed."

"You know, they wouldn't have lived anyway."

"No. They didn't want to let Zach leave, either. He said one of the rangers, an old guy with a belly over his belt, got all puffed up and stood in front of the doors with his hand on his gun. You know Zach, though."

"I did," she said. It was strange to imagine her eldest brother with children old enough to have children. He was twenty-three when she ran away, not even mated yet. Generations had been sown in her absence, had sprouted up and been mowed down as if never here at all. "Pretty Pox," Arie mused. She thought about her neighbor's baby, how beautifully flushed and ruddy he looked the day he died in her front yard. The striking beauty of the dead was remarked on without fail during the few days that news could still be accessed. That, and the ruthless efficiency of the virus. The last numbers she heard before the world went dark was a kill rate of over 90 percent. She did the math: seven of her thirteen siblings survived. "Near half of us still here," she said. "Long odds."

Handy got to his feet with a grunt. "I'd like to have a knock of that shine you used on her leg this morning."

"Yeah," she said. "It's back on the shelf over there." He made his way in the dark without any trouble. She heard him pull a cork, sniff, and pull another. Sniff again. Then he was getting a mug from the work table, moving around the attic as though he'd been here for months, sure-footed and almost silent. "You see in the dark, Brother?"

He chuckled under his breath. "A little. Not owl. Dog, maybe. Want some?"

"No. And go easy. All I have is all I have." The attic was stuffy after a long day and with the three of them shut in. "I'm going up top a minute," she said.

"What about the watcher?"

"I'll have a look first. I always do."

She had the sky panel open and the ladder standing when he said something so low she almost didn't hear. "What's that?"

"Why did you leave her in the bedroom like that?" he said. "To let her lie there and...and spoil away."

"Ah," Arie said, "Granny." She stepped onto the ladder and took a deep breath of the cool night air. A gibbous moon, waxing and well past the meridian, put the time somewhere after midnight. "That was her idea."

On the roof, a damp chill rushed over her skin. She savored the sensation. As Handy had said, there were several small animals working over the bodies of the dead dogs. The low, fat moon provided plenty of light. She took her time with the binoculars but saw nothing. She laid them aside and busied herself with small tasks, things she would have done during the day if she hadn't been otherwise occupied—checking the filter on the water barrel, pulling a few weeds, turning the compost pile. When her joints began to thrum in protest of the temperature she knew she had to go back inside or risk being very stiff come morning.

She stood in the one sheltered corner where angle met angle, looking west. Full moon in three days. She wondered if she'd be able to slip out for the ritual, if Handy would interfere. She wished them gone, Renna and Handy, though it was unthinkable that the girl could travel anytime soon. She closed her eyes and counted, calculating how soon she could send them away. "My life is my own," she whispered. She imagined the mandala in front of her. Her hands rose and traced the labyrinth in the air.

The old woman was just visible in the moonlight, standing in a shallow corner. During the time since he first discovered her here, he had only seen her out during daylight. He couldn't quite see her setup, but clearly the roof was crucial territory, and he was fairly sure she had supplies there, perhaps food. She had rarely come out at night—he'd only seen her do it twice before—and those were brief appearances, hardly visible as she scurried and stooped, gathered and retreated. Tonight, though—this was something new. Her hands moved in the air before her, as if conducting some strange music or making a painting.

He squatted in the scrub, well back in the trees, and watched. Talus leaned heavily into his thigh, dividing her attention between the old woman on the roof and the little feast of dead dog going on in the street. She made no sound, Talus, didn't even pant. The upright points of her ears pricked forward each time various scavengers squabbled over the corpses. Other than that, she remained motionless. The young man, the one who had killed the wild dogs with a slingshot, was nowhere to be seen. In the attic, apparently.

Except for the rhythmic movement of her arms and hands, the old woman's slender body was still and straight. Moonlight caught here and there on her profile and in the waves and curls of her hair, which fell past her waist. Earlier today there had been a lot of yowling and weeping from inside that house. A female voice. After all that, he hadn't expected to see the old woman again.

But this afternoon she had appeared on the roof, ready to help the young man sling rocks. Watching her solitary habits all this time, he'd not imagined she might find an ally. A mean aim, that one. And a timely kill. The dogs now being picked over by night creatures had been pressing him for weeks, edging in on his camp. The wild ones were harder and harder to drive back lately. In their early days in the woods, he'd been able to let Talus go on the roam when they were out. No more of that now. She had learned quickly to shake her puppyish exuberance and stick by his flank.

She understood the least twitch of his fingers and the minutest click of his tongue.

He watched the woman a few moments more. His place in the woods had suited for summer, but it wouldn't work through winter. Too wet, and too many tracks closing in. Not just dog, either. A few days ago he found mountain lion prints just outside his perimeter line. The thought, sitting here in the dark, made him want to peer into the trees behind him, perhaps to see a pair of green eyes reflecting the moon. Something watching him watch the old woman.

If she could acquire one confederate, she might acquire more than one. Time was getting thin—he'd have to make a move, sooner rather than later.

The instant he stood upright, Talus rose too, seeming to intuit his intentions before he knew them himself. She turned toward camp, a full stride ahead, attentive but relaxed. She'd alert him to threat. His crawly sense of menace faded as he formulated a plan.

3

FOR THREE DAYS THEY STAYED PUT. Each time the old poultices came off Renna's leg, the healing had advanced, and although she slept almost constantly, the fever had finally broken into sweats and passed. Arie and Handy went onto the roof only twice a day, once in the twilight of sunrise to empty the swill bucket and get fresh water, and again at sunset to collect what they needed from the garden boxes. Both of them did intermittent perimeter scans with the binoculars, but they saw nothing unexpected. Arie thought even the animals were particularly quiet, as though the killing of the wild dogs had dampened their usual vocal exuberance.

They kept watch in shifts. Handy insisted on going downstairs once each night for a quick look out the windows. "Someone could get close and us not know it," he told her. "Better to take a look than not know." She argued that she had managed quite well all this time by leaving the downstairs mostly to itself and not taking that risk, but he was immovable in his quiet way. It was clear that he wasn't seeking her permission. They kept the doors downstairs blocked shut.

Arie and Handy were still out on the roof in the dim morning of the fourth day when Renna woke up. "Hello?" Her voice was scratchy and tentative, faint from down in the attic. "Who's there?"

Arie was clearing the rough filter on the water collector. "Go down," she told Handy. "Before she starts yelling." She rapped the filter—layers of polyester batting held taut in the double ring of an old plastic embroidery hoop—against the edge of one garden box. The filter had collected the usual mass of leaf fragments, tiny pebbles, and random small insects from the gutters and roof runoff.

"Yeah, we don't want her waking the neighbors at this hour," Handy said. It was cold enough that his breath made pale steam when he spoke. He knelt over the rope ladder, checking for fraying or loose knots. Arie was continually surprised at the way he silently went about these sorts of tasks without prompting on her part, as if he could guess what needed tending to before she could mention it. At this remark, she glanced up. The first blue light in the east showed the tiny smirk on his face.

"What a relief," she said. She fitted the filter back into place. "I've been holding my breath hoping a comedian would show up here."

Handy took the larger container Arie had filled from the jerry can. "How's the supply?"

"Fair," she said. There had been another light rain shower, but the three of them were going through stored water even faster than she had expected. "There's a barrel behind the house if push comes to shove."

"Are you there?" Renna called again.

"Hold up, we're coming," Handy said. He maneuvered himself onto the ladder with the water container in one arm. Arie pulled a young dandelion out from among the beet greens and tucked it in her pocket to eat later. She took a last long look at the street and tree line, and followed Handy down.

Renna was propped on an elbow, squinting at the open sky panel. Her dark hair flared out around her head, despite the loose braid Arie had made of it.

"So, you're awake," Arie said. "Do you know us?"

"I think—" She squinted a bit, as if trying to recall a bit of historical trivia. Her eyes, huge in her gaunt face, wandered from Arie to Handy and back to Arie again. "You were in the woods," she said to Handy. "On the night it rained, you helped me. And you were—" She blinked up at Arie. "You were mad at me?" She shook her head. "You hit me, right?"

"I did. To quiet you."

"Okay," she said, not seeming at all disturbed by the fact. "Can I have food?"

"Good you have an appetite," Arie said. She stowed the water and flipped a tattered bath towel from the top of a plastic milk crate. The crate was full of apples, windfalls mostly, small and blemished. "I'll mash you up a couple of these," she told Renna. "It won't be cooked sauce, but they're good." She tossed one to Handy. "Try that," she said. "You might have to eat around a wormhole. Not fussy, are you?"

Handy took a tremendous bite out of it. "I've eaten a worm or two," he said around a mouthful. He sat on the floor a couple of feet from Renna, facing sideways and sneaking surreptitious looks at her.

Arie brought the dish of pulverized fruit. "Looks to me like you can probably feed yourself today," she said. "Let's get you sitting up some. Handy, be handy and help me." Renna laughed, a rusty sound, then put a hand over her mouth as though he might react badly. "Don't fret," Arie told her. "Like a lamb, this one."

Together they eased Renna into a semi-sitting position, propping her against a nearby support and tucking blankets behind her. She moaned some through gritted teeth when they first lifted her forward, and by the time she sat upright there was a thin sheen of sweat on her pale forehead and upper lip. Arie handed her the bowl. Despite shaking hands, Renna got the first spoonful to her lips and began to eat in earnest, clutching the spoon in her fist like a young child.

"Go easy," Arie said. "You've only had liquids the past couple of days."

"It's good," Renna said, a little breathless.

"A lot of people had backyard apple trees in these older neighborhoods," Arie said. "There are three still bearing fruit right around here, though I don't know how long that will last." She held up her own apple and turned it speculatively. "Food apples were a purely human notion from the start. So they're dying out, like us."

"We still have the orchard on God's Land," Handy said. "Twelve trees."

Renna, licking the last bit of food from the bowl, stopped and looked at him. "What's that?"

"Home," he said. Now he looked at her directly, and everything Arie suspected about his feelings were in plain evidence on his face. "Mine and Ariela's. Yours too, maybe."

Arie plucked the dish and spoon from Renna and gave her own apple core to Handy. "You know what to do with these," she said. She wiped her fingers on her apron. "My home is here. Handy's home is quite a trip from here," she said, "and if you're to travel with him, we'll have to get you on your feet again. Let's practice a little." She motioned to Handy. "Take the bad side."

"But I can't," Renna said. "I'm hurt."

"You're rather remarkably healed, actually," Arie said. She had an arm snugged behind Renna's shoulder blades, and the girl's right elbow clasped with her other hand. "All of the bites, except for that worst one, have closed up dry and clean." She patted Renna's back. "That's due to your youth and the good earth's bountiful help. Now," she said, hurrying on before Renna could gather enough momentum to fight them, "on the count of three, Handy and I are going to lift you up, and you're going to get that good leg under you and push. One, two—"

"Wait, I—"

"Three," Arie said. Renna was upright before she could protest further, with Handy doing the greater share of the lifting to compensate for her bad leg. She swayed a little in their arms.

"Dizzy," she said. Her voice was thick and unsteady.

"You've been lying down for days," Arie said. "That's just your heart working against gravity again." They stood still with Renna between them, letting her get used to standing. She let her head fall to one side so that it rested on Handy's shoulder. Arie pretended not to notice. After a minute or so passed, Arie patted her back again. "Still dizzy?"

"Better, I think," Renna said.

"Stand up straight, then. We're going to take a little walk."

"I can't. It hurts too much," she moaned.

"No doubt it does," said Arie. She shook the brown bottle of Indica tincture—now half gone—and uncorked it. "Take a little of this. It'll help." She expected Renna to object or at least ask what it was, but she sipped from the bottle without a question. "Don't you wonder what it is?" Arie asked her.

"Yes," said Renna, wincing a little at the taste of it.

"What if it was poison?"

"Is it?" she asked, not looking as if she cared.

"No. It's medicine," Arie said. "Helps with pain. Not that it matters after you drink, eh? You're just as dead, if you ask about it after."

Renna blinked at her. "Why would you poison me now?"

Handy stifled a small laugh, and Arie shot him a look. "Here now," she said. She got a firm hold on Renna's arm and shoulders and took a smallish step forward, forcing Renna to come along—Handy too—or risk toppling forward.

"Ow!" Renna wailed. Handy was doing so much of the work for her that Renna's right side barely touched the floor.

"Quiet down," Arie said, "and take another step. That medicine you just took will hit in a minute. Lean hard on us and make your good leg do the work." She poked Handy in the bicep. "Don't do it all for her," she said. "Unless you plan on carrying her piggyback all the way to God's Land."

He nodded. Arie forced them into another step. Then another. Renna's face contorted, and she made a soft sound of effort and pain each time she had to move her right leg, but she stopped yelling, perhaps remembering the slap Arie had given her on the first day.

"That big bite got down to muscle," Arie said as they inched their way across the attic floor. "That's the one that's giving you the real hurt. It's knitting together and trying to work for you at the same time. It's stiff." Renna nodded slightly, saying nothing. She was close to panting and her breath smelled of acetone, strong enough to overpower the odor of her unwashed hair. "But if you don't work it," Arie added, "it's going to wither on you. Maybe never heal right."

"Please, can I stop for just a minute?" Renna said, sounding as though she'd just finished a footrace.

"Sure," Arie said. They'd made it about six feet and were almost to the makeshift sofa. "Catch your breath a bit and we'll settle you over there." She pointed at the car seat.

The rhythmic sun-shadow pattern of the spinning turbine vent dappled the floor at Renna's feet. She painstakingly inched forward the toes of her right foot, out from under the loose skirt that Arie had put on her, and into the fluttering reflection. "That's pretty," she whispered. The light and shade fled over her dirty, bony foot. Somewhere outside, a blue jay scolded.

"Take a deep breath," Arie said. "Almost there." They got to the sofa and eased her down until she sat on Handy's bedding. "There," Arie told her. "You'll be ready to run in no time." She realized how dire that sounded under the circumstances and amended. "Or dance the watusi."

Renna looked up, arming sweat from her forehead. "Dance...what?"

Arie shook her head. "It was a thing my granny used to say. They did it in the time before the Pink, a long time before I was born. I'm going to check your hip, so you go ahead and lay over for a minute." Renna did so in stiff little increments. She sighed and closed her eyes.

Arie pulled Handy aside. "She needs more food. Did you smell her breath?"

He nodded. "What was that?"

"It's her body eating itself. Healing uses up a lot of power, and she's been too out of it to do much more than take bone broth." She lowered her voice. "What's needed most is some fresh meat. She needs the protein."

"I can go for it."

Arie gave him a level stare. "Stop a minute and think with your best mind, not whatever passes for a man's mind when a fertile woman is in the room."

He looked at the floor and scratched one ear. "You fancy yourself a mind-reader, sister. It wears."

"I'll concern myself with your delicate feelings later. Right now I want your carefullest estimation about going out there alone. Do you calculate it's a reasonable move, or are you showing off?"

He ticked off reasons on his fingers. "It's been a full three days and nights since you saw someone. We've set a watch round the clock, from the roof and from down below, and have seen no threat since." He paused, looking at her carefully. The ambient morning light falling through the narrow east-facing window caught in his pale blue-green eyes.

"Bone in your throat?" she said. "Say the rest."

"We don't know what it was you saw. Could have been a person, but—"

"But you think not?" She searched his face. "My gut has been a fine guide since the Pink."

"I think we don't know," he said again. "Maybe it was a person but not a threat. A woman alone, or a man working to stay hid. On my way here I saw plenty. Even youngsters abroad at times, fourteen, fifteen years old—could have been like that."

Arie looked at her mandala, traced it with her eyes. It was quiet inside, quiet outside. "Yes," she said. "I know what I saw. It was human, and it was full-grown. But I don't know what it meant. It hasn't moved on us in all these days, and that sort of hesitation doesn't seem likely for a desperate person." She paused again, thinking. "My notion is that it saw the dead dogs, maybe saw us kill the dogs, and has judged us not worth the effort." She put her hands on her hips and looked up at him. "Yes," she said again. "I think it weighs to the good for you to go out. We're of one mind on it?"

He dipped his chin in agreement. "We need the fresh meat for the road home, too. For all of us."

"Repeating a thing doesn't make it so, William. Once you and she depart, I'll be fine. But yes, you'll want some extra meat to dry for jerky—I reckon a week or so and we'll be able to accouter you and she'll be fit to walk by herself." She said this last in a near whisper. "You know where the snares are. Set them, and set the fish snares, too, before you come back. Take this." She tucked a worn burlap sack into his belt, then took his hand and traced on his palm the directions from the main path to her fishing spot. "Anything you can't bring back in one piece, leave down there, back in the trees. Bringing a carcass into the streets up here is a dinner bell to everything with legs." She rolled his hand into a fist and squeezed it between hers. "Try not to leave sign," she said. When he took a breath to speak, she shook her head. "I know you know it. I know you're careful. But I have to say the words."

He put his free hand to her face and stroked a hard, warm thumb over one cheekbone, light as a passing thought, and dropped the hand before she could react. "It's all right, Ariela," he told her. "I hear you. I'll be back before dark, no matter what."

She opened the sky panel and stood at the bottom of the ladder. "You should take the slingshot."

He stopped at the top, as usual, for a quick scan. The air coming in was quite cool and damp, though the sun was out and it was getting on toward mid-morning. Arie was certain that, before many more days passed, wet weather would set in for the duration. It was one more reason to get these two quickly out and on their way. Otherwise she might end up stuck with them for weeks to come while the coastal climate served up its usual late-autumn slops.

"Better we keep the sling here with you," Handy said. "I have my knives, and I'll hack a quick spear from that dead rhododendron." He pointed down into the yard. Arie knew it was a good choice. Old rhodies produced a great many long branches that were reasonably straight. The wood was hard enough to be effective but not so hard that Handy couldn't carve a rough point in a hurry.

Arie went onto the roof with him. He let down the rope ladder and went over the side. Once on the ground, he wove the ladder into the bushes. While he chose a four-foot-long branch and whittled the narrower end into a wicked point, Arie checked the street with the binoculars. There was virtually nothing left of the dead dogs, so thoroughly picked over were the carcasses—even their bones had been largely carried away, leaving only dark stains and flattened patches of stiff hide here and there to mark the place where they died.

Spear over one shoulder, Handy paused at the gap in the overgrown fence, taking plenty of time to gauge the street, and set off toward the river path in an easy, loping trot. Arie watched until he disappeared into the trees. An unexpected hollow space tried to open itself behind her breastbone when she lost sight of him, and she yanked her consciousness back. There's the trap, she thought. Damnable species blindness—I see and respond to my own. She stood. Tonight was the full moon, and she was determined to get out for the ritual. Having Renna awake would be a fine distraction for Handy. She would make it work, even if it meant going on the sly.

Back in the attic, she decided to leave the sky panel open for a while. Renna had maneuvered herself back into a semi-sitting position, and she hummed a little tune, pulling her fingers through her hair, working out knots. The tincture was still in her system.

"You ought to use a comb for that," Arie said. She fetched one.

"Thank you," Renna said. "I forget your name."

"It's Arie. You remember his?" She inclined her head toward the open sky panel.

"Handy," Renna said. "Your brother."

"Who saved your life."

"You look too old to be his sister." More humming.

Arie gathered what she needed to tend Renna's wound. The comment made her smile. "I am too old," she said. "But it's true anyway. Give me that." She took the comb from Renna and worked it through the hair on the back of Renna's head. "What you really need is a bath in the river, but that's a few days off. A bucketful will have to do."

"I used to have a bathtub. A long time ago."

"Of course you did," she said. "We all had tubs. How old are you?"

Renna was quiet. "I forget."

"That doesn't sound likely."

"What year is it?"

Arie kept combing. "What year do you think?"

Renna looked into her lap. "How long since everyone died?"

"Twenty months. Almost twenty-one."

Renna counted silently on her fingers. "Then I'm still nineteen. My birthday is in December. I'm a Christmas baby."

"Christmas," Arie said. The word hung in the air between them, a wistful oddity. "Well, you're nobody's baby now, I suppose."

"Arie," Renna said, "do you know why this happened?"

"Why? Oh girl, that's a confounding little word. You'd do well give up on why. The good world manages itself fine without why. When we're gone, we'll take why with us, along with all the black answers it drags behind it."

Renna stared, her face bleak and exhausted. Arie rested a hand on her knobby shoulder. "Never mind now," she said. "I'm going to warm some water, a bucketful, and we'll get you washed."

Arie had her undress a little at a time, exposing only as much skin as necessary to the cool air in the attic. She began with Renna's bad leg and hip, so that the two bandaged areas were washed while the water was clean. At first, Renna did nothing to help, just sat still while Arie tended her, limbs limp and pliable as a rag doll. "Look down here," she told Renna, "where you were bit."

"I don't want to see it."

"Too damned bad," said Arie. She put two fingers under Renna's chin so that the girl had to look her in the eye. "This is your body," she said. "Not mine, nor anyone else's. It's time you started doing for yourself. Your body," she said again. "Your life is your own."

Renna chewed her top lip, but she twisted around to look at her hip and thigh. "Oh," she said, and gingerly touched the deep, pink spots that were already mostly healed. "I thought it would be more awful."

"It was plenty awful when you got here. You're a quick healer. That's your age. Here now." She handed Renna the rag and chunk of soap.

She scrubbed her face, neck, and upper body. Arie helped with her hair, pouring the wash water through while Renna bent over a second basin, and she gave her a stiff brush to work on her deeply grimed hands and feet. Finally, while Arie turned her back, Renna squatted over the bucket and washed between her legs.

"Pee in that bucket when you're clean," Arie said. "It'll save me a trip later."

"All done," she said. Arie had given her clean clothes: a sweatshirt and soft old set of pajama bottoms. When she turned to take the bucket of bath water—now so opaque with soap scum and the dirt of the body it resembled the swirling murk of a disturbed creek bottom—Renna looked like a child brought in from a downpour. The clothes, though not over-large, looked voluminous on her. Her wet hair clung to her face and neck in dark strings and dampened black splotches on the shoulders of the green sweatshirt. She huddled on the Packard seat, shivering. Dark smudges of exhaustion showed beneath her eyes.

"Wrap up in Handy's sleeping bag. And pull up that hood—keep your head warm." She set the bucket of swill by the back wall to be taken topside later. "How did those apples sit with you? Any bellyache?"

"No. I'm hungry, though."

"Yes," Arie said. "I can smell it on you. Here." She handed Renna a chunk of rabbit jerky. "You need the protein while you heal," she said. "Easy does it. Small nibbles, and chew until it's liquid in your mouth. Then swallow."

Renna bit off a corner of the pale meat. "It's good," she said. "Kind of sweet."

"I always enjoyed a rabbit." Arie took a piece of jerky for herself and rolled the remainder back in its paper wrapping. "There are a great many rabbits these days. I've tried to think why that is—seems like all the extra dogs and coyotes would have knocked their numbers back, but I keep finding them in my snares."

"God is providing for you."

"Is that so?"

Renna nodded and chewed.

"The last time we spoke together of God, you had a very different opinion." She opened her mouth to tell Renna what she'd screamed at Arie that first morning: *God will fuck you.* But looking at her gaunt, earnest face, Arie thought better of it. "I won't look sideways at the bounty either way," she said.

"This is a good place," Renna said. "It was your house?"

"My grandmother's. But yes, mine after she died."

Renna's gaze travelled over the tall shelves—boxes, baskets, bottles, piles of goods from top to bottom. "You have everything in here."

"It's been plenty," Arie allowed. "Up until now."

"I went in so many houses. I hardly found a thing." She twiddled the bit of jerky between thumb and forefinger. "Well, sometimes there was something, small stuff like what you'd drop and not notice under the couch. But mostly it was piles of..." She shrugged.

"All the things we couldn't live without." Arie looked at the shelves, too. Years of accumulating that started long before the Pink happened.

"I found this giant box of microwave popcorn once. I tried to hold the first bag over a fire." Renna laughed, an utterly infectious and unexpected sound in the attic. "Oh my gosh, it was so stupid," she said. "I was holding it up with one of those giant barbeque things." She mimed the scissors action of tongs. "I thought if I sort of, you know, toasted it—"

"Like a marshmallow," Arie said, knowing how the misplaced attempt must have ended.

Renna laughed again. "Like a marshmallow. The grease in it made the whole bag just...whoosh. A torch. I dropped it right in the fire," she said, grinning as though telling a story about a camping trip gone wrong instead of a desperate act of hunger. "It started popping. All these burning pieces of popcorn were flying out everywhere. I got three burn holes in my sweater. But I found a few pieces later that weren't too black."

"You've been alone all this time?"

The girl said nothing at first. She nibbled around the edges of her jerky, making a smaller and smaller bit, then put the last of it in her mouth. She licked her fingertips with delicate precision, like a cat cleaning itself. Not looking at Arie, she shook her head. "No, not all the time."

Arie sat very still. "So you've seen others. Been with them?"

"Yes."

"Near here?"

"Pretty near." Renna was almost whispering now.

The tiny white hairs on Arie's arms stood up. "How near?" she said, matching Renna's quiet voice. A wind was kicking up outside, and the old stove vent began its thin metallic clatter. "How many?"

At first Renna sat silently, and Arie thought she might clam up altogether. But she leaned back on the old car seat and crossed her arms tightly over her scant chest. "The high school," she said. "They have a sort of—" She paused. "Like a village, I guess."

That small sense of alarm deepened. "A village?" Arie asked. The local high school was four miles away, as the crow flew.

"No," Renna said, "not a village exactly. More like where they put people during the twenties, those places for terrorists."

Arie stared at her. "The peace camps?" Renna was talking about the Muslim internment that took place shortly after the 2024 elections. "Those happened before you were born."

"My dad showed me pictures."

"You're telling me someone has turned the high school into a sort of prison." Arie couldn't picture it. She hadn't thought there were enough people left alive in town to group together so specifically.

"They make you think it's a good place," Renna said. "That's how they get you in. It seems safer." She swiped at a tear with the back of one hand.

Arie knelt on the floor in front of her. "How many?" she said. "How many people are there?"

Renna brushed away another tear, but her face looked set. "I don't know for sure," she said. "There were seven, I guess, when I...when I left." She counted on her fingers, mouthing silently to herself. "Yeah, seven men in the main building. And some women. But in the bunkers, I don't know."

"Bunkers?"

She nodded. "That's what they started calling the portable buildings. The music room, the typing room, and that long skinny building where the science classrooms were."

Settling on Renna's uninjured side, Arie sat close enough that their shoulders and elbows and hips touched. "People are kept there?"

"I don't know how many," she said again.

"You were kept there, though."

"Not in the bunkers. I was always in the main building."

"You weren't captive, then? You were part of their group?"

Renna rested her chin in the palm of one hand. "I left," she said, and pressed her long fingers across her lips, literally keeping her own mouth shut.

"Yes you did," said Arie. "And here you are." She wouldn't push Renna about it now, but she had to get a sense of how many people had been pulled into the high school compound, discover what might be going on there—whether they had supplies, how large a problem they were to her.

From the open sky panel, over the sound of the rising wind, there was the slightest thump against the edge of the roof. "Here's Handy," she said. "Fish for lunch, maybe. More healing-up food for you." When he started down the ladder, she stood ready to help him carry things in.

He was much larger than Handy. In the instant it took for Arie to register the intruder, he dropped into the attic in a single fluid move, landing squarely between the women and the ladder. She tensed, body poised to find an escape, traitor mind yelling at her to get between the man and the girl. But the Packard seat rested squarely over the inside hatch, and her knife lay useless on the work table. *Stupid*, she thought in that endless moment. She reached for her short spear. Before she had even tightened her grip on the handle, he had crossed the space between them and yanked it from her belt, cutting the fleshy pad beneath her thumb as he did. Renna scrambled awkwardly off the seat and tried to scoot into the dark recesses under the eaves.

"Stop," he said. Despite his deft maneuvering, there was a faint quaver in his voice. He pulled Arie in front of him, short spear in one hand, his free hand crossed over her collarbone so that he gripped her opposite shoulder. His chin grazed the top of her head so that her hair caught in his short beard. He smelled of campfire and damp living, rough living.

Renna froze, face averted, staring off into the unseeable places around the deep edges of the room.

"You're not moving well," he said. "You go crawling around up here and you'll end up with wood in your hands and knees. That, or fall through the ceiling. I saw through the windows downstairs. You'd break your neck in that mess."

"Conditions have declined," said Arie, her voice steady, quiet. "No prize, this place. Better if you move on."

He raised the short spear closer to Arie's upper body. "Get back over here," he said to Renna, "before something happens that we can't undo." He motioned to the Packard seat with a jerk of his head. When he did, the blade of the short spear, honed to the thinnest possible edge, made a whisper of contact with Arie's throat. It wasn't deliberate; he didn't appear even to realize what was happening. But she felt the fine sting, a delicate slash probably no wider than a hair's breadth, and the beginning trickle of blood, warm on her skin. The soft flesh under her old chin was a small protection, like the wattles of a turtle. Watching Renna crouch in the dark, Arie thought that up against Renna's smooth neck the blade would get up to real mischief.

"You're cutting me," Arie said, voice firm and declamatory. "If that's your intention, you may just as well do it properly." Before he could react, she grasped his forearm with both hands and simultaneously lifted her chin, banging the top of her head into his jaw. "I am only a sojourner. Pilgrim, will you give me rest?" She tried to pull the blade closer. He cried out and shoved her away. With her low center of gravity and practiced sense of balance, Arie stumbled only a little. She faced him, knees bent slightly, ready to run, or pounce.

"Arie?" said Renna behind her. "Are you hurt?"

"Just an accident, I think," Arie said, not taking her eyes off the man.

He stared at her, slack-jawed. "What the hell is wrong with you?" Under the thick scruff of beard his face was pale and damp. He looked to be in his late twenties, though the deep lines etched between his dark eyes may have put him closer to Handy's age.

"Wrong with me?" Arie said. She smiled, and there was an atavistic shift in his posture, a tiny shrinking away. "I'm suffering an overabundance of company," she said, "and I'm waiting to see if it's terminal." She looked him over with slow deliberation, crown of head to cuff of jeans. "You don't seem entirely well, either. You're sweating."

He armed his forehead reflexively with one sleeve. "Enough," he said. "No matter what you try, I can grab that one before she gets halfway out." His voice sounded far more tired than menacing. "Tell her to get over here."

He was right, of course; no matter how Arie might distract or waylay the man, Renna couldn't exactly make a run for it. Why was Arie primed to protect her anyway? The impulse filled her with a niggling fury. All these years she'd practiced it: manage herself. Leave others to manage themselves. "My life is my own," she said. "And this girl's is hers," said Arie. "Not for me to interfere."

"I'm interfering," he said, "and I'm done asking." He raised the blade of the short spear with a hand that had begun to shake in earnest.

"Don't," said Renna. "I'll come out." She did, ducking back into the middle of the space in an ungainly, crabwise scuttle and back onto the sofa.

"Better," he said. The expression on his face, far from being the black threat that he seemed hell-bent on projecting, was one of weary frustration. Whatever his plan had been when he jumped inside, it was definitely not going as expected. "You, too," he told Arie.

She settled herself on the Packard seat. Renna grimaced at the sight of Arie's collar and shirtfront. "Oh damn, you're really bleeding."

"It's not bad," Arie said.

The man pulled a coiled length of nylon cord from his jacket pocket and tossed it into Renna's lap.

"Tie her wrists with one end of it," he said. "If you leave any slack, I'll tighten it, and I can't promise she'll have a lot of feeling in her hands after that."

Arie held out her hands side by side. She strained to catch any sound of Handy, but the tinny rhythm of the stove vent and the wind in the trees around the house were all she could hear. The open sky panel and her knife on the work table tugged at her attention, so she nailed her gaze on the intruder.

"Not like that," the man said to Arie. "Put the insides of your wrists together."

She rotated her forearms, face placid, not taking her eyes off him. The cut part of her thumb was a raw inch, ugly but not bleeding much. Renna saw it and hesitated.

"Go ahead," Arie said.

Renna fumbled with the loop of cord, paying out a length from one end. She bent over Arie's hands, winding the rope in careful arcs and struggling with the long remainder that was now puddled in both their laps and draped onto the floor. "Is this hurting you?" she said.

"Move away from her," he said.

"She's an old woman. You cut her." Renna's voice was rising. "Look at the blood on her, you pig."

"Stop—" Arie began, but before she could say more the man strode forward. He pushed Renna against the seat back and held her there, his big fingertips pressing against her collarbones.

"Yes," he said. He was breathing heavily, searching Renna's face. "Stop." Renna went quiet, and Arie thought she might drop her eyes, but she sat rigidly, glaring as though she'd like to bite him.

He held her a moment longer, then sighed and took his hand away. Where each finger had been was a round, pink impression in the pale skin of Renna's chest. Tears, more rage than fear, Arie thought, now brimmed in her eyes.

With a small step backward, he looked bemusedly at his open palm. "Don't you know that I could break your neck with one hand and put out her eye with the other?" His voice was utterly without rancor, casual: Did the mail come yet? Shall we order pizza? Do you think it will rain? He almost seemed to be asking himself the question. He placed the hand over his heart, and for just a moment closed his eyes. This caused him to sway tiredly, and he shook himself.

"Make some room," he told Renna. She scooted away from Arie, favoring her right hip. He quickly ran the cord from Arie to Renna and tied Renna's wrists, then looped the remainder around the back frame of the car seat, knotting it with a hard tug that made the old springs squall. He checked Arie's hands; the binding was apparently snug enough to satisfy him. With the two women secured, he climbed the ladder, Arie's weapon in one fist. He cocked an ear, listening, and eased up to look around the roof. Renna reached for Arie's arm and squeezed, no doubt hoping that Handy was out there waiting. Nothing happened.

Back inside, he looked around, getting his bearings. His eyebrows went up, and he hurried to the table. Arie figured she was about to lose her knife, but instead he reached for the plastic crate of apples, still pulled out and uncovered. He picked up two, one in each hand, and ate them in huge, gobbling bites, not bothering to spare the cores but eating them whole.

"Really good," he said, mouth full. He took a third and ate more slowly this time. As he chewed, he examined the short spear, getting a close look at its business end. "Did you make this," he asked Arie, "or did he?"

"It's mine," Arie said. "My weapon, my work." Her heart sank a little. He must already have seen Handy. But she kept the concern out of her voice. "My place. No he here, though. Just us." She gestured with her bound hands. "All in decline, as I said. You saw for yourself. Man big as you really will fall through the ceiling. Best watch your step."

"Ah," he said. "So I may just as well move on, is that it? Nothing here worth having?"

"It does for one small woman near to death and one crippled-up girl no use to anyone. We can maybe find you something for the road. But this place? There's surely better."

"Better?" he said, and made a derisive sound. "I guess you've been tucked up in here for the duration." He secured the short spear under his own belt—which gave Arie an angry jolt to the gut—and patted its handle, tightly wrapped with sinew. "Here's a thing not in decline. All this," he said, gesturing at the shelves and boxes and baskets of goods, "is about staying alive." Swallowing the last of the apple, he came close to Arie and Renna and squatted down, wiping his hands on the knees of his pants. "I've been watching you on and off for a pretty long time," he said. "I've tried to be patient and I've tried to be careful. I know your coming and goings, and I'm not buying your sob story. No more bullshit," he said. "Where is he?" Perhaps he meant to sound stern, but what Arie heard in his tone was entreaty.

"Gone," Arie said. "On to greener pastures."

"No," he said, shaking his head. "I saw the two of you, up there slinging rocks together, tag-teaming to take out those dogs." He ran a hand through his short black hair, making it stand up in greasy shocks. "Thanks for that, by the way. I'm pretty sure they were getting up the nerve to eat us."

"They already tried," Arie said, laying her palm on Renna's thigh. "Made an appetizer of her. She'll not walk again."

"Is that so?" He studied Arie's face. "It would be great if we could be straight with each other, wouldn't it?"

Arie stayed silent.

"I could tell you that I'm only trying to get myself safe. That I could be of help here—maybe we could be of help to each other," he said, and shook his head again. "But you have no reason to trust me and I have a hunch it's not be in my best interest to buy everything you tell me." He glanced at Renna then back at Arie. "I'm not so sure she's as helpless as you're letting on. And I don't think your slingshot buddy is gone for good."

"You think it's a lie?" Renna said. "Look here, at me. See for yourself." She turned sideways, facing Arie, and there was something on her face, a bright, desperate hope that made all of Arie's senses rise to full alert. Renna used her tied hands to yank her skirt up nearly to the waist. She was bare under her clothes. Even in the dimming midday light the bite marks, in their various states of healing, stood out garishly on the taut, pale skin of her leg and buttock. The bandaged area on her hip had seeped pink and yellow fluids and had a grotesque caved-in look. "Want me to peel the bandage off for you?" she said. He stared at her ruined flank, mild revulsion on his face, and to Arie's surprise, Renna laughed.

It was at that moment, while the intruder's attention was caught, that Arie saw from the corner of her eye what Renna must have seen first: a flicker of movement at one corner of the sky panel.

Handy.

Arie tensed. Everything seemed to happen at once. He flung a handful of stones into the attic. They banged in, rattling into corners, bouncing against wall and floor and ladder. At the same time, he must have thrown a handful at the turbine vent. They clanged and clattered against the spinning metal. The intruder, still squatting slightly, recoiled. He raised his elbow in a warding-off gesture, and Renna drove her foot squarely into the side of his head, her heel slamming him in the eye. Arie heard Handy hit the floor of the attic, but she couldn't wait for him. She dove from the Packard seat and fell on top of the man, pulling Renna with her by the cord holding them. He was already on one knee, pushing himself up and bringing Arie with him as if she weighed nothing. Renna was dragged onto the floor, landing on her bad side. She howled, but braced her feet against the rough attic floor, using her weight like an anchor. Arie clung to him and managed to throw her arms over his head. He pushed her off, but Arie pulled backward on the cord, now at his throat. It all happened in seconds. Then Handy was there with a river rock in his hand. The man twisted his chin up, trying to reach around the cord that was biting deeply into his flesh, and Handy hit him squarely in the jaw. He swung so hard that he fell forward, ending up on his knees next to Arie. The stone flew across the attic and crashed into the outside wall with a percussive thud. Blood flew from the man's mouth; he slumped to all fours and over on his side, unconscious. The split skin of his face bled freely, quickly creating a small pool under his head.

They all sat there for a moment, panting. Renna lifted her head and howled again, not in pain this time. Triumph. Arie, her breath coming in shaky tatters, stared. She had a terrible momentary sense that the girl would dart her head forward and bite the man. Renna yelled again, not so loud the second time, then leaned her head back on the car seat and started to cry. From far down in the gulch came a thin answering call from one of the rightful inheritors.

4

HE WAS OUT COLD. Handy held his knife at the man's throat while Arie and Renna untied themselves.

"Help me pull him," he said. He and Arie dragged the man by the armpits, dead weight, to an upright post. While Handy trussed him hand and foot, Arie washed and wrapped the gash on her hand and swabbed at the small one on her throat as well. One thing was certain in the new world after the Pink: every small break in the skin was a septic threat in this post-penicillin era. She stripped out of her bloody shirt and pulled on a clean one, guzzled a full mug of water and part of another. The rest she carried to Renna, who drank greedily. Arie thought she'd have to scrape her off the floor in a heap of anxiety, but she was sitting up, looking clear, watching Handy tie the intruder's ankles together. Plugged in, thought Arie, with a single wistful pang for the careless luxury of electricity in the walls.

"Good thing you got back when you did," Renna told Handy

He gave the rope a final firm tug. Hands on knees, he leaned there for a moment and sighed. His long ponytail pointed at the floor, a straight brown line. "I was up there for a couple of minutes," he said.

"Couldn't judge when to move, with him holding that blade. We all got lucky." He straightened stiffly and hobbled to the water jug. "He left the rope ladder hanging," he said between sips. "When I saw that, I figured it was trouble. Arie, you're all right?

"Fine, if I can keep this clean," she said, holding up her hand, now wrapped in a strip of rag. "Are you limping?"

"Landed funny," he said, slapping his left thigh. "My ankle. It's fine."

"Baby Moses, what a motley crew we are," Arie said. "Can you manage that panel?" she asked Handy. "Let's bolt ourselves in before one of his friends comes visiting."

"What do we do with him?" Renna said, studying the intruder. His head slumped almost to his breastbone and the scalp wound where Handy hit him had bled copiously, leaving a gruesome stain down his face and the front of his jacket.

"We'll decide that when he wakes up," said Handy. He climbed topside, navigating the rungs slowly, favoring his ankle.

"First thing is to make sure he's not ready to die anyway," said Arie. She got down near him and looked over the gash on his head. His hair was clumped with gouts of drying blood. She used a rag to push it away from the cut, wanting to avoid getting too much of his blood on her. The rock had done damage—the scalp had a cut at least three inches long and the flesh all around it was swelling, a dark red-and-purple mess. The laceration still actively bled but was clearly beginning to clot over. "He'll live," she said. "Though he'll have a hell of a headache when he wakes."

"Good," said Renna. "I hope his brain is scrambled."

At the work table and shelves, Arie gathered several items into her pockets. "That's an evil thing to wish on another with the world as it is," she said mildly. The light of early afternoon was pale and soft. She hated to shut them inside already, but it had to be done. Handy's movements were barely audible above them.

Renna made a small sound of derision. "Worse than what he had planned a minute ago? And I doubt he was going to make it quick."

"Hard to say unless he tells us so," said Arie. "I don't believe I saw murder on his face. If he meant to kill us, we'd likely be dead." She gave a little half-shrug. "A mercy, maybe."

"You're pretty anxious to die, aren't you."

"My life is a gift," Arie said, "but it's a finite one, and I've already had more of it than most." She settled herself next to the intruder, spread a clean cloth, and laid the items from her pocket in a neat row: small scissors, thread, needle, and a bottle of rubbing alcohol.

"We'd probably both be dead already if he was."

Arie used the scissors and cut sticky wads of hair away from the gash in his scalp, laying the bloody bundles in a neat pile in his lap. With a wet cloth, she wiped around the long cut to get a good look what she was doing. The man's steady breathing faltered a couple of times as she worked. "He'll be awake before I'm done with him," Arie said.

"Why are you helping him?" Renna said. "Let him sit there and bleed. That's what he did to you. His life is his own, right?"

Arie was dampening a fresh cloth with alcohol. She paused when Renna said this. "Well," she said. "Look who's paying attention." She examined Renna's angry face. "You're right. His life is his own." She cocked her head and looked speculatively at the intruder. His breathing was steady again. The gash was white and naked where she had snipped the hair away and wiped the skin clean. A fine tendril of blood spilled over the lip of the cut and trickled toward his beard. "But he's here, Renna. He's in here with me, just like you are." She smiled wanly. "You're here. Handy's here. Now him. I don't like it, but here you all are." She put a little more alcohol on the cloth and steadied herself next to the man. "You've all run riot into my life, and something's being required of me. Don't expect me to explain what I don't yet understand. Now let me see to this trouble."

She knew she needed to do this part quickly. She braced his head with one hand and laid the alcohol-dampened cloth directly over the wound, holding it there under the flat of her hand. Just as she expected, this revived the intruder. He uttered a groan that trailed up into a thin, breathy squeal. He tried to move his head away from her, but she held him firmly between her two hands. Handy had wrapped a few turns of the rope around his chest, and there was little room for him to maneuver. He struggled to open his eyes, still making noise through gritted teeth.

"Hurts like hell, I reckon," Arie said.

He squinted hard, one eye marking her, one squeezed shut. He tried again to pull away, but it was obvious that the effort caused him even more pain. "You're not getting out from under me, so you may just as well save yourself some hurt and hold still." She could feel it in the palms of her hands, how the muscles in his jaw and neck relaxed. He closed his eyes again, but his breathing was still quick and disturbed. "Better," she said. "You can't see it, but you're laid open good on your melon. I'm going to stitch it." He chuffed once, like a dog will do when it's thinking of barking, but he remained still. Arie was threading her needle when Handy came inside.

"He awake?" He made his way slowly down the ladder, one hand clutching the bulging tow sack.

"More or less," said Arie, "but he's trying to behave. What did you bring?"

He opened the bag and held up his catch. "No way," Renna said, and laughed. Arie glanced around at him. In the uncertain light she could just make out a pile of dark feathers.

"Caught a bird, did you?"

"Bird, my foot," said Handy.

"Looks like bird from here, unless fish have gotten feathers," she said, turning attention back to her needle. She'd chosen a small one and thought for a moment she might have to ask Handy to help her. But she managed to get the thread—a brilliant shade of turquoise, as it happened—into the tiny eye.

"You're teasing us," said Renna. "That's a chicken."

"That's two chickens," said Handy. "I couldn't believe it. I was stoked when I found one in the first trap, but when I went to the next trap and found a second, I thought I might be having a dream. What are the odds?"

"Slim to none," said Arie. She dipped the length of thread into the bottle of alcohol and gave it a second to wet through. "I've heard cockcrow now and then, but haven't ever seen one when I'm out. You think they're fit to eat?"

"Damn right they're edible," said Handy. "Sister, these girls were still breathing when I found them. They hadn't even been caught long enough to stop thrashing."

"Oh my gosh, we're going to have a chicken dinner," Renna said. "Doesn't that make your mouth water just to think about it?"

"I guess you'd better get to pulling feathers," said Arie. "Hand those to her," she told Handy, "and after you bolt the sky panel I need some help with this job." She pulled the dripping thread out of the alcohol and capped the bottle securely.

Handy picked up both chickens by their feet and brought them to Renna. "Ever done this?"

"Kind of," she said. "If you count a blue jay and two pigeons."

"Close enough," said Handy. "Some of the feathers will get hard to pull because the muscles are tightening up. I didn't get much of a chance to bleed them. Try not to tear the meat. I'll yank out whatever you can't manage." He spread the rough tow sack and laid the birds atop it. Renna scooted off the car seat. She pulled the birds between her knees and went to work.

Arie turned her attention back to the intruder. "I'm going to sew up your head," she said. She spoke quietly. "I'm not trying to hurt you on purpose, and it will go better for both of us if you don't fight me."

The man turned his head, a small slow movement, and he opened both eyes. "Do it," he said. His speech was thickly slurred but understandable.

"Shall I have my brother hold your head?"

Handy was standing next to Arie, holding one of the kerosene lamps. The man looked up at him, moving only his eyes. "No thanks," he said, voice a husky whisper.

Arie patted him on the shoulder. "Hang on, then, and let's be done here." She motioned for Handy to bring the light close, and she got up on her knees, leaning against the man's shoulder for balance. When she took the first stitch, he flinched and squeezed his eyes closed again but did not try to pull away from her.

Arie worked methodically, pulling the edges of skin together with her left hand and making as careful a job with the needle as she could. "I don't know if you'll win any beauty contests when I'm done here," she said. "My main practice has been keeping the pockets in my clothes and adding patches to the elbows of my shirts." Near the end of the gash the skin got ragged. "I'm going to have to trim a little flap you have hanging," she said, still using the same low, soothing voice. She let the needle dangle a moment so she could wipe the blades of her scissors, and she snipped the problem piece away. The man winced harder and made a surprised sound. There was a fresh trickle of blood; Arie pressed the rag to it. "Almost done," she said.

Two more stitches finished the job. The brilliant turquoise thread looked weirdly festive against the sewn wound, but the gash was neatly closed. Using the same strip of rag she'd used to bandage her own hand, she wound a dressing around his head, covering her handiwork and keeping his dirty hair from getting near the stitches. She took Handy's arm and got to her feet. "I imagine you're thirsty," she said to the man. He said nothing.

"Hey," Handy said. He knocked the toe of his boot against the man's bound feet. "You want some water?"

"Yes," he whispered.

"Get it for him," Arie told Handy. "Put some tincture in it."

"You sure you want to waste good medicine?" Renna said. She didn't look up from the bird in her hands. A reddish feather hung in her hair like a copper leaf.

Arie turned on her. "Mind your plucking," she snapped. "I wasted plenty on you, didn't I?"

Renna kept her head bent over her task and said nothing else.

Arie gathered up the bloody hair she'd set in his lap and tossed it on the heap of feathers Renna was making. Everything else she'd used went back where it belonged. While Renna worked and Handy gave the intruder water, patiently waiting between each small sip, Arie stopped at the mandala. It was days since she'd stood at the labyrinth, although she'd traced it with her eyes dozens of times. She put her finger in the outside ring and moved it along the familiar path. The wood, smooth and glossy with the oil of her skin and the pressure of her touch, felt like warm stone, as though she'd long ago worn away the grain entirely. A sense of comfort dropped over her, a falling away of the troubles all around this dim and stuffy room, as if she were here alone, her finger meandering toward the labyrinth center and out again.

"Where should we cook them?"

She started. Handy was standing right next to her. She hadn't sensed him there at all. Had she been sleeping? Surely not. But she was leaning against the wall, her cheek pressed to the pattern of the mandala and her hand splayed there between her bosom and the boards. She straightened and felt the little pins-and-needles sense of a limb falling asleep.

"The chickens are clean," he said. He spoke quietly and didn't look directly at her. "Shall we spit them?"

"Spit them. Yes," she said. She rubbed her face with both hands. "Sorry," she said. "I can't believe I dropped off to sleep standing here."

"It's been a bad day."

"Aren't they all?"

He smiled. "Some are not so bad. Now: cook in here, or outside?" He had one chicken in each hand, and he hoisted them to chest height. They were pale and rather scrawny, but a bounty nonetheless.

"In here would probably be the smart thing to do, but this grate is so small, I'm afraid we'd burn them."

Handy considered the little fireplace. "We could only cook them one at a time in here—it'll take forever. Outside I can break them down and spit the halves, roast them on the pit all at once. We'll have the fire put out and be eating right quick."

They went up together. Arie laid the fire, adding a fat measure of kindling to start building a quick bed of coals. Handy did a perimeter scan while she worked.

"Fat lot of good all our watching did us," she said, "in the end. The minute you went into the woods, he made a move. Was watching us all along."

"We had to take the chance," he said.

"Yes, we did." The little fire blazed in the pit, already hot and hungry. She fed in more twigs and small splits of cut wood, relishing the heat on her face and hands. "And here he is with us," she said.

Handy moved from spot to spot, checking with the binoculars. "I'm going down," he said. He paid the rope ladder over the edge of the roof.

Arie looked up from the fire. "I wish you wouldn't," she said. Having the rope ladder hanging made her feel jumpy. "Can't you check from inside?"

He shook his head. "I don't want him seeing that hatch," he said. "You keep watch here at the ladder. I'll be quick." He was already over the side and going down.

Arie laid on a little more wood and then squatted at the edge of the roof, looking into the bramble where the rope ladder dangled. Handy looked up and gave a little nod. Knife in hand, he crept close to the house, looking in all directions and glancing in through unboarded windows. He moved around the corner to the front of the house and disappeared. Her body tensed when she lost sight of him, just as it had when she watched him head into the woods earlier. From where she waited, she saw their small cookfire had diminished; she hurried to it, added more fuel, and returned to her post. After what seemed a very long and silent wait, Handy finally returned, sidling behind the brambles to hurry up the rungs, agile as a monkey.

"Nothing," he said.

"Like always?" She returned to the fire. The bed of coals was ready enough. Handy pulled up the ladder and joined her. He split each of the chickens into halves and skewered each one onto a thin metal spit that fit on a rack above the pit. "That's still over-hot," Arie said. "Mind you turn it, or they'll be black before they're cooked through." She left him to cooking and tended the garden. When she stirred the compost basket, it looked dark and broken down enough to throw a thin layer over the soil. A half dozen bright-red worms, whose prolific parents she'd dug at the river and added to the compost by hand, waved momentarily in the open air, slowly burrowing under to add their effort to the garden.

Handy rotated the spit every few seconds. The small amount of fat the chickens sported had begun to melt, dripping into the embers with bright sizzles. The smell was already bringing back her own memories of family meals long gone. As a child, she'd helped make chicken dinner every Sunday. The little boys chased and dispatched the pullets, the little girls plucked, then the older sisters did the gutting and cooking, all while Mammy Delonda supervised from a comfortable and leisurely distance. The smell of the roasting birds opened some old transit in her mind, and she had a sudden clear memory of the Sunday she'd first been allowed to move from plucking—smelly and tedious— to preparation with Lulu and Mercy.

"We'll probably have to kill him," Handy said. As always, his voice was low and even.

"Kill him. That's a leap, Brother."

"No." He turned the spit a quarter-revolution.

The low clouds that had hung in all day were thinned enough that Arie could see ribbons of pale blue. There would be a beautiful sunset. "Rest is not mine to give," she said. "We aren't his judges, are we? I'm not the author of his life, but you'll make me his executioner?"

"He set his own fate in motion when he climbed that ladder and broke in."

"You broke in, too."

The cook fire lit Handy's face and reflected yellow in his pale eyes. "I did. And I set my fate."

"I might have killed you. Might have let Renna die, for sure. She was close to it when you got her here."

He tended their meal and said nothing.

"We can't choose that for him," Arie said. She loosened the bandage on her hand partway and straightened it, rewound it. Her heartbeat had quickened and the little cut throbbed in time. "Handy," she said. He looked at her. "Not yet. We'll give him a chance."

"A chance," he said. "To do what, exactly?"

"I may be a fool," she said. "In fact, I assure you I am a fool. But I want your word that we'll make this decision together. Hand me your knife." She speared the meat at the leg joints. The juices ran clear and hissed in the coals, now brilliant white and yellow in the late afternoon. "These are cooked," she said.

They each took a whole chicken on a plate, and Arie dropped the chipped and dented dome lid of an old barbeque grill over the fire pit. At the sky panel she prepared to go down, but Handy put out an arm, blocking her. "I won't stand by and let him hurt either of you," he said. "If something goes badly, if there's no time for discussion, I'll kill him."

"My life is—"

"Don't say it." He stared at her, their faces inches apart. "Your life is not only yours alone." The dark scar on her inner arm, the null sign carved there years ago, was just visible at the edge of her sleeve. He tapped it briefly. If she hadn't been holding the plate of meat, she would have jerked her arm away. "This doesn't change it, Ariela. Your life is mine, too."

She glared at him and swallowed a hundred retorts. "Here comes dinner," she called into the attic.

The tincture and the promise of cooked chicken had brought the man around. His face was more swollen, the bruises darker, but when Arie and Handy got inside, bolting the sky panel behind them, he was sitting up, head erect, eyes open.

"How's the pain?" Arie said. She put the steaming plates on the work table and lit a couple of candles.

"Feels..." His voice was a wooden croak. He coughed, eyes squeezed tight, made a small moan. "Feels like someone hit me in the head with a rock."

"Just in the nick of time, too," said Arie. She wiped the blade of her knife and cut the halves of one chicken into the familiar parts of long-gone suppers: thighs, drumsticks, wings, breast, and back. "Renna," she said, "Handy's going to help you walk over here for your meal." The girl had already done more moving around in one day than Arie would have thought possible, but she was determined to push Renna to the limit of herself, so they could both learn where that limit was. "You, now," she said to the man. "I suppose you'd like some of this." She nodded at the food.

He squinted at her. When she said nothing, he must have decided she meant it. "Yes."

"Attacking innocent people whetted your appetite, did it?" she said.

Renna had made it to the table, leaning on Handy's arm. She shot a look of contempt at the man, but to Arie's relief she kept her mouth shut.

"I didn't intend to—" His mouth opened and closed it again, flailing to explain. "It wasn't meant to be an attack," he said.

"Funny, it sure looked like an attack when I got here," said Handy. He was helping Renna settle herself back on the sofa. He closed the distance in two strides and squatted in front of the man, eye to eye. "I looked in from up there and saw two women tied up, one with blood on her, and you with a spear." He straightened. "That's just your way of getting to know a neighbor, I guess." He helped himself to an entire roasted half-bird. He took a tremendous bite from the breast and made a little sigh of pleasure before sitting down by Renna, who was already gnawing on the gristled knob at the end of the drumstick. Handy pulled the drumstick off his own portion and put it on her plate. She smiled at him and kept eating.

Arie watched their captive a minute. He sat still, looking at his own feet. "I've earned my daily bread," she told him, "and I mean to have it. You, though." She took up the back piece, not bothering with a plate. "You're going to have to barter for your supper." She pulled loose the tail, plump and brown, and laughed. "My favorite," she said, holding it up to admire. "Our grandfather taught me to love this bit," she said to Handy. When she bit through the browned skin, the yielding fat and bits of meat melted in her mouth. Unexpectedly, her eyes stung with tears. She turned slightly so the man would not see this. "Pop always pulled the tail off a roasted chicken, or the turkey at Thanksgiving, just as soon as Granny put it on the table." She glanced at Handy, who was busily creating a little pile of chicken bones. "Do you know Thanksgiving?" she asked.

Renna looked up as if Arie were dimwitted. "Of course I do." She picked up the leg bone again, snapped it neatly in two and began picking at the marrow inside.

"I was asking Handy," said Arie. "We weren't raised to celebrate it."

"I know Thanksgiving," he said. "We went into town often enough." He wiped his mouth with his forearm. "I went with Morgan once when I was, oh, maybe eight or nine, and we had to pick up rice and oats and some other stuff from Nilsen's. When we drove past the school, the little kids' school by the bridge, there were all these turkey drawings put up in the windows. I couldn't figure that out," he said.

Arie snuck a glance at the intruder. He had stopped staring at his feet and was watching Handy, who ate while he talked. The man sat completely still, but Arie saw him, just once, lick his lips when Handy took a bite of food.

"I made those," said Renna. She held up a greasy hand, palm open and fingers splayed. "First you traced the head." She touched her thumb. "Then you traced the feathers." She touched each finger. "After that, you colored it. A turkey."

"I didn't know that, though," said Handy. "We ate a turkey sometimes, but we didn't make a holiday for it. That day when we pulled into the parking lot at Nilsen's, I asked Morgan if the school was a store where people got their chickens. He looked at me like I was daft."

Renna laughed. "No Thanksgiving," she said, shaking her head. "That's too bad."

Handy shrugged and kept eating, but he was clearly pleased at her attention.

"What Grandpa always said," said Arie, "when he pulled off the tail and put it on his plate was, 'That's for me. The pope's nose.' It was the sort of thing people weren't supposed to say back then, but he'd learned it from his own father, and it stuck, I guess. I didn't know for the longest time what he could mean by that—the pope's nose." She snorted. "What did I know of a pope? Or of the Catholic Church, or even of Rome, for that matter. Do you know Rome, William?"

He didn't look at her. "I don't imagine it matters now," he said, "if I can't walk there."

Arie wiped her hands on her apron. The meat was warm in her belly, and the perfectly familiar taste of it gave her an odd contentment. She dropped the bones into a small cook pot to make broth with later and placed a meaty thigh on a pocked and creased metal pie plate. Marie Callender's was embossed across the discolored bottom. She approached the man. "There's some talk that has to happen," she said.

His eyes went from her face to the plate in her hands. "Fair enough," he said.

"What's fair might have been to cut your throat and throw you in the woods to make a meal for something with fur or feathers." She nodded at the meat she held. "Mought be it's only a fair trade, eh? We eat them, after all."

He held his peace.

"I'm not promising you won't end up on the menu, understand." She smiled. "Not our menu. We've not sunk to that depravity. But there is a world of appetite that would be delighted to have you. Meantime, though, I'm going to give you this plate, and in exchange I expect you to answer my questions. Are we clear?"

"Yes."

"I'm likely to know a lie," she said. "I have an eye for faces. Always have." This was true. Of course, she hadn't had the chance to read many faces in the past two years, but he didn't know it, nor would he likely believe her anyway. She put the plate of chicken in his lap.

He picked it up, awkward with his hands tied, and managed to grab hold with his long fingers and get it to his mouth. He took such a massive bite that she could hear the crunch of bone between his teeth. It obviously pained him to chew, but he kept at it that way, making small grunting sounds as he ate.

"I want your name," said Arie.

He paused mid-bite. It seemed to cost him some effort to stop. He laid down the food. "Curran," he said. "My name is Curran. May I have some more water?"

Arie glanced at Handy. Handy refilled the mug and set it by him. When he tried to reach for it, the plate slid off his legs, tumbling the remains of the chicken onto the floor. Arie put it back on his plate and helped him drink the water. He took several deep swallows and belched.

"Don't mention it," she said lightly. "Now Curran. Tell me what the blue hell you intended here today, leaping in and scaring everyone witless. Because you know who does such a thing? Hm?"

He watched her, long fingers clutching the edge of the pie tin.

"A marauder, Curran. A cunning invader with black intentions breaks into a home and purposely terrifies those within." She stared at him. "Your actions betray you as a marauder."

"I accept the wisdom of that," he said.

Arie stood. "Do you, now?" She looked at Handy and Renna, side by side on the sofa again, perfectly still, watching her. "Curran concurs. He is a terrorist."

"No," he said. He leaned his head, gently, against the post. "I had to do it that way."

Arie rose and pulled her single hard-backed chair over so that all of them were in a rough circle. "No yourself," she said. "You did not."

"You jumped in here to scare us," Renna said. "Don't lie. You knew we were here—you said so. You crashed in and cut her, you cut her throat." She was leaning forward, eyes blazing. "An old woman. A girl who can't walk. You cut Arie and you tied us and you said—" She leaned on Handy's shoulder and got herself to a standing position. He stood to help, but Renna waved him off. She managed two halting, awkward steps, unassisted. "You put a blade to her throat," she said. "You said you'd take her eye out. That's what you did. Tell me you didn't. Tell me that."

They all waited. Curran put his chin down and closed his eyes.

Renna's fists were clenched and shaking. "Tell me!" she shouted.

"I didn't know who was here until I came in," he said. "Not for sure. I saw him leave, and I took a chance." His voice was thin, a little slurred. "I saw you killing those dogs the other day, saw you hurling rocks, and—"

"And you figured we might be ready to kill you, too," said Handy. He waited until Curran looked his way. "You were right," he said in his soft and steady voice. "It looks like you should have stayed clear."

Renna swayed a little, and Handy helped her sit again. He gathered the remains of their plates and dumped them in the pot as Arie had. He hunkered down close to Curran. "Looks like one more shot to the side of your head will do for you."

"We had to get inside," Curran said. "If we stay out there, we're dead anyway."

Handy jerked his head around to look at Arie. "We, who?" he said. His face opened with agitation. "Hey." He darted forward and balled the front of Curran's jacket in his fist, gave it a rough shake. "Who else is with you?"

Curran lifted his tied arms in a weak warding-off gesture, and Handy slapped them aside. "My dog," Curran said. He stared up at Handy from his swollen, purpling face. "Just her. My dog, Talus."

Handy looked at Arie again, his face still worried and confused.

"Enough," Arie said. "Let go of him, Handy."

Handy shoved Curran just enough to bump his head on the post, making him groan.

"Off," Arie said, pulling Handy by the shoulder. He raised both hands to shoulder height, stepped away and paced as if those might get up to no good if he didn't keep them lifted. Arie hadn't seen him agitated this way since he'd first shown up in the woods. "Breathe," she told him. "This isn't helping." She leaned forward, resting her forearms across her knees. "I'm not convinced, Curran," she said. "What did you expect to accomplish breaking in here? As we used to say, what's in it for you?"

"I mean it," he said. "I've been living in the woods for weeks. I made us a camp."

"For you and your dog. What was the name?"

"Talus."

"But you haven't answered my question. Why did you break in here?"

"We're too exposed. It was working fine for a while—we've been out there for..." He frowned and shook his head. "All through the summer, however long that is. Four months, I guess." He had been watching Handy tread the attic, as if at any moment Handy might lunge. But now he looked squarely at Arie.

Despite the condition of his scalp and the awful bruising on the whole left side of his head and jaw, she could see that he was in his right mind and was desperate to make her listen.

"I'm sorry," he said.

She watched him.

"Ma'am, I swear to you on my life that I didn't mean to cut you. I wouldn't. Those things I said were bullshit." His expression was miserable with physical pain and what looked like bleak and hollow surrender. "I can barely make myself hunt for food," he said. He finally looked away from her. "If I didn't have Talus, I would have starved, probably. She's like a damned magic fairytale dog—going out for food and bringing it back for me."

"Where's your fairytale dog now?" said Handy, not pausing in his nervy circuit of the open center of the room. "Is she invisible, too?"

"I left her at our camp. I tied her up inside so she couldn't bust out and follow me." He swallowed. "If anything gets in, though, she'll—"

"She'll be eaten," finished Arie. "Man or beast. The beasts don't have a choice, really. They look for food, they find it, they eat."

"The dogs you killed have been pushing at us for a while. The first few times we saw them, they ran off when I yelled. But every time they got closer, even when I was throwing stuff and Talus was bushing out, ready to jump them." His voice was raspy, but he sat as straight as the rope would let him, looking from person to person as he spoke. "There was something bigger coming around, too. Mountain lion, I think. It's sneaky."

"Bears don't sneak," said Arie. "Maybe people."

"I don't think so," he said. "I set up trip alarms, a lot of them. It would be really hard for anyone to miss hitting one, day or night. I spent as much time stringing noisemakers through the bushes as I did looking for food." With deliberate care he picked up his water and drank. "Every once in a while we hear something bump into a string, but it's always just a little clatter like maybe a raccoon or something would make, and Talus barely pays any attention. In the last week, though, something bad has been in camp after dark. The noisemakers don't rattle, but all of a sudden Talus stands up and starts growling."

Arie watched him thoughtfully. Now that he was really talking, the man who had spoken of blinding her and snapping Renna's neck was nowhere in evidence. This was a frightened person, not a malevolent one. Handy seemed to be feeling it, too, at least a little. He'd finally stopped pacing. He stood close, though, and Arie could sense the nervous energy rolling off him. "Curran," she said, "how long have you been out there in your camp? Why are you in the woods?"

"Only since the start of summer, like I said."

"Why are you in the woods?" Arie repeated.

He hesitated. "I was with a group," he said finally.

"What group?" said Handy. "Where?"

"They were some guys I knew. A couple that I worked construction with here and there before the die-off. One from the apartment complex by my house. Just guys I've seen around all my life—you know how it is." His mouth tightened. "How it was. Small town. You do stuff after work and start seeing the same people. Beers and ping-pong at the Shanty, or league softball. The yard monkeys at McNealy's lumber."

"So you knew them, your group," Arie said.

"Only two of them, but yeah. When the pox first hit and things went south so quick, I didn't know what to do. I hid out at home for the first couple of days, trying to make the internet work, flipping channels on the TV and looking for something on the radio. I lived on the west side, in one of those shacky little three-room places with apartment buildings all around." He gazed into the shadows while he talked, his fingertips moving gingerly around the bandage on his head, picking at the dried blood in his hair. "It was a shit show. Three days, I guess, where you kept hearing yelling. Screaming. But a little less every day. Somebody in the building right behind my place kept crying and crying, the most awful sound I ever heard come out of a person. I think it was a woman, but I don't know. It would die down, and I'd think, finally. Thank God, finally. Then it would start again. Sometime on the third day it stopped. Stopped right in mid-howl. I knew what it meant." He pulled a little harder at his crusty hair and grimaced. "I didn't care. I was happy. The screaming stopped." His hands dropped into his lap.

There was movement in the corner of her eye, and Arie saw that Renna had gathered a blanket around her. The girl still watched Curran, but she had pulled her feet up and under the blanket so that only her head was visible. "How did you find your friends?" Arie asked. His face had gone a bit slack while he talked, and she was afraid he would try to fall asleep.

He looked at her. "Friends? At first. At least I thought we were. Two of them found me. I hadn't left the house at all. It was totally weird out there—you must have seen it."

"I did."

"People were looking for help, I guess. We all just expected somebody to come along and fix it. But nobody could. After the first day when it was nutjobs in the street, hollering and pounding on doors, gunshots—like every end-of-the-world movie you ever saw—I barricaded myself. Shoved furniture up against the two doors, put a bookcase and my box spring and mattress in front of the windows. Before everything went down, that little house always made me stir crazy. I wanted out." He shook his head. "Man, when it all hit the fan, I wanted to pull those walls in around me. I don't remember exactly when Darius and Little Mikey showed up. Two weeks, maybe. All I remember is being hungry. I knew enough to cook up what little I had in the fridge before the power went out, but that wasn't much, and I didn't have a lot in the cupboards, either. By the time those guys came and hauled me out, I was trying to ration some old hot dog buns and a jar of green olives. Oh, and some steak sauce."

Handy stepped forward and pulled Curran's hands away from his head by his bound wrists. "If you don't tell us about your group right now, I'm going to haul you up on that roof and throw your ass in the street."

"Okay," Curran said, voice placatory. "Sorry, yeah. When Darius and Mikey got me out, they told me they had a place, and it was good, safe, so I went. Who wouldn't? They were carrying weapons, and I knew both of them. They were good guys. It felt like a...like a good thing."

"Someone in charge again," said Arie.

"Right. I didn't know guns. I wasn't that guy. I was the guy with a phone in my pocket, not a gun. Or a

Taser. Hell, I used to carry around one of those little emergency pepper spray keychains and hold it in my hand when I was walking home from the bowling alley."

"I guess you learned a little about knives later," said Renna. "About how to cut old women."

"Let him finish," said Handy.

Curran threw another miserable glance at Arie, at her bandaged hand. "They had a shopping cart of stuff, and they told me we couldn't go straight back. They were scavenging. When they got into my neighborhood, Little Mikey remembered my place, and they stopped. As soon as they got me to open the door, it was like a done deal, like of course I was coming with them. So I did. I wanted to. They ransacked my place for usables, added them to the cart, and after they fed me some peanut butter crackers and fruit snacks, we hit it. I didn't have a weapon, so it was my job to push the cart. We stopped at a lot of places. Darius would wait outside with me while Little Mikey went in. Once he knew it was secure, he'd whistle, and Darius would go inside while I stayed by the cart. They gave me a golf club to use if anyone came around. Whatever they could find, they'd load up, and we'd take off again."

"You didn't see anybody else?" said Handy.

Curran kept his face averted. "There were a couple of times. I heard them..." There was a struggle on his face, as if the words were a physical thing he had to expel. "Yeah, there were people. They never did let me come in with them," he said, "and if there was any sort of trouble from inside, they'd come out with a story—how someone came at them with a knife, or how they tried to help someone who refused to leave and it got heated."

"And you believed them," said Arie.

"I wanted to," Curran said. "I knew them from before, from doing roofing and shooting pool, so yeah—I wanted to believe them. I started wondering why no one else would want to come with us. Hadn't anyone else run out of food? Didn't they want to get somewhere safe with other people? But these guys had an answer for everything. Finally somebody was calling the shots, and that's what I wanted, for someone to take charge of the mess. It took us until way after dark to get there, even though it was only three miles from my house."

Outside, the sun must have finally broken through the overcast. A long trapezoid of yellow appeared through the pebbled window at the far west side of the attic, lighting the space even into the narrowest spots under the eaves. It fell directly on the place where Arie sat.

"Curran," Arie said. The incandescent brightness bounced off the floor and lit her face, made her white-gray hair luminous. Curran stared at her. "Where did they take you?" she said, quite sure she knew.

"The high school. They've taken over the whole place."

"What's your name?" said Renna. The blanket had dropped from around her head and shoulders. She stared at Curran, leaning forward on the Packard seat, mouth open slightly. Arie had expected her to react with revulsion or fear, but this was something very different, expectant and intense.

For a long moment the two of them stared each other down. "My name is Curran," he said finally.

"You said you built houses before the sickness. You worked on roofs, right?"

Curran nodded.

"Joe," Renna said. She sat back, nodding. "You were a Joe."

There was a long pause as they continued to look at each other. The understanding passed between them was palpable. "My name," he said again, "is Curran."

"My name is Renna," she said. She turned to Arie. "We need to untie him."

Handy looked around at her. "No."

She lifted her chin in a defiant gesture. "Yes," she said. "He's not going to hurt us."

"He already did hurt you." He turned to Arie. "He cut you and tied you and threatened you. What is this?"

Arie stood. The bar of sunlight was still there, but already retreating across the floor. She was sorry to see it go, but the day was on its way out. It was the full moon tonight, and if the sky stayed cloudless, it would be fat and yellow when it rose. "I believe they know each other," she said. "We're going to trust her instinct and his promises." She studied Handy's good face, the internal battle to believe her clear on his features. "Cut him loose."

It was about an hour before Curran could trust his balance. Before Handy would agree to untie him, he made a deliberate sweep to secure their weapons—knives, short spear, slingshot. He even dug back in the corner of the attic after the rock he'd used to hit Curran and put it on the top of Arie's supply shelf.

Curran got to his feet, swaying, one hand on his head, and stood there for a full minute with his eyes closed.

"Are you going to keep your feet?" Arie said.

"I'm just dizzy."

"That's your heart sending blood back to your head," said Renna, mimicking what Arie had told her that morning.

"Clever," said Arie.

Renna ignored her. "You can sit here with me," she told Curran, indicating the place next to her on the car seat.

Curran nodded. "Thanks. I need to stand, though." He leaned down to get his cup of water. Bending over made him stumble slightly. Handy was standing between Curran and Renna, and when Curran stumbled he shifted his weight slightly, as if to catch hold. Arie couldn't tell if it was an instinct to help Curran, or to preempt him from moving toward Renna, but she knew he was trying to trust, and she felt a small surge of pride for him.

"I have to get back to Talus," he said. "It's not safe for her, tied up like she is."

"It doesn't sound safe for you, either," said Renna. She looked at Handy, then at Arie. "He should stay here," she said.

"There is no room," said Arie. "Look around, Renna. We are close to tripping over each other with three of us, and we're going through supplies too quickly already. Four plus a dog? No." She turned to Curran. "I'm sorry," she said. "But clumped up in a bigger and bigger group makes us a bigger and bigger target. You and Handy are leaving soon anyway," she said to Renna. "Perhaps Curran will go with you."

"Go where?" said Curran.

"To Handy and Arie's home place," said Renna. "What's it called?" she asked Handy.

"God's Land," Handy said, still terse and watchful.

"It's Handy's home place," said Arie. "I've not seen it nor claimed it for forty years. As soon as Renna can walk well, they'll be going, and I will be living here alone again." She looked from face to face. "Alone," she said again.

"If I just had somewhere to stay for a few days," Curran said, "a safer place for Talus and me to scout from." He looked at Arie. "Please," he said. "I won't use your supplies, I swear it. I can help you while I'm here, and when Handy and Renna are ready to go, Talus and I will leave, too. No matter what."

"Arie," Renna said. She managed to get to her feet again and limped over. "He can help us. He—" She hesitated, looking at Curran for a moment. "He knows things. About the people at the high school."

"What about the high school?" said Handy.

"A lot," said Curran. "Things you should know, Arie, if you're staying on."

Handy assessed Curran for a moment and nodded. "Sister," he said to Arie. A lot of the coarse tension had drained out of his demeanor. His voice had returned to its characteristic gentle lisp. "I think we should hear him out. He and the dog could stay downstairs." He searched her face with his eyes. "I'll help him make it suitable for the short term. But this is your decision. Whatever you want to do."

It was what they all wanted. She could see it on every face. Having Curran downstairs increased their possible visibility and risk of detection, but it might be offset by having another set of eyes and the early warning system of the dog. When Handy and Renna did set off for God's Land, they'd be safer with three than with two.

"You have supplies to bring here?" she asked.

"I do," he said. "Not a lot. Not like this." His eyes swept the work table and her tall shelves. "But if Handy comes with me, the two of us can carry back just about all of it."

Arie stepped close to Curran. He was more than a head taller, and she had to lift her face to look at him, but he took a compensatory half-step back. "You can stay," she said. "But when I tell you it's time to go, then it is time to go. Ready or not, new camp or not. When I tell you it's time to leave, that's exactly what's going to happen, or so help me there will be a blood-flowing tussle between us."

Curran nodded. "Agreed."

She squeezed his shoulder. "Handy," she said, "I'm going with Curran to his camp."

"What—"

"Let's not run this round and round, shall we?" She was already pulling on a heavy flannel shirt and stocking cap. She slid her arms through the straps of her carry basket. "It doesn't make sense any other way. If there is more trouble here, I want you with Renna."

It was clear there would be no arguing with her. Handy helped them leave through the sky panel, and when they'd lowered themselves into the yard, he pulled up the rope ladder. Arie and Curran waited at the corner of the house; Handy made a quick scan of the area and gave them the all-clear. They crossed the crazzled asphalt, once upon a time called Eleventh Street, and cut into the trees between the houses where Arie's neighbors lay a long time dead, their rooms now home to raccoons and mice, spiders and yellowjackets.

The woods here were new, scrubby second-growth that had once been mostly made up of massive redwood trees. Most of those were cut for timber long before Arie was born. She and Lulu and Mercy, on those rare visits to Granny with Mammy Delonda, had been allowed to play here, with earnest promises that they would not come back muddy from the trickle of a creek that piddled along at the bottom of the ravine year-round.

All these decades later, that ravine was now a river bottom. The dire warnings of rising sea levels hadn't meant much when she was growing up, even though it was pretty easy to see the trouble in progress whenever they made a trip into town. The bay took over more and more pastureland, freshwater sloughs became estuaries and salt marshes, and dozens of miniscule creeks that served as watershed runoff from the hilly wet woods became full-fledged rivers. Her grandparents' house, once a ten-minute drive from the beach, was now almost waterfront property. If not for the deep gulch, she might have ended up underwater altogether.

Curran was getting around surprisingly well in spite of the gash on his head, setting a strong pace, no doubt worried about his dog. They walked in silence for some time, him slightly ahead to show her the way. Arie kept the short spear in her hand, and she was happy to see that he was trying to be vigilant. He stepped around twigs and avoided snagging the undergrowth. But Arie could see exactly where they were going. If she'd wandered into this part of the woods earlier, she would have followed it straight to his camp. "You've made a trail," she said. Though she spoke softly, her voice was startling out here.

He looked around himself and back at her, not slowing. "I try not to walk exactly the same way every time," he said.

"Nevertheless," she said. "Tomorrow you and Handy should come out together and confuse things."

"Good idea."

When they were about a quarter mile in, he stopped and pointed into the bushes. "See the noisemakers?" He'd done a good job with these. The first string of empty cans and lids and miscellaneous detritus was placed strategically, low enough to trip but camouflaged by undergrowth. Once he'd pointed them out, she noticed lines of twine and what looked like green dental floss were strung with great care, like the work of a huge and busy spider. "I'll point them out as we go," he said. True to the story he'd told them, there were a great many noise traps. He alerted her to each one just before they reached it, not saying anything, only pointing and stepping around or over the obstacle, leading the way. Not once did he fail to get them quietly through his handiwork, even though daylight was rapidly diminishing this far into the trees.

There was one final spot where they needed to squeeze through an especially dense phalanx of underbrush, and then they came to his place quite unexpectedly. It took Arie a moment to realize they'd arrived. She'd expected some sort of tent or cabin, perhaps a weather-eaten shed or even an abandoned vehicle. What she didn't expect was an enormous redwood stump, probably twenty-five feet around at the base, made into a house. The body of the tree had broken away some unknowable time ago and lay nearby, a huge, disintegrating log completely covered with ferns and lichen. From inside the stump came a short, plaintive whine. Curran smiled and drew the post on a neatly made wooden hasp attached to an even more neatly made door, and pulled it open. The first thing Arie saw when she looked into that little square doorway was the smiling doggy face of Talus.

"Hey there," said Curran. He had to duck slightly to step inside. A length of twisted wire, relic of the early computer age, tethered the dog to a U-shaped nail pounded into the wall of the enclosure. Talus licked at Curran's face when he bent to untie the cord from her collar, then she bolted out of the stump to squat and pee a few feet away. She ran back to Curran, ears back, tail thumping.

"How's my best girl?" Curran said. He squatted next to the dog and rubbed her roughly from head to rump. She grinned at him, panting, long tongue out. He put his arms around her and put his face into her neck. "I was worried about you," he murmured. She stopped panting and began to sniff vigorously at the bandage on his head, especially in the place where Arie had sewn his scalp back together. "No worries," he said. "Just a little trouble I got myself into." He got to his feet, still a bit wobbly in the transition from down to up. "Say hello to this lady, Talus."

The dog's ears perked forward. She immediately got still and attentive, her brown eyes looking directly into Arie's. "She's a wonder," Arie said. For the second time that day she felt the sting of close tears. It had been decades since she'd been in the company of a good dog. "Hello, Talus," she said, bending slightly toward her. The dog's ears relaxed again, and she lifted an enormous front paw, swiping lightly at the air between them in an unmistakable gesture of accord. Arie took the proffered paw without a moment's hesitation. The pads of that warm foot were rough, the nails long. "What a great good thing you are," Arie whispered. Talus's tongue-wagging, tail-wagging smile returned.

Curran had a pleasantly bemused expression. "I've never actually seen her with anyone but me," he said. "I was a little worried—she's protective."

"She's smarter than we are," said Arie. "I trust her endorsement of you more than anything you've told me so far." She looked into the massive hollow stump. "Let's take what we can and get gone before it's black night out here."

"I'll get a light," he said. He ducked through the door, and Arie waited, not wanting to block what little light the open port provided. There was the small clink and rasp of a lighter, then Curran was putting flame to mantle on a fat-bellied old lantern. It blazed up orange and quickly intensified into a hissing yellow-white.

The little round room jumped into being around him, and Arie stepped inside. Talus, who had taken the moment to make a zigzagging circuit of the clearing around the stump, nose to the ground, returned and positioned herself at the door. She stood, tail wagging slowly, carefully watching Curran for a moment and then having a look outside.

Arie stood in the middle of the space and turned a full circle. What he'd created was remarkable. The inside walls had been planed so that the velvety surface shone burgundy in the lantern light. There were shelves built directly into the walls, where he'd stowed his usables—a couple of dishes and utensils, a ridiculously ornate beer stein, and a smattering of canned food. But there were also many small items that could only have been arranged for his interest and amusement—a glass jar filled with tiny redwood seed cones, a bird's nest with the remnants of little brown and white eggs still in it.

Under the shelves was a small table attached to the wall with hinges so that it sat on two legs and could be folded up out of the way. A stone fire ring, the rocks blackened on their inside edges from much use, was positioned near the far wall. There, the open top of the stump rose and narrowed into a natural chimney to draw smoke up and out. It was a crude fix; the ceiling was sooty, and the stump retained a heavy smell of fire. He had created a sort of carpet with a patchwork of canvas tarps and what looked like a nylon shower curtain that sported bright geometric blocks of color.

Most incongruous of all, and therefore wonderful, was a rocking chair. It was Windsor-styled, wide through the seat and solid despite the many slender rungs adorning the back and arms. On the backrest at head height was the embossed image of a tree, and beneath it Stanford University, painted in delicate red script. A book lay open, face down on the table, and several more sat in piles around the chair, their pages and paper covers plump-looking in the damp air. Arie crossed to the table and turned the book to see its cover, careful not to lose his page. She looked at Curran, who was watching her inspect his home.

"I'll be damned," she said, and then she laughed delightedly. "I thought for sure it would be a Jack London tale, but shame on me for assuming. The Great Gatsby, Curran. It boggles the mind."

He smiled, a little sheepish. He was gathering cans and various small tools onto the table. "I was never a reader before," he said. He added a short stack of clothing to the pile, moving methodically around the room, picking up some things, rejecting others. "But when there's nothing else to do but worry and wait for some new crap to go down, books start looking like the best idea anyone ever had."

Arie slipped out of the straps of her carry basket and began layering in articles of clothing with cans of food and tools—a hatchet, eating utensils, a heavy copper saucepot. "I was always a fool for a book," she said. "I reckon you'll want all of these?" She tucked all six books into the basket without waiting for his response.

"Remember I said that my old house used to make me nuts before the die-off?" He stopped gathering and put his hands on his hips, looking around the stump. "I've never felt like that in here. Not once. I wish—"

"You don't," said Arie. She tested the weight of the carry basket and added a folded towel—garish with a cartoon starfish, still thick and unfrayed—as a cover over all. "This is full," she said. "Put the rest in these." She tossed him two sacks she'd brought along. "Wishing is dabbling in what-if, that fool's errand. What-if will lead you by the nose into suffering. If you follow it, Curran my friend, you are not paying any attention to your life."

"Yes," he said. He tied the second bag closed.

"Steady this for me," she said, balancing the basket on his table.

"Let me carry it."

"Better if I do it. Lift it, is all." He did, and she put her arms through the straps. She made some minor adjustments of balance. "I want us both as mobile as we can be on the return trip. I want my hands free, and yours, too." She took the two bags from him. "Get that wire you had Talus rigged up to." Hearing her name, Talus poked her head inside. Arie smiled at her affable expression, but when Curran started working out the knot at the nail, the dog ducked her head and took several steps backward. "Putting distance between you," said Arie. "She's not going to let you batten her again."

The cable's soft plastic jacket made a stubborn knot, but he finally wrenched it loose. "What now?"

She had him bind the two bags together at arm's length, doubling the wire between them. "Take that towel off the top of my carrier," she said. This she folded into a padded rectangle and draped it across his neck and across his shoulders like a shawl. "Now yoke those bags over." He did as she said, so they hung on either side between armpit and waist. "It's bulky," she said, "but you can keep a weapon in your hand." She remembered what he'd said earlier about not being that guy. "Curran, do I need to unpack your hatchet, too?"

"No." From a single shelf hung above the door, he brought down a machete. In the steady light of the lantern the length of blade was partially rusted and the wood handle cracked, but the cutting edge gleamed with fresh honing.

"Better," she said. She looked around the snug space, which was still appealing even with his supplies stripped out. "This thing you made—it's still a real thing in the world." She rested a palm on the thick wall nearest her, and unconsciously her finger traced a labyrinth on the meticulously smoothed surface.

"What is that," he said, "the pattern you're making? I saw you on the roof." He faltered, then went on. "I've been watching your house for a while. You probably figured that."

Arie's hand fell away from the wall. "I saw you," she said. "Saw your shadow, anyway, easing into the trees. The day we had to kill the wild dogs. Saw her, too." She looked at Talus, sitting quietly outside, patient as a stone, it seemed.

"This was a different time," Curran said. "When you were on the roof alone. It was near dark, and you were doing that with your hand." He moved his own finger in a rhythmic imitation.

"That's mine," said Arie. "A sacred thing." She assessed him levelly, a dare in her expression, and she was pleased when he didn't back down under it.

"I get it," he said. He took the lantern up by its handle. "Ready," he said. They stepped out. He set the peg in the door latch and extinguished the light. The little clearing went dark and made the bits of visible sky a pale gray. "Talus will be our eyes," Curran said.

The dog was already right at his flank, alert and quiet.

They didn't speak at all on the trip back. They moved slowly at first, cautious about hitting one of the noisemakers. Farther from his camp they picked up a little speed. Arie stayed close this time, and Curran was mindful of her. Every few minutes he glanced over his shoulder to see that he hadn't gotten ahead. Crickets and frogs were starting to sing, and between treetops Arie spotted small bats stitching the early-evening air. Mostly it was quiet, the sound of their footsteps muffled and rhythmic.

Curran stopped so abruptly that Arie stumbled into his broad back. Then she could hear Talus growling quietly. She was looking back in the direction they'd just come from. Her rear haunch was lowered and tense, legs braced. Even in the near-dark, Arie could see that the heavy ruff of fur around her neck stood on end. All three remained frozen in place, Arie and Curran both looking in all directions, Talus staring behind them. Her growl intensified.

"We have to move," Arie whispered urgently. She pushed at Curran's shoulder. "Go, go." The minute he did, Talus turned and hurried ahead. Despite their load of goods and Curran's head injury, they set into a shambling jog. Arie could hear the fuel sloshing in the lantern, and she felt things shifting in the carry basket. She hoped the weight and bouncing wouldn't tear the bottom out, but the goods would do them no good at all if they didn't reach the house.

Talus ran ahead and waited for them to catch up, then she raced back to follow Arie and growl into the dark woods. She did this repeatedly, until finally the trees thinned and Arie saw first the houses on the far side of the gulch, then the space between the houses. The full moon had just risen, huge and yellow at the horizon, making the sky around it a deep purple. In its light, the old power poles—still standing sentry after all their long disuse—threw thin, spidery shadows over everything.

Curran was flagging. Arie put her arm through his. "Here we are." Both panting heavily, they rushed across the street and into the backyard. Talus turned at the edge of the woods and barked several times, hunching with her claws planted in the tall grass. It was a deep snarl, a warning to whatever was behind them. Curran whistled, a single sharp chirp. The dog whirled immediately and sprinted to him. As they passed into the backyard, Arie pounded on the wall of the house. Handy was already letting down the rope ladder. Curran motioned her ahead of him and she started up.

"Handy," she shouted. "Go downstairs, quick. Get the back door open." He disappeared, and she heard him run across the roof. "Follow me," she called to Curran. "Talus will be all right. We'll let her in down below." As she pulled herself hand-over-hand, Arie heard Curran tell the dog to stay.

The straps on the basket dug painfully into her shoulders and threatened to pull her backward off the ladder, but she finally got to the top and hauled herself up and over the edge. She let the basket fall off her. The binoculars were sitting near the sky panel where Handy had left them. She snatched them up and scooted up to the roof peak. It was a precarious spot but afforded the best visibility. She trained the binoculars first on the place where they had come out of the woods. Nothing there. She scanned up the street and down to the end of the cul-de-sac. Not a single thing moved except the cartwheeling bats, now clearly visible, hunting blind in the moonlight.

Curran got to the top and dropped his bags just as Arie had and pulled the rope ladder up. It clattered enormously against the side of the house.

"Arie," Renna called from inside. "Are you all right?"

Arie showed herself at the sky panel. "Quiet," she hissed. "We're fine." She clambered down, and Curran came right behind her. "Close that hatch," she told him. He did, and threw the bolt. He was wide-eyed and looked ready to collapse. The bandage on his head was stained with blood, and Arie hoped none of the stitches had torn loose under it. "Over here," she said. The sofa sat sideways, and the inside hatch was pulled aside. "Climb down through here," she said. "It will be a squeeze. There are shelves—feel with your feet."

Curran did as she said. His big shoulders were indeed a snug fit. Once he was down in the closet she saw how dark it was. "Hold on," she said. "I'll bring a light." She lit one of the votives and reached the cracked saucer and candle down to him. He was so tall that he could easily reach into the open hatch from inside the small closet. "Follow the hallway out," she told him. "Bear right toward the back of the house. You'll hear Handy. And watch your step—as you said, conditions have deteriorated."

"Thanks." He moved out of the little bedroom in the narrow circle of light the stubby candle threw at his feet.

Arie sat back on the floor and heaved an exhausted sigh. A complicated rustle and scrape made her look up; Renna eased across the floor in her careful half-crawl, holding a cup of water aloft, judiciously working to not spill it.

"Here you go."

Arie, touched by the small kindness, drank and sighed again. Most nights, by the time she climbed into her bedroll, she felt a sort of satisfied no-age tired. Right now her joints and back and the throb in her cut hand were proclaiming every one of her fifty-two years, and a couple of extra decades tacked on for good measure. "How's the supply in here?" she asked, wiggling the empty cup.

"Handy got some more from outside," she said. She put her slender arm around Arie's shoulders. It was an intimate gesture, and Arie wanted to shrug her off. That old resistance to touch didn't mind giving, but it hated to receive. She let Renna's arm rest where it was. "Are you all right?" she asked again. "What happened?"

"We're fine, I think," Arie said. "Something was behind us in the woods, but we didn't see anything."

Renna's eyes widened. "What do you think it was? People?"

Arie patted Renna's knee. "Let's get you back over to your bed," she said. She got to her feet with some effort and helped Renna up. With Arie to steady her on her bad side, she was actually moving pretty well. "I don't think it was a person," she said. "Talus, Curran's dog, she was awfully frightened."

Renna eased herself onto the car seat, making room for Arie. "Maybe it was a bear," she said. She'd knotted her long hair behind her head so that wavy tendrils hung down around the sides of her face. Despite her hollow cheeks, Arie thought her remarkably lovely.

"Not a bear," she said. "Bears won't come near a dog, especially a big dog like Talus. And they aren't stealthy. Not this sort of stealthy."

Then they both heard the click of Talus's long claws on the hardwood floor below. There was a soft burst of male laughter—two voices—and Renna's face spread with a smile of simple relief.

"They're in," she said, and hugged Arie.

5

I T WAS NEARLY MIDNIGHT, and Arie didn't
need the windup clock to tell her so. The moon
was acting on her like a magnet.

Renna had been asleep for hours. She had taken
over the sofa and was rolled in her blanket like a
sausage. She hadn't moved a muscle or made a sound
for so long that it was almost as though she wasn't
there at all. This day, which began with a forced march
across the attic and was topped off with Curran's
troubling entrance into their world, had exhausted the
girl. But Arie also thought that having two men
standing guard—Handy on the roof and Curran in the
rooms of ruin—had allowed her to drop into a deeper
sleep, maybe deeper than any she had had in a very
long time.

Everything Arie needed for the ritual was in her
pockets or tucked into her belt. She crossed as silently
as she could, wanting not to alert Curran down
below—though she thought Talus would certainly
hear. The sky panel was unbolted; she went up top and
carefully closed it behind her to keep a little warmth
inside.

"Can't sleep?" Handy sat in the single corner,
bundled much as Renna was. He leaned on the raised

platform where the jerry can sat, knife in hand.

"I haven't aimed for sleep yet," she said.

After she'd gotten Curran back to the house, Handy had helped him set up a spot to sleep in Arie's old bedroom. The dog, as delighted with Handy as he had been with Arie, had taken her time sniffing around the house. Arie shooed her in with Curran and told him to keep Talus closed in the room until they could clean up broken glass and anything else that might hurt her. She didn't need the dog to take an interest in Granny's closed bedroom door—not yet.

"Everything's quiet up here," said Handy. "You should rest, Sister."

"I have a thing to do," she said. "You'll not like it, and I'll not explain it. I have an errand by the river."

"Not now," he said, quiet voice perplexed. "You don't mean to go out there in the dark."

"Yes, that's what I mean."

He threw off the blanket from around his shoulders and stood. Arie took two steps backward and drew her short spear. "If you try to stop me, all you'll accomplish is waking everyone else or making me mark you with this blade. And Handy," she said, her voice conversational, "I've bound up enough open flesh in the past few days—I don't want to make more work for myself with you."

He sank back to a sitting position and rested his forehead in one hand. "Ariela," he said. Her name came out in a long, weary sigh. "Something was in those woods tonight. It chased you and him. Right up to the house, damn near."

Her heart hurt a little to hear the fatigue in his voice. "I'll tell you a true thing, little brother: there is something in those woods every night. Who knows: tonight may be the night it eats me." She let down the rope ladder and stepped over the edge of the roof. "Or maybe not. If not, I'll be back before dawn."

She took the short spear in hand and moved out of the backyard. Just as she stepped over the buckled sidewalk, she heard Handy overhead.

"I love you," he said. His words were as clear as if he were standing next to her. He stood at the roof peak, watching her go. His long hair fell around his shoulders, and the moon lit one side of his face; the other half was in black shadow. She lifted her spear in a salute and turned to the trees again, this time strolling to the end of the cul-de-sac, down the hill to the place of ritual.

Those first few steps into the woods were hard to make tonight. Her mind wanted to ping backward and see Talus braced for a fight, snarling at whatever had stalked them from Curran's camp. But she pushed through it, told herself that it felt like this every month when she had to pick her way along in the dark. The sense of eyes everywhere was part of the ritual, after all—the understanding at a cellular level that tonight each breath could so easily be the last one she pulled into her lungs, that the chorus of frogs and crickets, bats and screech owls might be the music that sang her out of this life.

When she broke through into the clearing, the tall grasses were like a still life—not even the slightest breeze moved them, and in this light they seemed painted there, silvery and still. Somewhere close by— she could no longer tell quite how far—there was a cemetery, the first one established when Eureka was made a town. Most of the headstones had sunk beneath ground level long before Arie had moved in with Granny, and now it was impossible to see even the taller monuments through the landscaping that had gone back to forest and meadow faster than anyone could have imagined possible. The cemetery had never been her intention, though. She was bound for the river, just on the other side of the clearing and down the bank.

She laughed out loud when she got there. It was cold, past dew point, but she didn't so much as slow down. She set the spear on the stony, leaf-littered bank, stripped out of her clothes, and strode into the river before her skin even registered the cool night air. The cold water made her breath catch, and before she was up to her knees she put her hands over her head and dove.

Gods, the shock of it! All last fall and winter it had been the same, often colder than it was tonight, and every time she wondered if it could be enough to stop her heart. True, winter wasn't what it once was, and winter here had always been a temperate thing. But when the night air was cold, forty-eight or fifty-degree water was a jolt. She had to fight her lizard brain when it yelled at her to get out, get out, get out of the water now. Instead, she stayed under, kicking for the middle, until finally her breath was gone. Up she came. She broke surface, panting and treading water. It wasn't very deep out here, perhaps eight or ten feet, but in the dark it seemed there might be a fathom yawning below her fluttering legs, deep enough for any number of mythic creatures to rise up and take her. She forced herself to lie over on her back and float, then she rolled onto her belly and did a neat breast stroke for shore.

Climbing out, the air seemed colder still. Atop her pile of clothes was Curran's beach towel. Even in the washed-out moonlight, the cartoon starfish was a bright shade of tangerine orange, its huge eyes blue and bordered with long, curling eyelashes. A girl starfish, then. "Appropriate," she said. The towel was bigger than she was and smelled strongly of Curran's smoky home in the woods. Arie wrapped herself two whole times around, covered from head to ankles. She let it warm and dry her for a few moments. With the towel over her head, the night sounds were muffled and sweet. At random intervals the water dimpled when some low-flying night critter skimmed the surface and was taken by a fish. Bats were everywhere, small silhouettes. The moon made for a good hunt.

Relatively comfortable now, Arie folded the towel on top of her clothes, felt for her folding knife in the pocket of her skirt, drew it out. It was the only thing she needed for the rest of the ritual.

Twenty yards upstream was a massive sandstone boulder. It sat half-in and half-out of the river, and in the daytime the water around its base teemed with fish. She found the first foothold, about two feet up, and hoisted herself. Her shoulders and knees were sore from carrying Curran's supplies earlier, but after that first step it was an easy climb. The top evened out to make a nearly flat surface. Smooth from eons of weather, there was a shallow declivity in the center, stained and spotted, that always looked to Arie like a well-worn mattress.

Minding her knees and elbows, she lay down on her back in the center space. The stone was cool under her. Bits of lichen made furry patches under her fingertips and shoulders, heels and buttocks. She pulled her wet hair from behind her and fanned it out across the rock. If she'd been able to see herself from above, she would seem to be a woman airborne, falling through space or weightless in orbit. The moon spared nothing. The wavy nimbus around her head and the thin thatch between her legs were silver. Every little goosebump threw a shadow so that her whole skin was a pointillistic wonder. Her belly was flat between her sharp hipbones, and her small breasts, though softer than they once were, were still round in the cool air. She spread her arms and legs like Michelangelo's Vitruvian Man and looked the moon full in its face.

"The month is gone, but I am not," she said. "I sojourn. My life is..." Her voice faltered. Unbidden, she heard Handy instead: Don't say it. She lifted her chin. "I sojourn. My life is my own," she shouted. She waited, consciously slowing her breathing. "I sojourn. My life is my own. I shall not give, neither shall I receive. Rest for me. Rest for the Mother." The tears that had tried to form twice during the long day just past finally came. They rolled into her hairline and ears, their wet trails hot, then cool. "Mother, I sojourn yet a while longer," she said. Her voice failed on the final word, and she was racked with sobs. She lifted her arms above her, palms up, reaching for the moon with her wrists cocked back. The dark scars, her pledge to the Mother, her only gift to the future, were deep purple. She cried until she was hoarse and her sinuses blocked, cried the way she had as a little girl, weeping with her head under the blanket so Daddy Mack wouldn't hear, wouldn't climb the stairs.

Handy. Renna.

How could they lodge themselves inside her this way? Even Curran. Talus. After all the months of solitude. Before that, too, the time alone between Granny's death and the day the Pretty Pox swept through like a scythe. She was desperate to have back the simple task of minding her own diminishing days. Everything else, and everyone—family, friends, neighbors—she had released to their own destiny. And now she found that, even in the midst of all her deliberate letting go, her heart was a traitor.

Admitting them all. Opening itself around them in love, despite her.

Finally, she sat up and wiped her face, turned her head and blew her nose onto the rock. Her hair was barely damp, a silky cool curtain down her back. She pulled her legs together, straight out in front, and opened her knife.

The marks ran in two neat rows down both thighs, small chevrons that resembled a child's line drawing of geese on the wing, arrows pointing at her feet. Twenty marks, one V for each month since the Pink had accomplished its work. Each leg had two rows of five; this month it was her right leg, and that would make twenty-one. The oldest Vs, high on her legs, were pale white lines. Each successive scar was a darker shade of pink or red; the one from last month was healed, although it still itched now and then.

She ran her palm over her thigh and visualized the new mark. She rubbed the spot with her thumb and made the cut. It had to be deep enough to bleed well and scar well. The sting was intense and caused an echo of sensation between her legs, a small clench of muscle that rarely happened to her anymore. The feel of the blood was like the feel of tears. It trickled down either side of her thigh and pattered onto the stone. It would be food for something. A few mosquitos gathered, and she let them light—they'd be food for fish or bat or crane fly soon, or simply dead in the first frost.

After the blood slowed and thickened, Arie got to her feet. She was stiff and sore, sluggish in all her movements. She closed the knife and climbed off the boulder. It was always harder getting down than going up, easier to slip when she was tired and drained. Before she dressed, she wrapped her leg with a fresh rag. She thought again what a motley group of wounded they all were: bitten, cut, and bashed. She felt settled, though, cleaned out. Once more bundled and done with the ritual for another month, she picked up a flat stone and, with a practiced flick of the wrist, skimmed it out over the placid surface of the river, breaking the reflection of the moon into dozens of moving ripples.

Up the bank and into the clearing, she considered her new circumstances. The cutting not only marked her with the passage of time. It lent the gift that narrows focus: pain that clarifies. She saw now that she didn't have to make herself responsible for the lives of everyone under her roof. Neither did she have to resist the strong sense of good company well kept. She would urge them to go, all of them together if they would, but only after they had a little time to heal and plan. If they were a gaudy target now, the five of them in her ramshackle hideout, they were also more—more eyes and ears, more muscle and sinew. Even more tooth and claw.

The meadow and the trees ahead were quieter, now that the moon had passed its zenith. The path into the woods was nearly invisible. This was the hardest moment, every month—swallowing dread and walking into the dark.

Ten feet from the place where the shadows obscured the trail, something huge fell from the treetops in a lowering arc, straight toward her. It was a great horned owl, utterly silent, and if it hadn't thrown a wide shadow in the later light of the moon, she would not have seen it coming. She ducked at the moment it passed over her, and the displaced air pressed against her face and neck. Turning, she watched the owl drop into the deep grass of the clearing, which closed over it like water over a stone. There was the sound of invisible struggle, thrashing and a sharp bleat of pain and terror that made the last singing crickets fall momentarily silent.

All meandering thought dropped into an urgent blank, and Arie hurried out of the clearing, away from whatever was dying in pain and blood behind her. She couldn't see anything in the trees, and she kept herself from breaking into a run only by an act of steely will. This was different than the return trip from Curran's camp—that had been like swatting away a fly compared to what she felt now. The path was as familiar to her in the dark as it was in broad daylight, but rather than counting her steps, as she normally did, she kept her hands clenched at her belt and hurried in a stiff-legged gait. She was somehow sure that if she held her hands out in front of her—as instinct demanded when rushing through the dark— she would touch something unexpected. Or it would touch her. It would be her own great horned owl, a set of smothering wings and rending talons she was destined to succumb to.

Curran moved around the downstairs, getting his bearings in the mess. When he'd gotten here this morning, nerving himself to get inside, the couple of furtive glances he'd had through the haphazardly covered windows had only partly conveyed the wreckage. Arie had warned him about keeping Talus out of it, and when he saw the amount of broken glass everywhere he was thankful she had.

He made a full circuit of the L-shaped living room and dining room. There were four windows; he cleared a trail to each one, using his feet and a mildewed throw pillow to push the mess aside, flinching a little at the sharp rattle and clatter it raised. Talus whined and scratched at the closed door of the bedroom, and he shushed her. Her claws made a fretful circuit away from the door, then back, but she stopped whimpering.

As he reached each window, he paused and looked out with the binoculars Handy had left him when he'd turned over the watch. On the east side of the house he paid special attention to the end of the street, looking for Arie to come out of the woods. His mind kept trying to create her out of nothing, but all he saw was the place where the cul-de-sac fell away, dark and more dark.

A low-grade nausea worked on him, partly from the persistent ache in his head and face, but watching for Arie was making it worse. When Handy shook him out of a profound sleep, the first thing he told him was that she was out there again, alone this time. He hadn't explained a thing, Handy, and his tone of voice made it clear that Curran would do best not to ask. He didn't.

Returning to his makeshift broom, he swept a path from the dining room into the kitchen, where the back door was. He barely glanced at the demolished garden window over the sink. So high above ground level, no one could access it without first finding something the size of a pickup truck to climb on, and even then they would have to navigate through a massive amount of glass and rubbish. The other window showed him only a corner of the wildly overgrown backyard.

Satisfied that he'd made it safe enough, he let Talus out of the little bedroom. She wandered into the hallway, nose to the floor, getting her bearings by smell as she always did. The only thing to see out the bedroom window was a rotting board fence, but he took a quick look anyway. The closet door stood ajar, and he knew the hatch in its ceiling was open, but there was no sound from up in the attic. Satisfied, he followed Talus. She stayed next to him as he made a second circuit of the windows, but when they passed the front entry she veered off. The ruined hulk of a steel tool chest lay on its side, blocking the door; bent posts, where its rolling casters had once been, stuck out to the side like the legs of a dead thing. Talus rose on her hind legs, braced her front paws against the toolbox, and sniffed vigorously. Then she dropped back to the floor and growled quietly as she paced, intermittently whining and scratching around the edges of the metal cabinet.

"Hey, knock it off," Curran said. The entry smelled of urine, but it was essentially bare, and he didn't hear anything. Just to be sure, he ducked down and looked out the peephole in the door. Nothing but a shadow-riven front stoop and the haggard street beyond it. "Come on," he told Talus. "Stay by me." She obeyed but still seemed agitated, and it made Curran jumpy. Still, he felt safer by far in this remnant of a house than he had for weeks in his own snug camp.

He could still hardly believe they had let him stay. Handy, especially, who'd been so recently angling to kill him. Without Arie, it wouldn't have mattered what Renna said—he'd likely be lying dead in the woods now if Arie hadn't said otherwise. Handy's esteem of her was palpable, and—despite her small stature and her age—Curran already felt an answering deference.

He positioned himself at the east window again, resting the uninjured side of his head against the wall. The shattered upper panes of the double-hung sash allowed in a cool breath of night air, most welcome in the fetid stink of these lower rooms. The funk was heaviest near the closed door in the hallway. Handy had explained that the windows in there were boarded shut and covered with vegetation on the outside anyway, of no use to their watch. Curran took him at his word. Since the world had ended, the smell of a dead thing was more than familiar, and as far as Curran was concerned, whatever was dead in that room could remain so in peace and privacy.

Talus sat close and leaned against him as she always did. He stroked her silky head with his free hand, and they waited. Something was bound to come out of the woods.

༄ ༅

Renna's dream began the same way every time. She was in her office, next door to the principal's. The tall windows were open, the aluminum blinds fully raised, and afternoon sun shone in. Final bell had just rung, so the shouts and laughter of kids leaving for the day drifted up, along with the ubiquitous hum of Utiboards and the air brake sigh of buses lining up in the roundabout next to the cafeteria. She loved this part of the day, when the phone rang infrequently, the final touches were already added to the next morning's bulletin, and she could actually drink a whole cup of coffee before it went cold on her desk.

She was putting things in order, as she did every day before she left: lingering inbox items few and neatly ordered, outbox full. As she poured a fresh batch of paperclips into a pretty ceramic holder, someone outside screamed. She dropped the holder and the small red box. The ceramic dish shattered, and paperclips flew, bouncing silver reflections all over Renna's little office. It was awful, that scream. When she tried to run to the window, her feet wouldn't move. But somehow she was already looking out. Dead teenagers lay in perfect, uniform rows on the green lawn, arms crossed over their chests, bodies as far as she could see, like a vast cemetery that had arranged corpses but forgotten the burial. Their eyes were closed, and their faces were radiantly pink. All of them looked asleep, except that a great many had bled from the nose and eyes. Packits and Utiboards and Solareads were tumbled around them like confetti.

She turned from the window. When she tried to lock her office door, her hands couldn't remember the trick. She rotated the thumb bolt, but no matter how many times the bolt clicked into place, the door fell open. She got to her knees and crawled across the cheap carpet into the little supply alcove. The paperclips she'd scattered clung to her sweaty palms. There were no windows in the alcove, no door either.

"Posie." A man's voice bellowed out in the hallway. "Where the fuck are you?"

A storage cupboard took up most of one wall. It had large sliding panels in the bottom third. Renna opened one of the panels. There were banker's boxes in there in stacks of two, marked with the relevant school years: 2047-48, 2048-49, 2049-50. Still in slow motion, she pulled the boxes out, stacked them neatly next to the wall.

Something slammed repeatedly in the hall, something heavy hitting the metal lockers that still lined both sides of the corridor. "Posie, answer me!" The banging got closer. Renna crawled into the bottom of the storage cupboard. She slid the little door all the way closed, shutting herself into complete dark. The cupboard smelled like cardboard and copier toner. She pulled her knees to her chest and wrapped her arms around her breasts. The office door that wouldn't lock crashed open. She held her breath.

అ ✍

Handy spread blankets on the floor next to the Packard seat. When he'd gotten too tired to watch anymore, he secured the rope ladder and went down into the house to wake Curran. He had explained about Arie, hoped hard that Curran would watch, would see Arie when she returned, and would let her in downstairs. But in case she had to call up to Handy, he propped the sky panel open a few inches. The setting moon shone in at the crack and transected the attic in a thin band, offering just enough light to see without a candle.

Renna thrashed once in her sleep, moving her arms and legs in a crawling motion. The bedding she'd rolled up in didn't give her much room to move. "Shh," she whispered, and curled herself into a ball, as much as she could, anyway.

He knelt next to her, watching her face. Her brows drew down, making parallel lines above her nose. He touched that spot with one fingertip, letting it rest there, then he traced it over her broad, satiny forehead. Her body relaxed, and she stopped fighting the blankets. "Best sleep now," he whispered.

Her dark eyes opened. Seeing him so close made her recoil at first. He straightened, and she recognized him. "Oh, it's you." She reached behind his neck to pull him close again. Her eyes were so dark that pupil and iris were indistinguishable. "I'm so glad it's you." When he leaned to kiss her, she slid her fingers into his long hair and held him there with both hands.

֍ ֍

Talus could smell the old dead woman hidden in the middle of the house and could smell the bad dog that had been inside at the front door, and the old dried fear-piss of the woman Talus had heard but not seen, the young woman who was now sleeping over their heads.

The man Curran was afraid. She could feel the fear in his hands. Maybe it was his injury that made him afraid, because this was not a bad place. This was a good place. The bad dog wouldn't come in here again. It had come around their place in the tree, had stood at a distance and made Talus's fur jump up. But it was dead now, that bad dog—dead out in the street, dead like the old woman in the closed room. Dead things weren't scary. A bear had been here, too, but bears were easy to frighten with a loud bark. She liked barking at bears, and at raccoons and blue jays. Not skunks, though. Best to stand behind something until a skunk went the other way.

She sat close to the feet of the man Curran. When she pressed herself against his leg his fear stink lessened. She stayed close, though she wanted very much to run through this new place. There were food smells, but not down here—only in the place over their heads. Talus could smell the cooked chicken. That smell had been on the man Curran tonight when he came back to their house in the tree. The chicken smell made water come to her mouth, and she licked her face in case something tasty was there on her fur.

Many good things had been here in this new place, not just food. Other people and other dogs. Good people and good dogs. A little bird, too. Strange to keep a little bird in the house. A man with a cigar had been here for a long time with the dead woman in the closed room. And the small old woman, the woman who came to the house in the tree with the man Curran—she had been in this place for a great many years. Her smell was the smell that touched everything here, was stronger than all the other smells, even the bear's. She wasn't inside with them now, though. Talus had heard her leave a while ago, during the time when Curran was sleeping. Perhaps she went out to find the big cat, to kill it.

Talus was afraid of the big cat. It had come around their house in the tree, too, like the bad dogs. It pissed on things close by and came around while they were inside at night. The big cat was not like a bear—it was quiet. It followed in the dark and watched from up in trees. Talus didn't think it was very afraid of dogs, not like a bear was afraid. Tonight, when they had walked from the house in the tree to the new smelly house, the big cat followed all the way. Even when Talus had made her fiercest growl and bark, it had stayed close. The cat didn't smell afraid. It had kits and smelled of milk. It smelled hungry.

The man Curran moved in a hurry to look out the window, and Talus scrambled to her feet. "She made it," he said. Even though his head was still making him sick, he was happy. Something good was going to happen.

అ ఆ

Arie finally came out at the top of the path and onto the street, sweating in the cold pre-dawn air. She slowed her pace, fighting the urge to look over her shoulder, but her eyes tracked the night sky anyway. Two blocks up, a single unmolested streetlight shone, still doing its duty for no one, and in its light the dead

neon sign at the corner grocery—Pat's Market—
reflected dully beneath it.

Setting foot on the weedy tangle of her yard
brought a flood of relief. The skeletal branches of the
maple tree seemed like a naked welcome home. She
slipped through the gap in the fence, thinking to signal
for the rope ladder to be let down.

Something moved out of the dark, directly at her,
and in the instant of contact she gasped and stumbled
sideways, groping for the short spear. But then Talus
was pressing against her leg, licking her hand.

"Here." It was Curran, speaking from the back
door.

"Damnation," she breathed. She made the little
detour under the old porch awning, and Curran
stepped aside. The door was only open about a foot;
Talus squeezed through first, and Arie followed. She
expected her feet to grit through the usual mess, but a
path had been cleared.

"Handy told me you were out," Curran said. The
dead hulk of the refrigerator now served as a blockade
and prevented the door from opening all the way. He
put his shoulder to it and muscled it back in place. A
length of rope secured on either side of the doorframe
functioned as a tie-down; Curran gave the knot a
mighty yank. The boards Handy had torn free earlier
to get Curran and Talus inside lay heaped in the
corner, and Arie made a mental note that they should
be carted upstairs to split for the fire.

"It's good Handy was able to wake you," she said.
"I wasn't sure but that you'd go comatose."

"I'm still here," he said.

"Glad of it. You did well on the watch," she said. "Both of you." She slapped Talus companionably on the rump, and the dog looked up, wagging her tail furiously. "It's another three hours or so until dawn," she told Curran, "and if I'm honest, there's no way I can stay awake. How's your head now?"

"Still hurts a bitch," he said."

"Wounds of war," she said. "Has it bled?" They were making their way down the dark hallway and into the little bedroom. Talus tarried again at Granny's door, but only to give it a single cursory sniff, her curiosity apparently satisfied.

Curran gingerly touched the stained bandage. "Seems fine," he said. "I can finish the night."

"I'll go up, then." She moved into the closet. The smell of the attic—kerosene lamp, apples beginning to ferment, crumbling insulation—took hold of her. "Tomorrow I'll see to it, that head, along with all our various infirmities." She braced her foot on the lower shelf. Curran put a hand on her arm.

"Why did you go out?" he whispered. "After what happened to us before—"

She waited, saying nothing. He took his hand away.

"It was time," she said, climbing.

In the attic, she found Handy and Renna asleep. Renna was still wrapped in her blankets on the car seat. Handy had made his bed on the floor beside her. He lay on his side, right arm curled under his head, left arm planted above him, fingers intertwined with Renna's. That's going to pain you later, Arie thought, when you wake up all pins and needles. Truth to tell, she had fully expected them to be sleeping under the same blanket tonight; it surprised her to see otherwise.

She let down the sky panel so that it closed all the way, and she threw the bolt. It was easy enough to find her own bedroll in the dark—she'd done it a great many times. In her habitual fashion, she tucked the short spear under her pillow. The slingshot and ammo bag were wherever Handy had left them; they were his concern tonight. She took off her apron, shook her hair out of its horsetail, and slid beneath the blankets.

The thin padding of her bed might just as well have been an eiderdown mattress, so heavy was her exhaustion. Falling into sleep as if launched from a catapult, she heard a soft, sonorous voice beneath her: There is a ship that sails the sea, she's loaded deep as deep can be. Curran, singing to Talus.

6

"SUNDAY BREAKFAST." They were on the roof together, all but Talus, and she'd been satisfied with a meal of her own and a nap in a patch of sunlight on the small bedroom floor. Even Renna was up top; it was a meticulous effort, but with a great deal of help, she'd managed it. "That's what we're going to call this," Arie said. "It may just as well be Sunday."

She'd been the first one awake. After a harrowing day and a night of scratch sleep, it was well into mid-morning when her bustling around had gotten everyone stirring. Now here they were, sitting on a blanket at the four corners of the compass, the sun warm and a fine meal ready. Renna angled herself to one side and used Handy's shoulder as a backrest. Handy looked simultaneously self-conscious and exalted, and Arie hoped this little dance didn't become a dangerous distraction. Curran had put the sun behind him but still squinted in the bright light, looking groggy and listless. They were all exceptionally quiet.

"Here, now," said Arie. She handed around plates, like she might at a social occasion in the time before. "Let's break bread. Every one of us needs mending and fuel." She had taken great care to make the victuals seem more than adequate. Diced apples tossed with dried blackberries made a sort of fruit salad. The last of the roasted chicken was shredded with slivers of carrot and chopped cabbage and rolled into flatbreads she'd cooked over the fire pit. She'd even gone to her dwindling store of home-canned food and opened a half-pint of plum jam and a quart of dilly beans. The beans stood in a neat green bundle in the jar. The garlicky, briny smell of them was a brilliant snap, a piece of every August she could remember before the world died, that feverish month when the summer garden flung a vast amount of food into the world before the earth tilted away from the sun again. She took one of the beans now, a long, crisp spear, and savored the acid tang of vinegar on her tongue. "Now, that's good," she said, smiling. She handed the jar to Curran, who helped himself and passed it to Handy. Handy fished out two and handed one to Renna.

"Like communion," said Renna. "With pickles."

"True enough," said Arie. She popped the rest of the dilly bean into her mouth and licked the sour juice off her fingers. "Last night it came clear to me what needs to happen here, quite clear. And one thing that we will do without fail is commune. Keep eating," she said. "I want you to fill your bellies for the day ahead. I can talk and breakfast at the same time—all you three need to do for now is chew and listen." She stood and wiped her hands on her apron. "I think better when I move." She put her hands on her hips and looked out over the yard and street.

The day was perfect, full of birdsong. A woodpecker thrummed somewhere nearby, the hollow rattle somehow a comfort. "This is the first time I've stood here and not given a tinker's damn what might see me," she said. There was the slightest intermittent breeze; it lifted a tendril of her white hair and rattled a few errant leaves in the corners of the roof. "By God, I feel like Peter Pan," she said. She lifted a fist and shook it at the street and the wide woods beyond. "Nuts to you, Captain Hook," she said. When she turned, all three of them sat stock-still, food in hand, staring. "Gods, what a failure of imagination," she said, waving them off. "Just hear me out." She began to walk from the rope ladder to the garden boxes, from the garden boxes to the jerry can, the jerry can to the sky panels—six paces one way, eight another, three, five—then around the circuit again.

"Strange, isn't it," Arie said, "what's happened in a day's time. Last full moon I was alone. Each of you was somewhere else. Yesterday, Curran, we thought you meant to kill us, and for a little while we came close to killing you." Curran nodded, silent, and Handy chewed contemplatively, gazing into the middle distance. Only Renna made eye contact, her breakfast set aside.

"From the first day, when we met in the clearing," Arie continued, "I've resisted. Resisted you, Brother, and you, too, Renna. That's been my way, the way I chose years before the Pink burned through. I chose the Null Folk, and the Null are anchorite in their ways. That's no secret."

Renna opened her mouth to speak, and Arie held up her two hands. "Wait, Renna. Let me say it all.

We'll commune, I promise, but not yet." She pondered just how to tell them what needed telling, what to say. What to withhold. She leaned between Handy and Curran and plucked one of the last dilly bean from the jar.

"The full moon is a holy time for me," she said. "I made it so and have kept it so." She'd brought up a stoneware pitcher, and she filled it now from the jerry can. Tucked out of the sun, the stored water was cool in her hands. She put the jar in the middle of the blanket and kept moving while they filled their cups. "I have no god. My devotion since I was old enough to choose has been to my true Mother, the earth, and to the great generative force of the universe, though it's a mystery." She finally stopped her wandering and came back to the blanket. She sat down again between Renna and Curran and straightened her apron over her lap. Renna poured Arie a cup of water, and she took a long, cool swallow. The unseasonable weather had warmed the asphalt shingles, making them smell faintly of tar and radiate heat like an afternoon sand dune.

"Like all pure devotion," she continued, voice quiet, "the ritual is also madness. I'm aware of it." She took another sip of water. "It's the madness of a single night each month that clarifies, that lends sanity and illumination to a life that might otherwise drive reason away altogether." She paused and looked at them— first Curran, then Renna, and finally Handy. Each one she measured, eye to eye. "Last night it was given to me to understand that I was pushing. I was wrong. My responsibility, and my gift, is to open." She turned both hands palm up. The cut on her thumb from the day before was uncovered, crusted and mending. "Curran," she said. "Renna. Handy. Your lives are your own, but your sojourn has intersected mine. I will embrace that for now—a temporary juncture." In the beat of silence that followed, a raven called nearby, a rusty croak like an unoiled gate falling open. "Whether we choose to traverse together from here is ours to decide, is it not?"

"Yes," said Renna. She touched Handy's arm.

"I think time is short, though. Do you feel it? We need to mark that feeling—we ignore it at our peril, I believe."

"We do," said Handy. "We're too visible." He looked at Curran. "You found us," he said. "You won't be the last."

"This whole area is on their agenda," said Curran.

"Agenda," said Arie. "You mean the group at the high school, yes?"

Curran nodded and rubbed at his eyes. "The Konungar," he said.

Handy frowned. "The what?"

"That's what they call themselves. Their leader is this guy Russell, and he has a thing about Iceland, talks about it constantly. He got them calling the school New Reykjavík, and the bosses are the Konungar—the Kings. A couple of weeks before I got out of there, Russell and—"

"Not now," said Arie. "I want to hear all of it, Curran. Forewarned is forearmed, and that's our aim. There's too much we don't know, and we can't keep bashing around, each of us keeping our own piece of the puzzle tucked in our pockets. Tonight you'll tell us whatever you can about the encampment. From you, too, Renna."

Renna paled, but nodded. "Whatever I can."

"Handy, I want to know from you what kind of journey it is between here and God's Land. It's only fair that everyone understand the trip they're in for." She cocked her head and gave him a level stare. "And what sort of place they're aiming at, too."

"It's likely different than you recall," he said.

"One hopes," she said drily. "I'll put in my nickel as well, and we'll see how the tale rounds out." She got to her feet again, tucked the short spear back into her belt. "But that blather can all wait. As long as we have sun, we're going to make hay." She perused the rooftop. "My strategy in these two-ish years was to stay invisible, a mouse in the wall—and a rotted wall in the bargain. Nothing here for anyone to want or wager on. For an old woman alone, it worked fine." She glanced around at them, each face expressing some species of sheepish guilt, and she made a little snort. "Oh, buck up," she said. "If the old woman can shift gears after all this time, it should be easy enough for the likes of you three. But we need to buy some time."

"How much time?" said Curran.

"Enough for your head to clear," said Arie.

"I could travel now," he said.

"But I can't," said Renna. Her face was creased with worry. "If I had to run..." Her voice broke.

"We're not leaving anyone," said Handy. He took Renna's hand in his two. "Arie's right. In a week, maybe a little longer, you'll be ready. And you, too," he told Curran. "I know how hard I hit you yesterday," he said. He was calm and conciliatory but—Arie was glad to hear—not apologetic. "It's a hard trip," he said. "We need to be sound before we go."

"This is exactly my point, Handy. Listen now," Arie said. She felt a great energy and could see that they were feeling it, too. "It's decided: a journey together. In order to make the journey, we must prepare, and quickly. To prepare well, we must be well, and to be well we must have some healing time, even if time is short. Do you see?"

They did.

"And at the heart of finding time, we must—must—have a safe place. It's essential that we make a small fortress. We're now visible, and visible equals vulnerable. As you said, Handy, Curran found us, so there's no reason to think that others won't. Today we fortify. Mouse in the wall is out. I want every one of you thinking about how we can best accomplish that."

"Let's do it," said Curran.

Arie stood and began picking up the leavings of their meal. "The first thing I'll do is see to everyone's bandages," she said. "If we don't look like the wretched leavings of a hospital waiting room, I don't know what. After I play doctor again, we'll get to work." She bustled around, scraping their few leftovers into a small bowl, which she handed to Curran. "Give this to Talus," she said. "My worms can go hungry for a few hours." She smiled around at them again, a pirate's grin. "I'm thinking castle keep. Can your imaginations go there? I believe we could pull that off."

≈ ≈

The rules were simple:

By daylight, mend and buttress. By lamplight, cohere and conspire.

Renna did her part in the attic. At first, with the weather so mild, she angled to stay up top. But after talking it over, they all agreed it was risky—if she needed to get inside and no one was there to help, she'd be stuck on the roof.

"While we shore things up down below," said Arie, "you'll be doing strategic planning for the trip and acting as quartermaster."

"A bean counter," Renna said. "Busy work."

"Yes, actually—someone needs to count the beans. Also the blankets, socks, tow sacks, and aspirins." Renna had just changed the bandage on her hip herself while Arie watched; now she was walking from one end of the attic to the other, working the muscles and using Handy's rhododendron stick to balance on. "Don't flatter yourself, either," Arie said. "No one around here is quite so precious that we can waste her on busy work. You're just grunt labor like the rest of us, honey. Here, now." She laid a piece of plywood, about two feet square, on the car seat. "You can use this as a lap desk." On the board, she placed two sharpened pencils and a straightedge. "This, she said, "is precious. You know that, though." She held up a spiral-bound notebook with a slightly dog-eared paper cover.

Renna stumped over and took the notebook, holding it reverently. "I do." She rested her palm on the bright-blue cover, Mead stamped there in white. She lowered herself onto the sofa and put the plywood across her lap, placed the notebook squarely in the center, and straightened the pencils and ruler. Then she covered her mouth with one hand. Arie thought she was laughing, but Renna looked up and had tears on her face. She tried to smile, but that only made fresh tears roll down her cheeks. "It's just—it's something normal. Do you know what I mean?"

"I know."

Renna picked up one of the pencils, sharpened to a fine, angular point with Arie's knife. She held it to her nose and inhaled. "Oh, I love that," she sighed. "The way the pencil sharpener smelled in school. In Mrs. Davis's second grade at Alice Birney Elementary. The sharpener was bolted on the wall at the back of the room, by the sink. It smelled like this. And like tempera paint." She shook her head and wiped her eyes with the back of her hand. "I always loved office supplies," she said, and laughed, a broken little sound. "I used to steal them from work."

Arie sat beside her. "Not enough here to steal, and you couldn't run far if you did," she said. "Handy'd come after you quick. Though I don't suppose you'd mind getting caught then, would you." Renna gave Arie an awkward sidelong look and kept silent. "No shame in it, girl," Arie said. "Thus was the world ever pushed forward, with that hunger. It's between you and him, at any rate." She thumped a knuckle on the cover of the notebook. "Let's put you to work. Here's what you'll do with this paper."

Renna would begin with a manifest of their supplies, including Curran's things from the stump house. "If we get a chance, we might make another quick run back there," Arie said. "We had to leave quite a few things that would be good to have on hand.

We'll cross that bridge down the road, though. For now, let's get clear on exactly what we have, and how much of it." What she thought, but didn't say, was that when the three of them were able to travel, they'd be able to more efficiently divide their stores between them—splitting out the best things to take on the road and what to leave for Arie. Over breakfast she had been careful not to say directly that she would not be going with them, and she intended to keep that information to her breast as long as she could. Her mind hadn't changed on that point.

"After you make the manifest," she said, "make a calendar, just a single month. I want us, all four, to have a quick point of reference. Best we set some concrete goals and stay on track. It makes the time pass, too."

"A calendar," Renna echoed. "But...what month is it?"

Arie knew from the flock of arrows cut into her own thighs that it was the end of October, but she didn't say so. "What month do you want it to be?" she said. "Gracious, girl, make one up if you've a notion. Who's left to tell you you're wrong? Make it twenty-eight days, is my advice. Every woman follows the moon in one way or another. But I leave those details to you."

Renna looked at her for a long moment and shrugged. "Okay," she said. She looked interested, the way a child looks when given permission to name a puppy or choose what to eat for supper, more engaged than Arie had seen her since the day she'd come out of her fever.

"And the last thing," she told her, "is crucial. You're going to make a map. For that, you'll need this." She handed Renna a folded square of brown paper. It was an old grocery sack, meticulously cut so that it opened up into a large rectangle.

"A map of what?" Renna said.

"As much of this corner of the world as you can," Arie said. She enumerated on her fingers. "The area around the school, our immediate vicinity, and the river through these woods. After that, work your way north as far as you can, and leave room for the hills out to the east."

Renna frowned at the unfolded brown paper, smoothing it with both hands. "Arie, I don't know how to make a map."

"Why not? Haven't you lived here all your life?"

"Yeah. I mean, I could draw you a map of my old neighborhood, but I don't know what to put in north of here. How do I know what...shape to make it? Or the size—the scale, I mean."

Arie patted her once on the back and got to her feet. "My goodness, who beat you over the head with rules?" she said. "Look around you, Renna." She spread her arms and gestured at the expanse of the attic. "Our whole life is a game of chance now. Take a chance. Do you think the map police are going to arrest you? In ancient times, cartographers dealt with the unknown by adding elaborate sea serpents and fanciful animals into their maps. Their art was not exactitude, it was knowledge and rumor combined with imagination. Learn as you go. Make it up, if you have to. Break rules, Renna. When we ally tonight, we'll all throw in to work up the map. Now I have to get down and help Handy and Curran."

Renna continued to stroke the paper sack, stared at it musingly.

"Don't forget to get up and move around as much as you can," Arie said. "Keep working your leg. And save the mapping until after you've worked on the other things. You'll give your mind a chance to wander with the idea while you count beans. Then, when you're ready to start, just do." She went to the inside hatch and started down. Curran and Handy were already hard at work together, and their mingled voices made a good sound. "Do what my granddad advised," she told Renna, "whenever he had a project going: do your best and caulk the rest."

"Do what?"

"You'll be fine," Arie said, working her way into the closet below.

Talus bounded in to greet her, dark eyes lit up with all the company and commotion. Arie squatted down for a moment and stroked the dog's head and neck. She was a handsome animal, and her heavy coat—gold and caramel, cloud pale and cinder dark—was silky under Arie's hand. In a crouch, Arie was so short and Talus so tall that they were face-to-face. She gave Arie a single, companionable lick on the jaw.

"Where are those men?" Arie said. She and Talus wandered down the hall and came out into the living room together. It had been less than two hours since they'd decided on a course of action, and already she was stunned by what Curran and Handy had accomplished.

Piles of debris had been sorted and consolidated. Upholstered furniture, most mildewed and vomiting stuffing, was set upright and pushed to one wall. The doors and drawers of every cupboard and closet leaned on end near the front door. Granny's antique dining table—all chrome and thick, indestructible Formica—was wiped clean and sported neat piles of cans, bottles, and a growing pile of coiled wire stripped from the backs of dead electronic devices. The black plastic cover from Pop's turntable was pulled loose to serve as a container for the silverware and kitchen implements that had been tossed everywhere.

On the countertop that separated the kitchen from the dining room was an accumulation of things that seemed like alien artifacts: a dented toaster, the drawers from a metal file cabinet, the ornate face and workings of a smashed grandfather clock, a huge branch of coral and a chunk of petrified wood, a dark-blue Webster's dictionary the size of a cinderblock, Pop's marble beer coasters, and Granny's pasta maker—which looked more like a medieval torture device than a kitchen gadget. A life-sized head made of solid teak, a souvenir from Granny and Pop's Peace Corps service in the Philippines, was placed squarely in the center of everything. It was the image of a young woman. Her eyes, blank and blind as a Greek statue, stared placidly. She had long, carved earrings, a flower behind her ear, wooden hair piled in a polished heap. The head weighed twelve pounds if it weighed an ounce, Arie knew—a perfectly useless thing from a life abundant with inadequate treasures.

"We haven't finished clearing the kitchen yet," said Handy, "but we're ready to start reinforcing. I found a mess of tools out in the garage."

"I dumped them out of that thing," said Arie, hooking a thumb at the roll-around tool chest wedged in at the front door. "I didn't need much more than what I already had in my little box. What are you going to do with these?" She held up a pair of heavy tin snips.

Curran was clearing up the last of the mess with a ratty push broom. The pile of sand, broken glass, gravel, and desiccated animal shit was considerable. "For the windows," he said. Talus sat off to one side, watching him work. "I'll cut some panels out of that thing," he said, nodding at the body of the metal file cabinet, "and the same with the washer and dryer. We'll tack the panels over the frames before we board them up."

"That's good," said Arie. "It'll be a light barrier, too. I don't know that you'll have enough for all the windows, so first cover the ones that face the street. And you need to make the front door as secure as you can. We're done using it."

"On it," said Curran. "Handy had a great idea."

"The fence," said Handy. "We're going to pull off some sections of the chain-length. There's plenty for every entry point. Once that stuff is pounded into the studs, we'll board it up, too."

Arie put her hands on her hips and looked around the room. It was strange to see it back in a certain rough order after so long. The midday sun showed black mildew that had climbed from baseboards to ceiling, especially on the east- and north-facing walls. "It'll be dark all day," she said. "But snug."

"We'll reinforce the back door but keep it usable," said Handy. "Maybe better to come and go from down here for now. Not give anyone else ideas about coming in through the roof." Arie could hear the smirk in his voice.

So could Curran, apparently. "Yeah, yeah," he said. "I'm a bad creeper. You'll be knocking me upside the head with that for a while, I guess."

Arie took the broom from Curran. "A pair of comedians," she said. "Because one just wasn't enough. Maybe you can work up a routine and take it on the road."

"You think?" said Curran. He looked at Handy. "What do you say—play the clubs in Philly?"

Handy gave him a long-suffering face and brushed his hair back with one arm. "Grab those bolt cutters. We'll go take the fence apart, Sister," he said. Better block the door while we're out there."

"Take Talus," she said. The dog jumped up at the mention of her name and grinned around at the three of them. "She's your lookout, aren't you?"

This was how they used up the rest of the day.

Arie dismantled the confusion in the kitchen, nearly puking when she bailed the swampy mess out of the sink. Afterward, though, the level of stink in the house registered at a much more tolerable level. The shattered garden window left a sizeable hole; even set high as it was, they'd have to use a couple of cupboard doors to cover it. For now, she relished the sunlight and fresh air coming in.

She carried the strange flotsam of the life before from the former breakfast bar and arranged it on the topmost shelves in the kitchen, using the huge dictionary as a stepstool. She could just as easily have tossed it all into the yard, but somehow putting everything in orderly rows on the shelves lent a curator's air, so that when she was finished the room resembled a museum of amusing artifacts, which she supposed they were. The tuneless plink and shimmy as the men took down the fence blended with the unintelligible timbre of their occasional conversation, creating an odd sense of homely satisfaction while she worked. A couple of times she went to the little bedroom and called up through the hatch to check on Renna, and Renna called back that things were coming along. She sounded pleasantly distracted, like anyone busy at a job of satisfying work.

Finally, when the sky had begun to dim and a fine coastal fog rolled in off the bay, Arie got the back door open and helped Curran and Handy haul in all the would-be ramparts. Before dark, they got the hole over the kitchen sink secured and most of the windows covered. The squares of thin metal they'd cut from the old appliances were wickedly sharp, and they warbled and thundered while being wrestled into place. There was still more to do down here, but when they were finished and the metal was boarded over, there was a palpable sense of security and satisfaction over a day well spent.

ॐ ॐ

"It would be best to hear from you first, Curran."

The men had gone to the roof to wash up and make a perimeter scan, and afterward they had once more taken their meal together. Once Curran had fed and settled Talus—who was none too happy to be left out of their company again, and proved it by sitting under the inside hatch and whining softly—he returned to the attic, and they settled themselves in a loose circle.

Curran, who sat backward on the single wooden chair, rubbed his palms on his thighs, considering. "I told you how things were for me when the die-off hit," he said. "You already know a whole lot more about me than I know about any of you."

"That's so," Arie agreed. "But what you know about the high school is the first thing we need to hear." She was sitting beside Renna on the Packard seat, and she patted her forearm. "Renna has a piece of that story, too, and maybe it will ease her telling of it if you go first, Curran." At the mention of the school, Arie felt Renna tense, but was reasonably confident she'd open up when the time came.

Curran took a deep breath. "Fair enough," he said. "Like I told you, the guys who first took over have turned it into a kind of prison—basically a concentration camp, I guess. My mistake was thinking that it would all be fine because I knew the two who brought me in." He gave a humorless little laugh. "Wrong."

He explained that from the very first night he was ushered into a long, one-story building and put in a room with eight other guys. It had once been a science lab, and with all the tables removed was fairly large, but with no windows it had a claustrophobic feel. The

room was outfitted with several bunk beds—five sets—
and each man had staked out a small space to hold a
change of clothes and little else. "When I got there that
first night, a bunch of them were hunched around a
table playing cards. There really wasn't much else to
do when we were locked in," he said. "The Joes were
very intense about pinochle."

"Joes," repeated Handy.

"All of us," said Curran. "All the guys like me who
did stuff from the trades. Plumbing, carpentry,
electrical—we were all Joe. The auto mechanics, too.
We were all Joe."

Within a couple of weeks, he'd gotten a pretty
clear handle on the setup. The bosses lived upstairs in
the main building of the high school. There were five
of them when Curran first arrived. Each had
commandeered a pair of rooms, all of which looked
out on the streets below. "Gave them a sightline and a
clear shot," he said.

"So they have guns," said Arie.

"A couple," said Curran. "Of course, that's one of
their priority forage targets—right after food and
people they can use."

Everyone else was segregated: the cooks—three
women and one man—lived in the rooms behind the
kitchen; each of them was a Bessie. A trio of men who
worked the gardens were Sams. A larger group of
them were called George, and included one old man,
two children, and a few hunched and sallow women
who had the telltale signs of prior addiction—missing
teeth, badly pocked skin, a certain dull and twitchy
hunch to their shoulders. The Georges were compelled
to do the most tedious and unpleasant jobs. They

cleaned the latrines and carried slops to the compost piles. They sorted scavenged clothing and made rags when that clothing gave out. They sweated over laundry tubs and mopped all the buildings every week. The Sams and Georges were kept in side-by-side portable buildings; like the science room and the back of the kitchen, there were no windows.

"How did they decide where to put you?" said Handy.

"I mentioned Russell before," he said. "The Konungar guys call him Chief. He's a real piece of work—uses the principal's office. Isn't that great?" His mouth tightened into a colorless line. "They haul you in, and Russell's sitting there behind the big desk like king shit. That's your 'entrance interview.' Very official. Everyone starts their first day at New Reykjavík talking to Russell." He combed the fingers of one hand through his short beard while he talked, making a small bristly sound. "The Chief has the final say on who works where. In my case, he had Darius and Little Mikey's word for it that I knew construction. So I was a Joe right from the start. That was...lucky, I guess." His face went somber, and the stream of words quit abruptly.

The moon was up again, a sliver shaved off since the night before, but bright enough to make the frogs sing. "Renna," said Arie. "What did they call you?"

On the sofa, Renna shifted slightly away from Arie. "Posie," she said. "There were four of us, so they—they had to share." She turned to Curran. "When I got out, there were seven bosses. They ran across a little group living in a house about a mile away. There were two new guys who got put in with the Joes, and two of the old Joes got promoted."

"So," Arie said, turning the conversation smoothly. She did a quick calculation. "Somewhere around thirty people. That's impressive. By my estimate, they've cast a net around ten percent of the people left in town. Maybe more."

"Ten percent?" said Renna. "You think there are only three hundred people left here, out of, what...twenty-seven thousand?" She stared at Arie, eyes large in the candlelight.

"Something like that. It's a damn rough estimate," said Arie. "Those first days, before everything went dark, they yelled a lot of numbers, but it was the usual horseshit. They didn't know. How could they? It was still knocking us down like bowling pins. Toward the end, though, one of the last things I heard was a guy on the radio. He kept repeating that almost everybody was dead. Almost everybody." She leaned forward with her elbows on her knees and stared at her feet.

"I couldn't shake that idea," she continued. "It was all I could think about for weeks, and I kept doing math—in my head, on paper, all day the numbers kept circling me in a cloud. That was when there were still a few people wandering around. I sat at that front window, and I kept a running tally of every person I laid eyes on. Then one day I didn't see anyone all day. This was maybe a week after the hit, and I made up my mind to go out.

"The next morning I got up at first light and walked five blocks west—that's about a half mile—and I worked my way back home. Knocked on every door, even if the red slash was on it, and mostly there was a whole lot of nothing. That pox mark didn't seem to mean much anyway—not many had time to fuss with it before the Pink slapped them dead. A couple of times I swore I heard something moving around inside, and twice I saw curtains move, someone peeking out at me, a shadow behind the glass. But not one door opened. Got up and did it all over again the next day in another direction, and more of the same.

"It was the fourth day when someone finally opened. He was just a boy, twelve I suppose. Maybe thirteen. Growled at me like a cornered animal, actually showed teeth, and he waved a big chef's knife at me. What was in that child's eyes was nothing but fear—it had hollowed him out and taken over."

Her words fell off, and for a little while they sat in the faint sound of the night world. When she recommenced, Arie's voice was rough with unshed tears. "I came back here and moved into this attic that same afternoon. In the ground I covered, there should have been well over a thousand people around. Do you know how many I counted?" She looked up at them. Curran had tears in his eyes, too, and when he lifted a hand to his mouth, Arie saw it trembling. "Eight," she said. "Eight people I glimpsed or heard shuffling behind closed doors. By my estimation, that works out to damn near everybody dead. If the kill rate was less than 99.99 percent, I'll be frigged."

"That sounds right to me," said Handy. "I was eight weeks getting here, and even going straight through the middle of Orick and Arcata I only saw a handful up and walking around. Lying dead everywhere was a different story—of those, I saw plenty."

"The way you went door-to-door is exactly how the bosses do it," said Curran. "There's a big conference room downstairs in the main building there, and they've got it rigged out like a war room, like pictures you used to see in books of generals moving their toy troops around. There's a map of Eureka pinned to the wall. They drew a grid over the whole thing, and they X out a box for every area they clear."

"How do you know all that?" said Renna. "They weren't exactly letting people roam around. Posies never got to leave the second floor, and every time I saw people outside, they were always herded in a tight bunch, walking with a boss."

"It was the remodel," said Curran. "Two of us Joes were doing the whole thing." He turned to Arie. "The bosses all got two rooms apiece upstairs, regular classrooms. They had us knocking archways between the rooms so each of them had a sort of suite. It was Little Mikey who got me that gig—I told you about him."

"An old bowling friend," said Arie.

"Something like that. He hadn't been a boss very long. After a few weeks, they got lax about watching us. Things had gone well, we'd been in and out of their rooms, in and out of the building with no troubles, and after a while there were so many other people to keep track of that they—" He shrugged. "I think they had us both tagged for promotion. They stopped paying attention."

"You were going to be a boss," said Arie.

"Maybe in someone's head," he said. "Not in mine. The first minute they dumped me in the room with the rest of the Joes, I was scoping my way out. The other Joe doing the remodel—I never did find out his real name—was a problem. Even though they weren't watching us themselves, they kept the two of us on a buddy system. Little Mikey had given me this pep talk about how the other bosses were eyeing me for promotion and to keep tabs on the other Joe because they weren't sure they could trust him. I figured they were giving him the same speech about me. It wasn't a half-bad way to work us." He got himself a cup of water, drank it in a few large gulps, and wiped his mouth on his sleeve.

"I saw into the conference room one day when we were carrying in framing materials. Only a peek, but three of them were huddled over the big table with their heads just about touching. It was weeks before I found a chance to get in there, but when I did it was obvious what they were up to. There was a halo of Xs on that map, a perfect ring. They'd make a green diagonal in the sections they planned to forage and then they'd finish the X with a red marker when it was done. That was the day I decided to run, and which direction to go in. Started packratting a cache of stuff in a downstairs supply closet that had a broken lock. Once I had enough to get me through a couple of days, I got down to the basement, smashed open a little side door, and hauled ass."

"How long before you found your hideout?" asked Arie.

"Two days. I saw which sector they were planning to scavenge next, so I went another direction. I slept in empty houses, found a few things to scavenge myself. Found Talus. She was locked in a garage. When I broke in, she was just standing there wagging her tail at me. For a second there I figured she'd take my throat out, but she was..." He smiled. "She was just Talus. When I tried to back out of the garage, she followed me like it had been her plan from the start. I didn't do anything to keep her. She kept me. I found the big stump that same day, and it sure seemed like Talus was my good omen."

Arie turned to Renna. "You and Curran did not meet at the high school."

Renna shook her head. "Never," she said. The bosses were..." She thought for a moment. "Possessive of us."

Arie stole a look at Handy. Throughout this conversation he'd kept his hands busy, shaving a wicked point onto another long branch he'd gathered from the yard. Two more lay at his feet. His face was half in shadow, and his long hair obscured his expression. It couldn't be easy for him to hear this, Arie thought, but better to know it than leave it to the rot of imagination.

"The Posies, we each had our own rooms down on the far end of the upstairs," Renna said. "It was blocked off to just those four rooms and a bathroom. There were two Bessies who brought our food, and one from the Georges who swapped out the buckets. They weren't allowed to speak to us, but I don't think they wanted to." She stared off into the shadows while she spoke, studiously avoiding eye contact with any of them. "This one Bessie, though—man, she hated our guts. The whole time she was bringing in food and taking out dirty dishes, she'd be muttering to herself. One day I heard her say, 'Must be nice.' I guess it was because we lived in our own rooms, and there were windows. I wanted to kick her in the face." She spoke through clenched teeth.

"You were two rats in the same maze," said Arie. "Stuck and wanting to bite." Renna looked at her. The ghost of rage was still evident, a well of pain, but she nodded. Like a child, she stretched out on the car seat and laid her head in Arie's lap. The weight of it pressed against the cut on Arie's thigh, making a small, bright pain. She put a hand on Renna's head and combed her fingers through the heavy dark hair, caught wholly off-guard by a bolt of feeling for her, the sisterly, motherly old feeling of family. "I'd like to know how you got away, Renna," she said.

"I killed a man," came the immediate reply. Handy and Curran were both brought up short, their faces a little stunned, and Arie felt a similar jolt. "His name was Brody."

"Oh, shit," said Curran. "Yeah, I remember him. Wiry, tall guy."

"And smelled bad," said Renna. "Worse than everyone else, I mean." She closed her eyes. "They weren't supposed to fall asleep with us," she said. "Lots of times they did, but only for a few minutes, after. Brody really fell asleep, pretty much every time. I'd wake him up on purpose and act like I was afraid for him to get caught, but I just wanted to get him out." She yawned expansively, and Arie could feel the girl's body settling, unwinding. "One night," Renna said, "when he was really under and snoring, I went through his pockets. He sometimes had candy or gum, and I was always a little bit hungry. He didn't have candy, he had a knife. I didn't even think about it. I killed him, and I ran."

"So," said Handy, "he smells a lot worse now." There was a beat, with only the quiet schist, schist sound of his carving. Then they all began to laugh. This was more than Talus could bear, being alone down below, and she voiced a long, plaintive whine that curled into a sad howl at its end.

"Talus is right," said Arie. "We've blown enough wind up here for tonight." She slid out from under Renna, who pulled the blanket around her and up to her chin. Arie bent and kissed Renna's cheek.

"I'll take first watch tonight," said Curran. He pulled the sky panel lead from the spring clip and lowered it, bolted it. "You all get some rest."

Handy laid the sharpened stick in his hand with the others he'd whittled, stood and brushed shavings from his arms and legs. "Give a thump when you're ready to be spelled," he told Curran. "I'll be right here." He indicated the spot on the floor next to the sofa.

"I reckon I'll sleep better tonight than I have for a while," said Arie. "Things are battened pretty damned snug down there. You boys got a hard start on it."

"Tomorrow we should have it finished," said Curran. "The whole thing solid." As he crossed to the inside hatch, he touched big, tentative fingers to Arie's shoulder. "Good night," he said.

Arie reached up and gave his hand a brusque squeeze. Like a big paw it was, rough and warm. "Watch well, Curran," she said.

"Tomorrow I have to show you my map," murmured Renna. "I need input."

"Not to worry," said Arie. When she saw that Handy was bedded down, she blew out the last candle. "We still have plenty of nattering to do. We'll all throw in on the map project."

She moved by instinct and by feel from the work table to the compost bucket at the back wall, and squatted for a piss. Washing her hands and face, drying them, she heard Handy and Renna's whispers—not the words, just the simple exchange of thoughts on breath. She was next to the mandala now, and she leaned on it, arms extended, palms flat on the wall. The labyrinthine ridges imprinted on her skin. "I sojourn." Mouthing the words. "We sojourn. My life is my own." This will always be true, she thought, her fingers moving into the smooth grooves of wood. "I shall give, and I shall receive, yet my life will forever be my own." The truth of it seeped through her, a warm rush like a shot of alcohol to the belly. "Rest for me," she whispered. "Rest for them." Circling in, out. "Rest for the Mother, in time."

In the far reaches of the night, the wee hours they once were called, Curran's signal to Handy roused her only partway. Her mind floated to the surface like a soap bubble. Down in the rooms of ruin. The thought was a whisper in her head. But they weren't a ruin now, were they, those rooms? She was aware of Handy rising, opening the sky panel and going up to watch. Chill damp fell into the attic with a smell like the ocean, and Arie curled on her side with the bedding drawn around her.

᷍ ᷍

By the end of the second day, the lower part of the house was closed tight, boards over the outsides of the windows as well as the insides. While Handy and Curran completed the heavy work and Renna finished cataloging supplies upstairs, Arie tackled the leftover mess. She cut the fabric from moldering upholstery into large scraps, segregated all the usable items piled on Granny's table into what she would keep for herself and what she would send with the others when they left. Remnant bits of wood she collected for fire-starting. Irretrievable trash she tossed onto a growing heap of refuse in the backyard. She swiped the ceilings free of cobwebs and brushed every last particle of debris from the corners.

When she was done, the floorboards, though scarred and pitted with rot in places, were clean. Even with the sun still above the horizon, the rooms were all dark. But for the first time since closing herself in, she felt she could use the lamps freely. Tonight they could even light Curran's bright lantern, and it would be imperceptible from outside.

"It doesn't look like the same house."

Arie turned. Handy stood surveying the space the same way she was doing, both of them with legs apart, hands on hips. "Nothing is the same," she said.

"Damned clean," he said, "for a place going on empty in a few days."

She studied him, as she had so many times since the day he appeared in the clearing by the river. His expression was innocuous, but she knew he was testing.

"I think it would be good for us to spread out some," she told him. There would be a time and place to make them see that, yes: they'd be leaving without her. But she wouldn't let him rush her there. "Renna could stand to get out of the attic. She's been a good sport, cooped up alone these last two days." She linked her arm through Handy's, and they followed the small light at the end of the corridor where Curran had lit his candle. "We'll have our meal down here tonight, and our talk, and you'll make a sleeping place. I'd like to have some privacy, too."

He stopped short. "Sister," he said. There was something stern in his tone, peremptory. She thought he was about to object, perhaps revert to the prissy posture he'd taken about Renna during those first days and spout one of Daddy Mack's many rules governing copulation and procreation. But instead, he placed one hand on Granny's bedroom door. "This must be tended," he said.

"Yes."

"It's the last thing."

"It is," she said. Talus had come to the door of the little bedroom and stood on the threshold, watching them. The wavering light turned her into a brushy silhouette with a wagging tail.

"I boarded the windows today, in and out," he said, "and I split the last kitchen cupboard face in three pieces to nail across here." He took her hand and moved it in the dark so that she could feel the rough barrier. "But it... she must be tended," he said again. "We can't leave her here like this." He paused. "It makes no sense, Ariela."

Arie sighed. "It has a sense you don't yet see. But I hear you. I'm not arguing, am I?" She pulled on his arm.

Curran had made a tidy space for himself and Talus in the little room, with a bed for each of them and a ragged metal folding chair for a nightstand. On it was set a votive candle, a comb, and his book: The Great Gatsby, with a black feather stuck between the pages to mark his place. Each time Arie had passed through today, going to or from the inside hatch, she was struck by the warmth of it, how it reminded her of his orderly house in the stump. He was stretched out now, one arm over his eyes, snoring lightly. They'd taken the bandage off that morning. The bright, turquoise thread Arie had used to stitch his head was now maroon with old blood, and his bruises were healing well—a ghastly rainbow of yellow, brown, and green.

Talus circled behind Arie and Handy and shoved her solid self between them. She put back her ears and vigorously licked their hands. Handy laughed and dropped to one knee. Talus gave his head and neck a thorough snuffle, and leaned her haunch against his shoulder so hard he fell sideways. "Hey, watch it," he said, and gave her a vigorous scratch on the rump. She slitted her eyes with pleasure.

"She's a treasure, isn't she," said Arie. The uncomplicated expression of happiness on Talus's face was echoed on Handy's, a rare smile that made him an extraordinary man to look at. The sorrowful sense of loss hit her again, the certainty of how much she would miss him when he took the road. This time, she didn't resist that little arrow. No more pushing. She let it pierce, let the small sting of it run all through her until it settled and faded. "Let Curran sleep a bit. He and I will trade the watch tonight," she said, starting her climb up. "You've earned a night off."

☙ ❧

They took their evening meal in the attic by the light of two candle stubs. When they were finished, Arie announced with a great flourish that they were going to have their chat tonight in the living room—all of them.

"Even me?" said Renna.

"Of course, you," said Arie. "What do you think all means? I saw how you were getting around today. I think you can manage the climb."

"I might need a spotter," she said.

"We won't let you fall."

The living room was alive with light. Handy had slipped downstairs before them and worked a minor miracle. Arie's wooden chair was there, and seats on the floor made from folded blankets wrapped around two upholstered cushions that had somehow survived in the rooms of ruin. He'd polished the chimneys of both kerosene lamps before putting the match to them. Curran's camp lantern hissed companionably, its white mantle throwing brilliant reflections on the chrome legs of the old dining table. Deep in the shadows of one corner, his bedding and Renna's were fashioned into a place for them to sleep.

Renna stared around her. She was radiant, her heart-shaped face all smiles in the warm room. To her delight, Handy had laundered

Granny's satin bathrobe, and she wore it now over her regular clothes; the pale peach color of it reflected a blush onto her skin. Her dark curls were piled loosely on top of her head, and Arie thought both men were having a great deal of difficulty not staring.

"I can't believe it," Renna said. "Like a real house."

Arie settled onto her chair. "Bare," she said, "but rather charming, Handy."

"You did this?" Renna asked him.

"We all did."

"Thank you," Renna said. She hugged Handy. "And look at you," she said to Talus, who was in a perfect fury of anticipation. She fell on the dog with a great deal of petting and cooing. After a solid minute of this new heaven, Talus disappeared into the little bedroom and returned with a chewed stick; she dropped it at Renna's feet and panted expectantly. Renna tossed the stick for the dog as if they were outside. It clattered onto the bare floor of the hallway.

Talus didn't move. Instead, she sat at full attention, staring at Curran. Curran jerked his chin up, and Talus leapt to her feet. When she returned, she gave the stick to Handy, who flung it into the kitchen. "Go get it," Handy urged, but she didn't even look away until she got the okay from Curran. Again, he made the motion with his chin. She galloped away like a gigantic puppy, claws scrabbling on the floor.

Arie said nothing. They were making too much noise. They were spending time and energy they couldn't afford. But they had all been so focused and worked so hard the past two days, she couldn't bear to once more be the voice of the pedant or the scold. So she waited. She held Renna's projects in her lap—the notebook, calendar, and brown paper map rolled into a soft tube.

Curran took a seat on the floor beside Arie, and when Talus returned she walked straight to him and flopped down, stretching to show her pale belly. "You're a shameless flirt," he told the dog, who rolled from one side to the other, tongue lolling. Handy helped Renna down onto one of the floor cushions, and he sat beside her on the other.

"Now that it's fixed up, it seems like a waste to leave," said Renna.

"Better to enjoy it right now than to miss it while you're still here," said Arie. "When I was a girl, when I first came to live here, I used to get into black funks, thrashing out old conversations and trying to make the past come out different than it had. I was filled to the brim with fury. I slammed doors and threw my shoes at the wall. When it would get bad that way, Granny would haul me outside to walk. Off we'd go— and she was damn fast, long-legged. I about had to run to keep up. No talking." She smiled. "I had no breath to spare for talking anyway.

"By the time we finally circled back to home, the fuss would be walked right out of me. I'd be sweating and breathing hard, and before we crossed the threshold, she'd put her hands on my shoulders and say the same thing: 'Arie, all you need to do is be here now.' Of course, I'd resist every last bit of it—it was my age. She was right, though. It's a fine way to shake what wants to chase you."

"We're not going to shake what wants to chase us unless we get our asses out of here," said Curran. He kept his eyes on Talus, who was dozing under his hand, and his voice was speculative, as if he were talking to himself.

"Absolutely right," said Arie. "My guess is that finding you and Renna is near the top of their list of priorities, the bosses."

"Maybe we should just go," said Renna. "I feel well enough. You said yourself that I was a lot better."

"I think she's right, Ariela," said Handy. "Even if we can't travel fast, we can put miles behind us."

Arie looked at Curran. "What about you?" she said. "Tell me the truth. Are you well enough to be out there?"

"I'm fine," he said. "The headache is gone."

"Dizzy?"

"No."

"You're hard to look at, though," said Handy. "I get a little dizzy when I see your face."

Curran laughed. "Big talk, Billy-boy. Enjoy my wounds while you can." He squared his hands at the sides of his head. "Couple of weeks and this face will be throwing you in the shade."

"Enough," said Arie. She held up Renna's calendar. "This is today," she said, pointing to the last box marked with an X. "I suggest we prepare for a departure here." She tapped the square two places forward.

"Wednesday," said Renna.

Arie looked at her, the ghost of a smile on her face. "Is it, now?"

"Yes. I started the calendar on Sunday," she said. "You said Sunday breakfast."

"Perfect," said Arie. "We might be able to leave tomorrow, but I'd like to have a whole day to prepare. Wednesday would be better."

"That seems right," said Handy. "Otherwise we'll be getting started late in the day, and we won't get far. Believe me, we don't want to be out gully-whomping in the dark."

"How far is it?" said Renna.

"Here," said Arie. She handed the rolled map to Renna. "Orient us."

Renna spread the brown paper on the floor between them. There was a rough approximation of the coast, a backward C-shape, complete with the north and south spits at the entrance to the bay. She'd added a simple grid pattern over the town with a few street names and drawn the old highway along the edge of the landmass. Arie was delighted to see a carefully made compass rose in the upper-right corner with a large, stylized N pointing north.

"This is great," said Curran, smoothing his hands over the paper.

"I didn't have a chance to fill in very much," said Renna, "but here's us." It was a small starred square with a margin of woods on two sides. "This is the river, obviously, and the high school is here. It's my best guess, distance-wise."

"They're about four miles away—close to five," said Arie. "You've proportioned it well. We'll use this relative distance as our scale for plotting the route north." She gave Handy a pencil. "Point the way."

Handy used the span of his hand to gauge an approximate distance. Seven measures north and three east, he drew a circle. "God's Land," he said. "Home." It sat by itself on the far edge of the map, far from the town grid, far from the coastline.

"Damn," said Curran. "That's a hike." All the joviality had fled the room in the very real face of what lay ahead of them.

"It's far," agreed Handy. He put a hand to his beard and pulled on it meditatively. "As the crow flies, maybe forty miles, but—"

"But we're not crows," said Renna.

"I was a long time getting here, maybe six weeks. The weather was still hot, but the leaves were about to color up. All of this here," he said, pointing to the empty area between the highway and the circle for home, "is rough travel. There are only two real roads, and they weren't much to speak of even before the world came down. Now they're a mess—torn up, washed out. I saw a couple of places that looked to be blown up. And where they look clear to travel, they're likely set with traps."

"What kind of traps?" said Renna.

"Any sort you can imagine," he said. "And a bunch you don't want to. What's left is to stay on the old logging roads."

"I'm surprised any are left," said Arie.

"Not many are," said Handy. "You can't even really use the word road—they're trails now. When you can find them. But cutting straight through the woods?" He shook his head. "That's tough sledding. A lot of steep climbing, a lot of wet slogs and poison oak."

"Cold, too," said Arie. "If it took you two months' travel during good weather and by yourself, it may take at least three to get back with extra bodies and foul weather coming. May even be snow by that time."

Curran, who was intently studying the map, got to his feet. Talus rolled her eyes to watch him; her tail thumped the floorboards, but she appeared perfectly content to stay stretched out where she was. "I get that this is your place," he said, leaning down to thump the God's Land circle with one big forefinger. "But that's a long-ass way to go from here." He rubbed the back of his neck with one hand, looking off into the shadowy kitchen. Dark skies had formed at midday, and even with the windows battened the sound of wind cranking up was plain. The tangled brush close to the house scraped the siding like a hundred enthusiastic fingernails. "It seems like the odds are that we could find a suitable place between here and there, something that's plenty off the radar of Russell and his team of assholes."

"Your life is your own, Curran," Arie said. "No one can make the choice for you."

"You haven't been out there," Handy told him.

"I was out there for months." Curran's voice sounded pissy and defensive.

"You were here," Handy said quietly. "It's not the same. You said yourself that you're shit with weapons and not much better at hunting. You were ready to settle into the attic for the winter." He was quiet for a moment, tracing his finger along Renna's rendition of Highway 101. "I'm not telling you what to do. I'm telling you it's a bad situation out there. We're safer together, and you're safer at the land. We all are."

"Curran," Renna said, "it's not like you're going to find a Holiday Inn and live happily ever after." She gave his sleeve a little tug. "Just come."

"I get it," said Curran. He squatted by the map again. "I'm not saying I don't want to go. Where we are now, this whole area is already a target, we all know that. And yeah—my skill set is, uh..." He rocked one hand in a seesawing gesture. "Very pre-plague. I'm going with you in two days, no question. But I want things clear between us. I won't promise to go all the way."

"Fair enough," said Handy.

"And I want to know what the hell God's Land is," Curran said. "Every time you say it, I get a little weirded out. No offense, but I...I don't do God."

Handy looked at Arie, seemed to be waiting for her to fill the void.

"That's also fair," she said, "and not easily explained." She gazed around the barren room, so changed in every respect—its old life wiped away, its demolition at her hands gone as well. The wind thrashed outside, and the lights of the kerosene lamps flickered so that their shadows rose and fell, faded and sharpened. "God's Land is the name my father gave the home place. Our father, I should say—Handy's and mine." At the sound of Arie's voice, Talus roused herself from her doze on the floor. She sidled up and laid her chin across Arie's lap. She stroked the dog's big head and marveled at the comforting warm weight of it.

"When he was a young man, our father came to believe he was called," she said.

"Called?" said Curran. "To what?"

"An anointing," Arie said. "Touched by God with glorious foreknowledge. Unique among men, chosen to create a new work on the earth by the strength of his will and the power of his loins." When Curran and Renna exchanged a glance, Arie laughed. "Oh, I know how it sounds," she said. "But those aren't my words, they're his—straight from the horse's mouth. And I heard them repeated so often I could recite them in my sleep. Mack McInnis was touched, all right. Crazy through and through.

"This was when he was barely in his teens, and the idea drove him. His family lived on a patch of dirt in the hills where three generations had grubbed out a subsistence living. There was no expectation that this tall boy with his strange manner would live any way other than how the rest of his clan was doing it—fixing up junk cars, raising hell in town Friday nights, and drinking away the rest of the weekend in front of the television. Meth was an epidemic in those days, and Daddy Mack often claimed that every one of them—all but him—used it on the regular, even his mother. To hear him tell it, there was a lot of bad skin and a distinctly low ratio of teeth to heads in the McInnis family. But his calling saved him from such a low fate.

"I won't go into the what-all of that delusion, or you'll still be sitting here and me talking when the sun comes up. Bottom line is, he believed he was chosen and that in the details God was damned specific. He quit school and went to work for two neighbors, doing rough field work and odd jobs. He was a tall, muscular boy. Handsome. All brawn and big ideas. Saved every red cent, and when his folks let on he ought to chip in for room and board, he set himself up in an abandoned shed up the road, a place so nasty you wouldn't use it to pen a goat. Cut all ties with the family. The day he turned twenty-one, he bought seventy acres outright and set up a tent.

"He chased his calling full bore, which first required building a house and finding a woman. He did both, and in short order. Of course, in reality the 'woman' he found was a girl. My mother, Delonda Merrit, was hiking in the redwoods with friends when she ran into Mack. All of fifteen and gullible as hell. Not overburdened with intelligence. Those two were an infernal match. Perfect for each other. She spent most of the next year running away from home—this home we're sitting in—and getting dragged back by Granny and Pop. Nothing would wise her up, though. She gave birth to her first child three days after her seventeenth birthday—our brother Zach. Oldest of fourteen, if you don't count two miscarriages and the one who died in the cradle."

"Fourteen," echoed Renna.

"Seven boys, seven girls. A perfect mystery of creation, ordained from the foundations of the universe, according to Daddy Mack," Arie said. "Ancient history, though. I ran off when I was a girl, about the age Mammy Delonda was when she signed on to play queen bee. I came here and lived with Granny and Pops. She used to say I was her chance to finish what she'd started."

"You still call it God's Land," said Curran.

"That's its name," said Handy.

"Why did you run away?" said Renna.

Arie caressed Talus's black snout and scratched behind her ears. "There's naught else I can add that matters now," she said. "Handy was the last born, some six years after I left the place. All I know now is what he tells me."

"The old man lived through it all," said Handy. "He's still on the land, and set me out to bring you home."

"As I said, I have your word for that, and you might have gleaned in our short acquaintance that a man on a mission doesn't hold much sway around here."

"You can be persuasive," he murmured. "May be it runs in the blood."

"So does being a smartass. What these two need from you, Brother, are the best reasons they should follow you."

"I trust him," said Renna. "I'd follow him out of here even if I didn't. Those..." She stopped, breathing hard. In the clear light of the burning lamps, Arie saw a brilliant flush spreading up her throat and onto her cheeks. "Those people running their little prison camp across the river are nuts, so it really doesn't matter what God's Land is like. Not to me. I'm going."

Handy took one of Renna's hands and pressed it to his lips. It was a sweet, courtly gesture that made Arie smile. First love at the end of the world, she thought.

"What we have there is a whole lot of people surviving," said Handy, "and they're family. We have some kind of resistance in the blood, I guess. Not everyone lived. Quite a lot of the little kids took the pox right off."

"That makes sense," said Curran. "If you do have some kind of immunity, it would get thinned out in the next generations."

"Three brothers are still alive there, and in good health, but two are Arie's elders." He looked at Curran. "Family alone isn't enough now. The old man believes it is, but he hasn't been off the land in decades. What's needed is able bodies, but trustworthy. The trip from there to here made that clear. The world's gone hard."

"The world," said Arie softly, "has not changed. Nor have people."

"I don't know," said Curran. "The guys who pulled me out of my empty house changed. When I first saw Little Mikey, I thought I was getting rescued by an old drinking buddy, the one who used to buy pitchers of beer and beat me at darts no matter how soused he got. I don't know what he is now, but he's changed, trust me."

"And you?" said Arie. "You might have ended up living in the main building with the bosses, two rooms of your very own and every night with a woman. Instead, you ran for the woods. Curran," she said, leaning toward him so that Talus had to finally move off her lap. "Lawlessness is here." She tapped two fingers hard on her sternum, making a muffled, hollow thump. "Before the Pink, we agreed on the surface to a rule of law. We pretended together that we were largely abiding by our consciences. We decided the only real problem among us was the outwardly renegade." She shook her head. "Not so. You've seen it firsthand. A great lot of people were restrained from their worst impulses only for fear of punishment. Now, the threat of shame is wiped out."

"No county jail, no problem?"

"That's right, Curran. They're following the dark thing that was in them all along."

"At the land we have plenty," said Handy. "There's water—springs, wells, creeks. Small livestock. Gardens."

"Holes in the hills," said Arie.

"That too."

"Daddy Mack was a big believer in preparing for Armageddon," Arie explained. "You might say he got a tad stocked up."

"So you learned it from him," said Renna. "All the stuff in the attic—you must have been setting that up for a long time."

"Granny and I both," Arie told her. "The handwriting was on the wall for years, I'd say." She closed her eyes, tired, wanting to get upstairs alone.

"What the land lacks is people," said Handy. "With so few left and fewer still to be trusted—we need each other."

Curran stood and stretched, rolled his head to work the kinks out. "So," he said, "tomorrow we pack, and next morning we get the hell out of Dodge."

Handy's smile, rare and transformative as always, was one of genuine relief. He got to his feet and clasped Curran's shoulder in wordless solidarity. Arie saw in the gesture how he must be missing his brothers, the men he'd been surrounded by all his life.

"I'll take first watch upstairs," said Arie. Her voice was raspy from all the talking, and when she stood she was stiff from the straight-backed chair. "You walking wounded need all the sleep you can get," she said, "and I'm going to get a start on sorting and packing. Handy, I'll wake you later. You hold on to this." She handed him the map. "With Renna's permission, of course."

Renna nodded. "I'm done with my part."

"And an admirable job," said Arie. "Sleep well, all."

"Wait, Arie," Renna said. "I'll walk you."

Arie took the handle of the camp lantern. "Come on," she said. They moved together in the yellow-white circle of light. Renna limped, but not much, even after sitting on the floor all evening. "I'm amazed how fast you've gotten that leg back in order," Arie told her.

"I'm scared," Renna whispered. She took hold of Arie's elbow, and the cold of her fingers was a shock. "I'm happy, glad we're leaving, but also...I keep wishing we could stay here."

"If you weren't afraid, I'd think you'd lost your wits," said Arie. "Do you want me to tell you everything will be fine? I might be able to say it with a straight face."

Renna laughed, and Arie was glad to hear it. "No, don't say that. I guess I just had to tell someone. Say the words."

They were in the little bedroom now. "I think you could tell Handy," she said.

"I don't want him to think I'm weak. Or make him worry about me."

"He'll likely worry about you anyway," Arie said, "but weak? Handy already knows better, and so do I." She patted Renna's smooth cheek. "You can trust him with your secrets, girl. Take this now. I can find my way without it." She handed Renna the lantern and climbed up into the dark attic, blessedly alone.

❧ ❧

Everything they possessed between the four of them was listed in Renna's log, every last plate and rag and bottle of tincture, the blankets and baskets and strings of leather britches. Seeing it all in Renna's precise handwriting was both a comfort and a concern—it made their stores real, and it made them finite. Arie could see at a glance where the gaps were, and the largest one was food. The three of them had to have more for their first two days going cross-country, when getting distance between themselves and the bosses was most important. Time spent foraging or hunting was time wasted. First thing in the morning, she and Handy would hit the woods, making a sweep of their snares and quick-salting whatever fish and small game they could manage in a hurry. This would at least give them meat for the first day or two of travel.

She went up top for a second perimeter check. The wind had relented a little, but on the roof it wanted to push her around. She stayed in a defensive hunch and scanned with the binoculars, first the yards, then the street. The moon was up, waning now and intermittently obscured by low, scudding clouds flying south to north. It was a threat of wet weather, one Arie hoped would pass over without harm. Satisfied with her check, she returned to the attic and let down the sky panel, glad for the relative warmth inside.

She'd cleared the work table of all her usual paraphernalia to make four piles to be carried: one each for Renna, Curran, and Handy, and a stash for Talus. As she sorted, she ticked off the items from

Renna's log and adjusted the diminished stores on her own shelves. Handy had his rucksack, and Pop's old nylon backpack would be a good fit for Curran. Renna couldn't carry much until she was fully healed, but Arie decided to send her with the carry basket, rigged with a tow-sack cover. As for Talus, Arie had cut a pillowcase and was reassembling it into a saddlebag to fit across the dog's broad back and tie like a harness at her chest and under her belly. It was quiet, straightforward work, satisfying.

They still didn't realize she wasn't coming along, and while she worked she chewed over the notion of when and how to tell. The less time they had for arguing, the better. If she could stave off that moment until they were ready to put foot to path, that's what she'd do. She wanted to part in peace, but part they would—even if she had to lock herself inside and threaten them off with the slingshot.

Alone here again, her provisions divided by four and a group of reprobates pressing in, she estimated her sojourn to be near its terminus. There was peace in it. If the interlopers breached the house, she'd make quick work with her short spear and save them the trouble. Be done, finally.

Like Granny, she intended to stay.

7

"**N**INE HOURS OF DAYLIGHT," Arie said, scraping a last spoonful of cooked oats from her bowl. "Maybe less, with this weather." They ate without speaking, only intermittent early birdsong to break the silence—and not much of that, either. The upper panel was thrown open to a barely visible sky, so thick with clouds it was hard to see that the sun had already cleared the horizon. The packs she'd filled during the night sat on the Packard seat like mute sentinels, and the diminished look of the attic was sobering them all.

"Did you stay up all night?" said Renna. She and Handy sat so close they were nearly entwined, as though they couldn't bear to put an inch of space between them. Arie was glad for it—better to start their journey bonded.

"No, Curran took a watch, too."

"Not much of one," he said. "It was practically dawn when you came after me."

"You needed your beauty sleep." Arie thought this might get a smile from them, but the weight of their departure hung heavy in the small space. "There's plenty we need to do before tomorrow," she said.

"Jobs all around. Some of it we can maybe do tonight, but far better if we finish and turn in early.

"I distributed the weightier supplies between you men. Everyone should have some basic items. Handy had some of this in his rucksack, but he needs replenishing. Renna, you're in charge here." She laid three wrapped bundles on the floor and unrolled them. "Make them like this," she said. "One for fire-starting, one for first aid, and one for hygiene. These should stay accessible."

Curran looked up. "Why not share out the supplies between us?" He pointed at the first-aid bundle. "Why have everyone carrying the same needles, thread, bandages, and...whatever these are," he said, pointing to a brown bottle of alcohol and one of Indica tincture.

"In case we're separated," said Handy. The void of response made the words seem to echo around the attic. "Or someone loses theirs," he added.

"Handy's right," Arie said. "With some things, more is better." She wrapped the bundles and gave them to Renna. "You'll need to tear and roll the bandages from this." She handed her a folded length of soft muslin. "Dry socks in the hygiene bundles—two pair each, along with the soap and clean rags. Add anything else you think you might need, but start there. Once that's done, go through all the extra bedding and make bedrolls. Granny was a fool for linens, so there's more than enough—we'll each have a bed to sleep on tonight, and one tied and ready to go for morning. By the time you're done with all that, we'll likely be ready for a noon meal. Use anything still left on the shelves."

Renna was looking at the packs on the car seat. "Where's yours?" she said.

"I'll take care of mine," said Arie, trying to sound nonchalant. "Don't forget, I had a jump on it last night." Renna looked satisfied with the answer, so Arie talked on, not even glancing in Handy's direction, certain he'd read her face like a book. "Curran," she said, "your first job is to fit this to Talus." She held up the makeshift saddlebags. "Better if she wears it most of the day with a small load so it doesn't take her by surprise tomorrow."

"She's been edgy this morning," he said. "I'll take her out later, let her run it off with the pack on."

"As long as she stays close," said Arie. "Poor thing is probably soaking up our nerves. Before you let her run, though—" She pulled a box from under the table and slid it across the floor to him. "Tarps," she said, "and a couple of old shower curtains. Figure out rain ponchos. Scissors are on the table. A circle with a hole for the head will work. Make them long enough to keep us dry, but not so long they trip us. You choose the specifics. The heaviest pieces are best saved as ground cover."

"And us?" said Handy. Arie finally dared to look at him, consciously armoring her face, willing him to see only the same impenetrable countenance she'd thrown at him the first day he showed up. What she saw was like looking in a mirror—the expression plain and blameless, revealing nothing but calm. Brother, aren't we a pair, she thought.

"I hesitate to say it, but we have to go out," she said.

"Out where?" said Renna. One hand, like a pale starfish, took hold of the hem of Handy's shirt.

"Getting outside the bosses' search grid is paramount," Arie said. "I know you feel it."

"We do," said Curran. "That's what's got Talus nerved up."

"My thinking is this," she said. "The first couple of days on foot it will be crucial to cover as much ground as possible, and my biggest concern is food. I've packed all the jerky, dried berries and beans, everything that travels light and keeps well. The longer it can be made to last, the better. That leaves hunting along the way. Handy's an excellent mark, but even when hunting is good, stopping long enough to clean and cook it wastes valuable time. Handy and I will go down to the river and make a quick sweep of the snares. My hope is we'll lay hands on some small game to quick-salt for the road, enough for a day or two."

"It's a good idea," said Handy. "When we get back, Curran and I can take Talus out and make a quick run through some of the houses on this block— see if there are any last supplies that suit us."

"Good," said Arie. "I think we can be fully packed and ready for tomorrow before the sun goes down." She looked up through the open panel at the threatening day. "And maybe before that sky cuts loose on us."

Curran let Handy and Arie out through the kitchen, and the last thing Arie saw before he closed the door and shoved the fridge back in place was Talus. The dog was already harnessed into her new saddlebags, and Curran was right—her playful side was nowhere in evidence. She watched them intently with her depthless brown eyes, ears alert, hindquarters still.

It was even colder out than Arie had expected. The onshore wind delivered a salty tang of low tide. It came in bitter gusts that nipped at her face and hands and blew a chill up under the hem of Granny's boiled wool coat. Several seagulls rode the air high overhead, wings still, surfing the current. After checking the street, they hurried toward the path into the gulch, each with a tow sack stuffed under one arm, hands in pockets, shoulders hunched against the wind.

Handy walked a couple of paces ahead of her, and Arie watched with amusement—and a small pang of sorrow—how perfectly matched their stride was, how each time she moved her head to look around her, his head moved in the same direction. She wondered if the younger siblings had been taught Daddy Mack's woodsing the same way she and the older kids had been, or if their similarities were less nurture and more nature. The wind twisted through the canopy, thrashing treetops back and forth in erratic bursts that were loud enough to discourage conversation. Arie was just as glad. She dreaded the exchange waiting for her, their response when she put her foot down about leaving. But it was Handy's reaction she dreaded most of all.

Without a word, they veered off to the fish snares, a distinct sense of careful hurry in all their movements. All the snares were sprung, but there was only one fish. Something had gotten to it—probably a bird, judging by the missing eyes and random chunks of flesh pulled out. Handy cut it loose and looked at Arie, a question. She shook her head—there was too much damage. By the time they cut around it, there wouldn't be enough meat left to justify the extra work. Arie's impulse was to reset the snares, but she resisted, maintaining a façade of leaving for just a little longer.

They doubled back to the path and half-trotted toward the clearing. Here the wind was an invisible tsunami in the head-high grass, flinging dead leaves everywhere in papery brown pinwheels. The first trap was empty. And the second. They skimmed the edge of the tree line from trap to trap, both of them wordless and frustrated. At the fourth post, finally, something dangled—but it was obvious from a distance that it was something small. A gray squirrel. Meaty, but even a fat squirrel wasn't enough to share between them, not even for a single meal. It was freshly dead, though—one thing to be grateful for.

Arie slipped the line and knelt to gut the animal. Handy looked around, weirdly antsy, chewing at his mustache and top lip. He crouched near Arie and put his head close to hers. "You finish this," he whispered. The instinct they both had to get this done quickly and quietly was, rather than reassuring, amplifying a sense of urgency. "I'm going to cut up through the trees and try to snag something else. Another squirrel. Maybe a quail."

She paused, knife in hand, looked at the day flinging itself in rattling gray chaos around them. She looked into his steady green eyes. His beard and hair streamed back in the wind. "This won't take me long, Brother," she said. "Meet me at the top of the path."

"Give me a slow count of five hundred. You can whistle?"

"I can."

"Two, short and loud. Whoever gets there first," he said. "Same in response."

"I'm cutting. Get on it," Arie told him. He took off in an easy jog. At the edge of the clearing he slowed to a walk and disappeared into the trees.

Her fingers were stiff with cold and it took a little longer to skin and gut the squirrel than usual, but it was a job she could manage in her sleep. The big margarine tub was in her tow sack, half filled with salt. She dropped the squirrel in, curling its body to fit. A sudden movement in the corner of her eye jerked her to attention. One of the last snares had sprung, and whatever was caught thrashed the small sapling back and forth. It felt like a gift, a little more meat for the road. She snapped the lid onto the plastic tub and gave it a gentle shake to cover the meat, hurried over to the fresh catch—all the while making that slow count in her head.

Closer to the flailing animal, Arie stopped short. It was a gray fox, straining and snarling. Even in its extremity, she saw the clear evidence of its illness. Three hundred ninety-eight. With only the short spear there was no way she could get near enough to kill it, and cutting it free was even more dangerous. No time. Tucking her chin into the collar of her coat, she hurried out of the clearing, into the woods and up the path.

Four hundred forty-six. Four hundred forty-seven. The trees thinned. Dead power lines became visible. The noise of the wind in the woods made a sudden thrashing to her right, her left. Behind her. She tried not to look. Had to look. The last three feet, four hundred eighty-two, heart skittering.

The top of the path. She stopped, breathed. Quieter up here. The house looked the same as always. The street was empty. Five hundred. She curled her tongue and whistled the signal. The sound was a sharp slap on the face of the day, but a brief one, swallowed by the wind. She listened—no response. Five hundred twenty-six.

Maybe I took longer than I thought. She looked at the house again. Perhaps Handy had gotten here first, gave up waiting and went inside. Her gut knew better—he'd have waited—but her reptile brain was urging her to take cover. Go, go, go.

Hurrying up the street, across the yard, alongside the house, she glanced repeatedly back over her shoulder. Each time she saw the same nothing—no Handy rushing to catch up, no one following at all.

"Curran," she said, rapping softly on the back door. Inside, the dead refrigerator was shoved aside in short, deliberate bursts, and Renna opened. Arie squeezed through and helped wrestle it back in place.

"Where's Handy?" Renna said.

Not here, then. Arie's heart sank. She secured the rope around the fridge. "We separated. He's...he'll be here any moment." Even in her own ears, the worry was plain in her voice. "Why are you watching this damned door alone? Where's Curran?"

Renna's face had gone deathly pale. "He got worried about the weather," she said. "He wanted to get Talus outside and check houses before it rained."

"Left you here alone? Damned fool," said Arie, slapping an open palm on the side of the refrigerator, hard enough to hurt. She was cursing herself and Handy as much as she was Curran.

"Only for a little while," Renna said, sounding young and defensive. "I told him it was all right." Her voice was swelling into a register of dread that Arie was afraid would blossom into panic if she didn't quell it.

"Never mind," Arie said. Her own pulse rushed dully in her temples. "I'll go up top for a look." Renna had brought down new bedrolls and laid them on the empty counter, but there was nothing immediately useful here. "Come up with me," she said, grabbing her arm. They hurried through the house, Renna limping slightly but keeping up, her dark eyes wide. "You need a weapon, and you need it on you all the time." How the hell am I just now telling her this? Arie thought. Damned fool. Damned fool.

She went up the inside hatch first, letting Renna negotiate the climb by herself. At the top of the ladder she grabbed the binoculars where they hung and went out the sky panel. If Curran and Talus were on this block, she might be able to see and signal them home. The wind was fierce on the exposed roof, making her eyes water. Her long hair flew around her in a wild silver tangle, and she had to brace her feet widely apart to keep from being pushed off balance. She peered into the overgrown yards around her. Children's play structures rotted and rusted. Blackberry vines and untended garden ivy buckled house siding and pushed through cracked window sashes. Useless vehicles sat neatly in most driveways, tires flat, batteries dead, gasoline contaminated and sour.

"Do you see them?" Renna was on the ladder so that just her head protruded from the sky panel. She squinted against the wind.

"Not yet," Arie said. She scuttle-hunched to the far edge, where the rope ladder lay in a heap. Her own yard was empty. She straightened enough to scan the path out of the gulch again. When she did, her gut went cold and she dropped the binoculars.

They had him.

"Hail, there." Four of them walked Handy out of the trees. The man who had called to her was in point position. Two others, one wearing a bright-orange knit cap and strapped with a compound bow, the other carrying a bulging canvas pack, pulled Handy along by the arms. A fourth man brought up the rear. He carried a brutal length of metal pipe over one shoulder and swiveled his head from side to side, keeping close watch in all directions.

Arie looked down at Renna. The girl's face was a gray mask of fear. Dropping onto one knee, she was, for a moment, out of their sight. "Find a knife," she hissed, "and stay down."

"Come on back, Gramma—we already saw you, no sense trying to cover up now."

Arie stood. She could hear Renna running through the attic, her pace stuttery and uneven. Arie didn't dare glance down again; she must hold the attention of these men as long as she could.

"Who are you?" She made her voice quaver slightly.

The lead man laughed, a simple, easy laugh, like a man watching a card trick. "It's pretty obvious, isn't it. We're the men who have your boy."

"My boy?" said Arie. "I don't have one. Never did. I'm Null." She was still in Granny's heavy coat. She pulled one sleeve past the elbow and bared the livid scar to them.

"A stinkin deader," muttered one of the two who held Handy by the arms.

She tried to get a look at Handy, but his head was down so that the curtain of his hair obscured his features. A few dark spatters of blood marked the front of his jacket. He was still solidly on his feet, but swaying a little.

The man shook his head and chuckled again. "Oh, he's yours. We saw you down there together." He gestured toward the gulch. "Let's not drag this out, my dear. Why, it's pure luck you happened to be standing up there. We're taking you both into protective custody. It's a dangerous world now. Safety in numbers. Don't worry," he said. He wasn't a large man—five feet six or seven, perhaps, and squarely built, lean but broad-shouldered. His iron-gray hair was curly and cropped short, and his face deeply tanned under a dark scruff of whiskers. "We'll pack your belongings, too. What's life without our precious keepsakes, after all?" He nodded at the man in the rear, who took his cudgel in both hands and broke rank. He cut into her front yard and out of sight.

"What's your name, young man?" Arie said, dialing up the frail and fussy tone in her voice. "I'd like to know who it is I'm speaking to. It's how I was raised."

The lead man smiled broadly, teeth large and even, very white in his tanned face. "I'm Russell," he said. "And you?"

"Minerva," said Arie.

"Charmed," he said. "Minerva, what do you say we stop this silly shouting back and forth? It's cold out here, and we have other business today."

"You're about to be sadly disappointed," she said. "Can't you see I'm living rough here?" Something clattered at her feet. It was the slingshot. Arie risked a flick of her eyes toward the sky panel. Renna clung to the ladder, the top of her head just below the opening. She lifted her right hand and showed Arie the knife.

A sudden volley of pounding commenced downstairs, heavy and deliberate. Renna gasped and nearly slipped off the ladder, knife and all. Arie ducked with an arm crossed over her head, feigning fear. With her other hand she snatched up the slingshot and stuffed it in her coat pocket. "Get down and cover the inside hatch," she whispered to Renna. The thudding blows below stopped, started again in a new place. The man with the pipe had moved from the front door to one of the living room windows.

"As you can hear, we're coming in one way or another," Russell called up. "You don't plan to fend off all four of us, do you? That could get…well, a little messy." He stepped over to Handy and jerked his head up by the hair.

Arie's fists clenched when she saw his face. His right eye was swollen shut and blackened. His nose, mashed to the side and obviously broken, was the source of the blood on his clothes. But then she saw his undamaged eye, clear and full of fury, and she knew he was shamming his stupor.

"This man is a pilgrim," she said, voice now strong and steady. The noise from below rose to a more frantic pitch, scraping and blows that Arie felt vibrating under her. "I offered him safe harbor from the weather last night, and in exchange he promised to help me find food this morning." She shook her head as if in disgust. "You should be ashamed."

"Gave it up for Lent," he said. He opened his mouth to say more, but the pipe-carrier stalked over. He put his head close to Russell's, gesticulated furiously at the house with his weapon. Russell threw his hands in the air and paced a few steps away. He looked at the woods for a moment, shaking his head.

Arie could see something in his posture, something capricious and ready to erupt. "I have supplies," she said. "Things you can take with you— medicine, tools. Let the young man go. It's none of his concern."

Russell faced her again. He was still smiling, but if there had been any humor in him, it was gone. "I truly prefer to reason my way around a disagreement," he said. "But you can't reason with a liar, and you're a liar, old woman. First you claim you're living rough. Woe is you. Now you offer a trade?" He gripped Handy by the hair again and pulled back viciously. "This one is no pilgrim. We asked him where to find you—several times. He played stupid." He cocked his head and looked speculatively at Handy's face. "Hell, he let us break his nose, Minerva. No pilgrim takes a beating for a stranger. I don't think Jesus himself would do that. Do you?" He nodded at the pipe carrier.

The man swung and hit Handy squarely in the midsection. He doubled over in a silent rictus of pain.

The instant their attention was turned, Arie ran to her ammo pile and dropped to her knees. With shaking hands, she loaded her empty coat pocket. Stones tumbled around her.

"Open up," Russell yelled. "You have one minute and then I'm going to beat him witless."

She pulled out the slingshot and stood with it next to her body, holding a stone in the other hand, desperately willing the shakes away.

"You're losing time," Russell said.

Handy pulled himself upright, arms wrapped around his wounded middle. His clear green eye looked straight into hers. "Sister!" he roared. The power in it was stunning. "I sojourn, Sister. My life is my own!"

The words of the catechism jolted her like an electrical shock. All the trembling fell out of her body, and she squared her feet. "I shall not give, neither shall I receive," she shouted, and brought up the sling.

Russell punched Handy in the face. He went down in the road, out cold. Arie fired. The rock hit Russell in the thigh. He staggered backward, clutching his leg. She drew another stone. "Renna," she yelled toward the sky panel. "You have to get out of the house right now. Hide outside—hurry."

The man who had been hauling on Handy's right arm now reached behind and fumbled with the compound bow. He fired too quickly, and the arrow flew wild, catching in the branches of a tree near the house.

"Save the arrows, you ass," Russell said through clenched teeth. He pointed at the one strapped with the bulky backpack. "Mikey," he said. "Burn it down. Cook the bitch."

Arie aimed at Mikey, who had pulled a brown bottle from his bag and was already stuffing a rag into its neck. She was about to fire when the man with the pipe turned on Handy and lifted the weapon over his head like someone about to split wood. She pivoted a few inches and let go as the pipe arced. The stone smashed into the man's elbow with an audible crunch. He screamed at the low sky, and the pipe flew from him, missing Handy's head by inches. She grabbed a fresh stone and reloaded.

Mikey had lit the rags in both bottles and was running at the house, arm cocked back. Arie swung and fired, but he was already out of range. The sound of shattering glass was followed by the immediate *whumph* of the explosion. A pall of black smoke and the smell of accelerant hit her at the same time. She ducked her head and hurried to the far edge of the roof, hoping for a glimpse of Renna's escape. Even with the pipe-carrier screaming in the street over his shattered arm, Arie could hear the fire, the old redwood siding of Granny's home catching and feeding the flames. Instead of Renna, she saw Mikey and his bag of mischief, backing away from the heat, another unlit bottle in hand. Behind him, Russell hobbled in a drag-step to where Handy lay, still unconscious.

Eyes stinging, she loaded the slingshot and stood straight. As she did, the man with the compound bow pointed behind Russell. "Look out!" he yelled, and stumbled up into the yard as a streak of gold and brown flew at Russell. Talus barreled into him. Russell hit the ground with the dog on top. Curran was right behind, machete in hand. He ran straight at Mikey, who threw out both arms in a warding-off motion.

"Whoa, Curran," Mikey managed, but Curran had grabbed the front of his jacket and yanked him forward. The bag slipped off his shoulder and into the weeds with a musical rattle.

"You sick fuck," Curran panted, and backhanded him a tremendous blow that sent Mikey sprawling. Russell thrashed frantically, trying to crawl out from beneath Talus, but she was seventy pounds of muscle and snarling fury. She battened on one hand, and he howled, hitting at her head with his other. The dog went for his face, and his cries turned into a terrified scream. Mr. Lead Pipe was now Mr. Broken Wing, face agog with an expression of yellow-gray retreat, tripping haphazardly into the trees. In the growing billows of black smoke, Arie clutched the slingshot and tried desperately to see everywhere at once, looking for a place to aim.

A flaming bottle arced overhead like a great burning bird and exploded behind her. Detonated fuel spread in brilliant gouts across the shingles. The light and heat of it was immediate and stupefying. Arie gagged on the stench of burning asphalt and wiped her streaming eyes with one hand. The man with the crossbow was holding a Zippo to another bomb. She spun the sling over her head and let go just as the rag ignited. The bottle erupted in his hand. He uttered a single shriek and was swallowed in fire. It bloomed around his head and arm, ran down his torso and onto the tall weeds around him. He spun and flailed and staggered, engulfed in a burning shroud of orange and yellow, grotesquely dazzling in the gray morning light. Arie turned away and retched. She clutched the heaped pile of the rope ladder and looked over the edge of the roof. The wall below was clear. She tossed the ladder down and was already over the side when Renna called for help.

She was still in the house.

Arie hesitated only a moment. Curran still struggled with Mikey. Handy was moving, trying to get to his hands and knees. Her eyes and nose streaming, Arie scrambled back up the rope rungs. The big jerry can sat three feet beyond the spreading flames. Skirting around the fire, she pulled off her coat as she went and threw it down, pulled the top off the jerry can and upended it. The dense fabric was drenched. Water ran between shingles toward the blaze, and the remaining fuel floated narrow runners of fire into the cracks. A little water still sloshed in the overturned jug; Arie splashed her face, drank a palmful, and wet her head with the rest.

"Help, somebody," Renna yelled. "I can't get out!" She was somewhere downstairs.

"I'm coming," Arie called. The soaked wool was so heavy it was hard to lift. She draped it over her head, and cool water poured through her hair, down her face and neck. Thin streams trickled out of the coat all around her feet. Three paces to the sky panel, and she climbed down into the attic.

It was dark and hot inside, getting smoky. Visible wisps rose through the slats of the defunct heating register. Arie held her breath and ran to the inside hatch. Lowering herself into the closet, feeling for the shelves with hands and feet, the smoke was much heavier. She could hear the fire.

"Renna, where are you?"

"In here. We have to get the window open."

Arie held the sleeve of her wet coat over her nose and mouth and crouched as low as she could. She stumbled down the hallway and into the living room. The smoke was so thick that she had to feel her way to where Renna huddled. The girl was making a terrible bronchial cough, interspersed with panicky whimpers. The burning siding lit the windows on the front of the house in a ghastly orange blare, like the light from some alien sunset. But the real trouble was fire inside. One of the Molotov cocktails had hit the garden window, one of the only ones not reinforced with sheet metal, and it was burning merry hell. Flames poured into the blasted opening and licked up the wall at the ceiling. The cupboards and countertops on that side of the room were catching.

"Help me get it open," Renna sobbed. Arie could see now that she was trying to tear the boards off with her bare hands. She'd managed to snap the bottom slat in its center. The two pieces dangled askew, and she was pulling on another, making the section of chain-link fastened there ring and clatter. She seemed to have no sense that she'd never get through the window the way it was reinforced.

"Come on," Arie said. "We have to get out the back door."

"We can't," Renna wheezed. "It's on fire." She doubled over in another choking cough.

"The door is still clear, Renna. We can make it."

There was a deep, concussive thud from the kitchen. Renna grabbed Arie. Her skin was slick with sweat. "It's them!" she said. "They're getting in."

Arie opened her coat and pulled Renna underneath with her. "No matter who it is," Arie said in her ear, "we have to go." She pulled her arm, and it was like trying to yank a marble sculpture. The crash came again, someone beating against the back door.

"Arie!" It was Curran.

"We're here," Arie shouted. "Renna, if we don't go now, we're dead. Move." This time when she pulled, Renna stumbled forward. They scrambled toward the conflagration, Arie forcing Renna into a stoop. Now they were both coughing. Even through the wet wool of the coat, the air seared her lungs and the taste of burning wood and paint and plastic was a miasma. Curran's pounding at the back door was now manic. The women, almost crawling, crossed the threshold into the fiery kitchen. One whole wall and part of the ceiling was fully consumed. The skin of Arie's legs shrank in the heat, and the wet coat felt as though it might begin to boil. The refrigerator was little more than a shadowy bulk ahead of them, made visible by the securing rope around it, now a fiery belt. Arie pulled them behind its far side. It provided only the smallest measure of relief from the agonizing heat. Both of them hacked and gasped in a desperate effort to get some air.

Everything seemed to happen in a single harrowing instant. The back door gave way with an enormous splintered crack. When it did, the fire roared with fresh oxygen. Flames rushed across the ceiling like a river in hell. Curran hit the refrigerator so hard it toppled forward and crashed to the floor. Arie shoved Renna toward the shattered opening. Curran grabbed the girl and pulled, dragging the coat with her. Arie, exposed and on all fours, got a hand over the doorsill when a burning chunk of ceiling fell. Most of it landed on the refrigerator, but one end of a charred timber struck her between the shoulder blades. It felt as though a block of ice had landed on her back, then her mind registered heat and she tried to scream. Suddenly Curran had her. He kicked away the debris and lifted her into his arms as if she weighed no more than a child.

Out in the street, Handy supported Renna, who choked and gagged. "It's her back," Curran panted. "Spread your jacket." Handy did, and Curran lowered Arie onto it, laying her on her uninjured left side. The burned place on her right back and shoulder was an agony of heat and outraged nerve endings. She was coughing, too, and every spasm sent a fresh surge of pain to the spot. "Water, Curran," she gasped. "Barrel in back, before it burns." He ran.

He had laid her so that she faced the yard and what had been her home since she was a green girl. Now it was a house-shaped block of flame rising from a wild verge of shoulder-high grass, naked trees, and enormous ragged shrubs. The mass of blackberry tangle that had shielded the rope ladder from view was wholly ablaze, its snarled branches glowing in skeletal fury. Talus paced back and forth at the crumbling edge of the street, alert and nervous, whining high in her throat. The body of the burned man lay curled and blackened on the far side of the yard, partially obscured in the tall weeds. A second body slumped several feet away, orange cap clearly visible. It was Mikey, not moving.

"Handy," Arie said, groping in his direction.

"Here," he said. He took her hand and gripped it tightly. A tiny raindrop splashed her face, then another. A few more pattered around them on the dirty, cracked asphalt. The acrid smell of fire was briefly eclipsed by the smell of new rain. Petrichor, Pop had called it, the fragrant chemical signal of the earth opening itself to water.

"Russell?"

"Ran into the woods. Looked like Talus took half his face off."

Curran reappeared, smeared with soot, jogging to them with an armful of cans and bottles, sloshing water. Talus barked once and trotted alongside. He knelt and set the containers on the ground between them, handed a bottle to Renna, who drank greedily. She gagged, spat, drank some more. Curran cupped his big hand under Arie's head and lifted her gently. He put a bottle to her lips. The water was slightly gritty and tasted of ash, but it was wet and wonderful. She took some more then motioned to her back. "Wet it." She rolled partway forward, and Curran poured water over the burn. The relief was sweet but brief. "How bad?" she wheezed.

"Blisters," said Curran. She could hear in his voice that it was worse than that.

Handy stripped out of his shirt. He folded it and wet it through with one of the cans of water. "Pour some more there," he told Curran, and as Curran rinsed the burned place again, Handy pulled Arie's torn shirt loose and laid his own wet one over the wound. It was heavy and cool. "It needs to stay covered," he said.

The freshening rain had turned into a fine drizzle. Curran took off his coat and gave it to Handy. "You're going to take a chill," he said.

Handy slipped it on. "We all are," he said. "We have to find shelter." He struggled to his feet. "They could be back."

"I know a place," Curran said. "Just for the night."

There was a tremendous crash inside the house, and the front bedroom window, Granny's bedroom, exploded outward. They all recoiled, and Renna covered her face with one arm. Glass and burning boards showered down on the yard, revealing a wall of flames in the bedroom.

Arie smiled. "Just so, Granny," she said, her voice nothing but a raspy croak.

Handy lifted her into a sitting position. He plucked his jacket up from the street, gave it a hard shake, and draped it gently over her shoulders. The weight on her livid skin, even with the makeshift bandage, was like being burned again, and she moaned.

Curran slid his arms beneath her, doing his best not to touch the bad shoulder, and stood, cradling her to him. The last thing she saw before slipping into a deep and blessed darkness was Talus. The dog was three paces ahead, leading the way between houses, back into the woods, back to Curran's house in the trees.

8

HE SAT IN HIS LAVISH RECEIVING ROOM, the entire space lit only by the faint gray pall of an overcast dusk. Lavish? Yes, by current standards. Tasteful. Appointed to suit his station in life: Chief of the Konungar.

Russell no longer made use of mirrors.

All of them he'd collected to decorate his rooms— and there were a great many—had either been quietly relegated to the barracks, strategically replaced by artwork, or smashed to fragments in the first early days of his recovery. Great care had been taken since then to shield him from his own ruin: lavatory mirrors painted over, blinds and curtains opened in the daytime, closed after dark.

He could see it now, though. His face.

Positioned in the chair directly opposite the uncovered window, even twelve feet away in the indistinct light, the damage was plain.

They could see it, too. It lurked, their seeing, behind every smile and pleasant nod that came a fraction of a second too slowly. The seeing flitted over their heads like a drunken bat each time a conversation fell to silence when he happened by them unexpectedly. The Posies were the worst. None of could adequately dissemble, none of them could offer him comfort—the comfort of their own feigned blindness. No matter how placid their expressions, their eyes were little mirrors, weren't they? He had to take them from behind, if he could bear to get even that close. Which was rare now.

Plain as the nose on your face, his mother had often said. *Dead as a doornail*, she said, too. Which she was.

Not much nose left anymore, Mom.

He stared as long as he could bear it, a fine sheen of sweat breaking out across his scalp and above the ragged remnant of his upper lip. With a plosive groan, he twisted away, nauseated. The dog. The teeth. He saw them in his fretful sleep, those many teeth, felt the dog's breath on his skin, on the surface of his eyeball, how wet and loud that snarl was with her muzzle at his ear.

Russell walked backward to the window and shut the drapes with his eyes closed.

A little better. He'd lasted at least a minute longer than he had the previous night. To see that ghost of a reflection and stay with it was his aim. No sweat. No desire to puke. It was good to have a goal.

A length of cloth, deep indigo shot through with delicate metallic threads, lay puddled where he'd dropped it at the foot of his bed. He twined it twice around his lower face, then up at an angle and over the crown of his head (folded just so—better to cover the dead eye). Tuck the end, and voilà. He didn't need a mirror for this. The soft weight of it was a comfort; a steadying measure of confidence fell into place when he was back under wraps.

It was full dark now. Time to sit at table with his council, most newly chosen, what with the recent deaths at the old woman's hovel. Streeter was gone, too, that fat man with his fat pipe, who ran when the shit hit the fan. The first day Russell was able to sit up and give orders, he'd made a summary judgment of treason—always a capital crime. For bolting in the face of danger. For cowardice, retreat. Desertion. Streeter was hanged.

He locked his rooms and strolled down the polished linoleum corridors, empty and echoing, to council chambers—the big conference room with its long oval table.

All seven of them were there, seated, quiet and expectant. His men. The Council of Konungar. Each one now wore a mask like Russell's, with the exception of that last piratical turn to cover the eye. When they turned to mark his entrance, the effect was an odd mashup: Wild West meets Timbuktu. They were allowed to choose the color, whatever they wanted as long as it was not garish, nothing that would draw particular attention. Most had chosen dark shades of green, black, brown, difficult to spot out in the woods. Russell's cloth alone had the sheen of silver running in its weft.

He stood at the head of the table for a moment, allowing them to absorb his relative position. Then he lifted a hand, pointed at the tactical map pinned to the wall and snapped his fingers. Two men (he wasn't sure who—since they'd adopted the head coverings it could be hard to tell at first glance) jumped immediately and spread the oversized plat on the table. Russell took his seat and nodded at the big man on his right. The man stood, causing everyone to crane their heads back, so tall was he. This was Doyle: mountainous, impassive, voice like stones grinding along a river bottom. An ideal proxy.

"No more supply patrols," Doyle said. "We're suspending broadcast scavenging runs. We have enough in storage now to see us through for months, if we ration it. We'll keep a skeleton crew here to mind the warm bodies and keep wheels turning," he said, "but most of us are going out." He tapped two huge fingertips on the upper right quadrant of the map. "We're certain they're traveling north," he said. "This is where we're going to find them."

They looked at the map under Doyle's meaty hand. They looked at each other over the folded borders of their scarves—brown eyes, blue eyes, muddy hazel.

"How can we know that?" asked one of them. He was young, nineteen or twenty, and when everyone turned to stare, the tops of his freckled ears flushed dark red.

"We have intelligence," said Doyle in his rumbling, bottomless voice. "Unlike yourself. Save your questions, cubby. Shut up and learn." A few uneasy chuckles rose and fell. "They have a small head start, but they have impediments that we don't," he said. "An old woman. A young one who doesn't know shit about rough living. A dog."

Russell stood and leaned over them, both hands on the table. The skin on his left hand was a map, too, one made of grisly interconnected scars.

"We're going to take them," he said. He spoke softly and the indigo wrap helped muffle the speech impediment caused by his wounds. "Every single one. Take them, and deal with them." He put his hands behind his back and let his good eye linger on each face. "Including the dog," he said. "Believe it."

9

THE SOUND OF RAIN. Shivering, her shoulder and back on fire. Renna coaxing, *Drink this, Arie. Drink.* Water. Broth, the taste of bone marrow. Sleep. Dreams of her sister Mercy, crying at the south gate as Arie walked away. A crackle of flames, then Handy, *You're safe, Sister, it's only to cook on.* Sweet brown eyes, cold nose, heavy pelt— Talus watching, licking her hand, stretched out along her side. Outside again: lying in Curran's arms, lying on a gently bouncing stretcher, trees like cathedral spires far overhead. Inside, somewhere. Curran singing, *There is a ship that sails the sea, she's loaded deep as deep can be.* Smell of mildew and mouse turds. Raised voices, men's voices, *Yes, but if we're caught out in the weather.* Renna with a soft cloth, washing her like a baby. Dreams of Granny in the bed with her, *We won't go anywhere.*

One morning, there were birds. Arie opened her eyes. She was in a bedroom. In a bed. The room was large, beautiful. Next to the bed were French doors that let out on a deck. The glass panes, though cloudy with dirt, offered a grand view of the trees. Narrow ribbons of morning sun stabbed through the branches A Steller's jay landed on the deck rail. He cocked his dark, crested head in several directions, hopped down onto the deck floor. He pecked at the piled needles, cones, and leaves, his plumage an otherworldly blue. Another jay landed, and they squabbled in their raucous way. On the floor next to Arie's bed, Talus lifted her head to see what the trouble was. She stood, stretched deeply, and stepped over to the French doors. One of the birds flew onto a nearby branch, but the other hopped brazenly about, keeping an eye on the dog behind the glass.

"Hey," said Arie. Her voice was a dry whistle. Talus looked and grinned her doggy grin, tongue out, big tail swinging. She came to the edge of the bed and stood. This put them eye-to-eye. "Aren't you a great good thing," said Arie. Talus put her forelegs on the bed and rested her muzzle on the mattress, looking out from under her black eyelashes. Arie reached, ran her palm over the silky face. The bad spot on her back was stiff and painful, as if some terrible thing would crack open if she moved too much. Talus let herself be stroked, and then she surged forward to give Arie a vigorous face-licking. She bounced off the bed and pushed open the partially closed bedroom door. In a moment, Arie heard Curran murmur. Talus barked once, twice, and Curran came shuffling into the bedroom, squinting against the sun now streaming across the floor.

"Hey," he said. "Is that you in there?"

"Still here."

He shook his head and smiled. "Your life is still your own."

"So it seems. Water?"

"Yep." He bent and kissed her cheek. "Be right back."

"Handy and Renna?" Arie rasped.

Curran stood at the door in sock feet, scratching the back of his head. His black hair had grown and mostly covered the place where she'd stitched his torn and naked scalp. His face was clear of all the residual bruises. Beyond the fact of healing, he looked changed to her. Older. "I'll get your entourage," he said.

For two weeks Arie's fever had run its course. Handy found chamomile and plantain in the ditches bordering the long gravel driveway that meandered up from the road. Renna bathed the burn in cool tea and gave it air until it scabbed over, then she covered it with plantain poultices, exactly as she had seen Arie do for her own dog bites. It had likely saved her.

Everything Arie knew now about those bleary, half-conscious days after the fire, she'd been told by the three of them, starting on the morning she woke up with Talus.

They had fled to Curran's house in the stump and stayed for two days, waiting for the first break in the rain. There were still a few usable items inside the place; the tarps and fabrics he'd used to cover the floor served to make Arie's stretcher. During those couple of days, both men had gone out under cover of dark, more concerned with human threat than with lion or bear. Back at the burned-out house, they had scavenged the black wreckage. The bodies of the two dead men were still there, picked over much as the wild dogs had been—scattered bones, torn and bloody clothing, a featureless skull wearing hair and an orange beanie.

"It was Little Mikey," Curran said. Telling this part, his face was more miserable than Arie had ever seen it.

"I thought as much."

"I killed him," he said. "Got on top and choked him." He held out his hands as he spoke, visibly shaking.

"Thank you for that," Arie said.

He balled his trembling hands into a single fist and nodded. "It was bad, seeing him like that, after—"

"No one came back for them." Arie shook her head. "Gods...not even to make a burial." She put her own hand over his two clenched ones and could feel his muscles thrumming. "Kings, my ass," she said.

As for salvage, there was little left in the smoking wreckage. The hundred-year-old redwood timbers had made glorious fuel. The site was little more than a pile of jagged black jackstraws heaped around exposed lead pipes and various humps and twists of metal—the steel tool chest, kitchen appliances, Granny's chrome dining table, the old hot water heater. But just as they were ready to give up and retreat into the woods, they stumbled across a wonderful thing: two of the three packs that Arie had made. While Arie had kept Russell busy from the roof, Renna managed to drag the packs down the inside hatch. She'd stashed them in the useless bathroom, which was nearly as far from the ignition point of the fire as it could be. Laid in the cast iron tub behind a closed door, the two packs ended up fully intact, no more the worse for wear than a great deal of smoke smell, greasy dark ash, and wet from the days of rain soaking through the rubble.

They were in a huge house, something a backcountry weed grower had commissioned far up a dirt road, lived in during construction but then abandoned—maybe a grow bust. Maybe the Pink. The finished area was a wonder, with its pale bamboo floors and natural stone fireplace. Those rooms boasted vivid hand-woven wall hangings from Guatemala and a display case of jade Buddhas, their milky translucent green so beautiful they were almost painful to look at. Nevertheless, depredation was everywhere. A falling branch had crashed through a bank of windows, allowing in all manner of weather and wildlife.

Most of the house was now rotted plywood, exposed lathing, and dangling silver runners of insulation. Huge banks of solar panels on the roof were connected to nothing and were buried under layers of rotting humus. Wind blew in through unfinished ducting and conduit. They'd hung whatever they could find to cordon off the mess, and still had four whole large, functional rooms to live in. Still, Arie was eager to put it at their backs.

Now the two women finished tying their bedrolls. Renna hummed a little tune while she worked—*Frère Jacques*—something she often did unconsciously these days. Talus galloped in from outside, smelling strongly of forest duff and unwashed dog. She wore the saddlebags Arie had made the night before the fire, and she looked ready for an adventure. Curran and Handy came in after her.

"Packs are ready," Handy said. "The sun's well up—better we move."

"One second," Curran said. He leaned Pop's old backpack, its faded blue now blotched and smeary gray, against his leg. He fumbled with a zippered front pouch and pulled out a square piece of wood. This he handed to Arie. "From your house," he said.

It was redwood, smooth and velvety to the touch. Six inches square, a half inch thick, the color of whiskey and old wine. Though it carried a trace of smoke smell, it was unburned. On the face, a mandala was etched, a small symmetrical path that wound in to a center point, out again. He'd somehow stained the meandering labyrinth a darker shade of red. On the back, two words carved in neat block letters: I SOJOURN.

She placed the gift flat against her chest and held it over her heart, over the place where the third null sign was etched into her skin. She looked up at him, wanting to say some word of thanks, but words failed. He smiled, satisfied, and hoisted the backpack onto his shoulder. "Come on, Talus," he said. They went out into the brightening day together.

Arie glanced around the enormous room. Her eyes lingered on the jade figurines, docile and transcendent on their glass shelves. The only things of theirs remaining were two tight bedrolls. "That's it, then," she said to Handy and Renna, who stood waiting for her. "Let's go."

Handy grabbed the bedrolls and they followed Arie out onto a huge flagstone veranda. The inside of the mammoth house was a half-finished shell, but no expense had been spared on the outside. Curran stood at the top of a stone stairway, throwing a stick for Talus. She chased it easily, as though her overloaded saddlebags were stuffed with feathers and cotton balls. Handy and Curran had tied their own bedrolls to their packs; Renna, who could now walk with barely a trace of limp, wore hers and Arie's, bound together across her shoulders.

Arie, finally able to bear the weight of Granny's old wool coat but not much else—not yet—took the sharpened walking stick Handy had made, one for each of them. The short spear was tucked through her belt, and Curran's gift snugged neatly into her coat pocket.

They walked abreast down the quarter-mile of gravel drive, stopping twenty feet from the gate that let out onto the frost-heaved and weed-raddled two-lane thoroughfare, once called Old Arcata Road. Handy eased up to the gate, looked for a long time in every direction. Though it was chilly, the vegetation all around them drenched and dripping, the sun shone in a remarkably clear sky. He motioned to them, and they all crossed the road, silent but for their gritty footsteps, throwing long shadows across the tired macadam.

Just visible across a wide, overgrown pasture was the highway. There were no morning commuters. No sixteen-wheeler ground its jake brake as it came across the bridge into town. No farmers hauled hay to their dairy cows, and not a single small plane cruised in the brilliant October sky. There was only birdsong and these five travelers. They climbed a short bank on the far side and made their own path into the trees beyond. They belonged to each other, and would travel north along the coast, then bear east as well as they were able.

North and east to God's Land.

TO THE READER

THANK YOU FOR READING *After the Pretty Pox.* ♥

- **If you enjoyed the story, please leave an honest reader review** on Amazon or Goodreads. A review only takes a minute to write, yet the results are invaluable! Your rating makes the book visible to more readers, and more reviews means better promotional opportunities for the author.

- **Dear Reader, do keep in touch.** Subscribe to the newsletter at www.carlabaku.com. I'd love to hear from you. Subscribers get first news of forthcoming books, fun giveaways, and more.

- When subscribing, you might just decide to join the ***Bodacious Vanguard***—my virtual "street team" of fabulousness! The Vanguard gets free ARCs (advance reader copies) of new books, contributes early reader reviews, and enjoys exclusive content. Are you one of the Bodacious?

Until next time:
Make peace, share love, read books.

Coming soon!

SHADOW ROAD
After the Pretty Pox: Book Two

In this first sequel to *After the Pretty Pox*, Arie and her close-knit band travel on foot, finding their way to Arie's childhood home in the mountains. Battling the hardships of this exposed life, Arie, Handy, Renna, Curran, and good Talus will come face to face with other survivors of The Pink. How radically has the world has changed, out on the *Shadow Road*?

Available Fall 2016

ACKNOWLEDGEMENTS

First thanks go to first readers: Allen Chamberlain, Christina Gillen, Jamie Jennings, and Sylvia Mann. Their critical input, observations, and encouragement were constructive, spot on, and eminently useful. Even though he's a very good guy, Randy George lent me his middle name for a very bad dude—I'm afraid we haven't seen the last of Russell, Chief of the Konungar.

Another big thank you to cover designer Dominika Hlinková with Inspired Cover Designs: talented, intuitive and *so* patient; and to the hardworking team at Red Adept Editing for pointing out where I zigged when I should have zagged. Dale at Biolitestove.com helped me with a question about their cool little biomass-powered camp stoves; and Brandon L. Browne, Associate Professor of Geology at Humboldt State University, took the time to tell me all about the composition of boulders in and around the Humboldt County area—complete with amazing color photos. Giant huzzahs to the Bodacious Vanguard for their enthusiastic support: readers rock the world, and *my* readers are simply the best.

As always, the biggest thank you is reserved for Mr. B, who believes. My hero.

ABOUT THE AUTHOR

 August Ansel is the pen name (and alter ego) of author Carla Baku. It's August who is forever wedging beloved dog-eared novels by Shirley Jackson, Peter Straub, and Joe Hill in among the works of Toni Morrison and Tobias Wolff. Working from a tiny garret overlooking the lovely Myrtle Grove Cemetery, August prefers to write novels longhand while sipping bitterly strong tea and wearing an atrocious pair of bedroom slippers.

Readers are most welcome to peruse all August Ansel (and Carla Baku) books at www.carlabaku.com, and to follow on Facebook: CarlaBaku.AugustAnsel and Twitter: @augustansel.